MAN FROM DURANGO

Center Point
Large Print

Also by Lauran Paine and available from
Center Point Large Print:

Beyond Fort Mims
Ute Peak Country
Way of the Outlaw
The Plains of Laramie
Guns in Wyoming

**This Large Print Book carries the
Seal of Approval of N.A.V.H.**

MAN FROM DURANGO

— A Western Duo —

LAURAN PAINE

CENTER POINT LARGE PRINT
THORNDIKE, MAINE

This Center Point Large Print edition is published
in the year 2013 by arrangement with
Golden West Literary Agency.

The text of this Large Print edition is unabridged.
In other aspects, this book may vary
from the original edition.
Printed in the United States of America
on permanent paper.
Set in 16-point Times New Roman type.

ISBN: 978-1-61173-871-1

Library of Congress Cataloging-in-Publication Data

Paine, Lauran.
Man from Durango : a Western duo / Lauran Paine. —
   Center Point Large Print edition.
pages cm.
ISBN 978-1-61173-871-1 (Library binding : alk. paper)
1. Large type books. I. Title.
PS3566.A34M36 2013
813′.54—dc23
                                        2013012362

Contents

Prairie Guns

I

They worked at the planting, with their guns against the stone row. A year ago they had been on their new claim but a week; they were building a home, when a group of horsemen had come up. They were rough men in boots, butternut shirts, and wide hats, armed heavily with carbines slung from their saddles and holstered handguns at their waists.

A grizzled, rough, and scornful man—he was Colton Miller, a cowman, they would remember him—had called sharply downward: "Do you know this is free-graze land?"

Buff Brady, a hot proud man, answered back: "We know this is homestead land and we got a right to be here."

"You damned clodhoppers, you'll find out whether you got a right to be here or not! You'll be buried here."

The horsemen had wheeled and ridden off. From then on the partners had kept their weapons close. Around them other homesteaders had come to take up land, to erect log houses or burrow into the prairie like gophers, to make soddies. It became a common thing for men to die in their fields, shot from ambush. Violence struck all around Buff Brady and Luther Hart, and, while they frequently

9

found tracks made by night riders upon their land, they were not themselves molested.

So they worked at the planting with their guns against the stone row, with the overhead sky swept clean by spring sunshine and the swelling of new life all around them.

Luther Hart was a heavy-boned young man with an easy grace, wide mouth, and a fearless look around the eyes. He had been a top hand for some of the largest cow outfits in the Southwest, but here in the Colorado plains country few knew this. To his neighbors he was just another squatter— another dirt-farming homesteader.

Buff Brady, Luther's partner of many years, was also a former top hand. But Buff had been something else, too, once; he had been an outlaw. But that was a long time ago. Now Buff was simply a man who had claimed 160 acres of former free-graze land. His claim adjoined Luther's 160, and with it the old riding partners had a fine parcel of rich grass and deep loam land. They meant to work hard until they could acquire more land. Their ultimate goal was to own two striving, adjoining cow outfits.

It was a common enough dream. Every cowboy at one time or another considered striking out on his own, making a home, building a cow herd, taking a brood woman, and raising up his own riders. To most riders, though, it was never more than a dream. A few tried it, but the back-breaking toil, the poverty, the restrictions—but most of all the scorn—made them give it up. Those who clung to this grinding way, though, came in time to resemble the emigrants, the Easterners, the dirt farmers, until other riders could not recognize them as former members of the range brotherhood, and that was how it was with Luther and Buff Brady. No one, not even the other hoe men, thought of them as anything other than a couple of young bucks trying to get a start in the plains country.

So, with guns handy, they worked this good spring day away, stopping only occasionally to speak when they passed one another in the furrows. The afternoon moved on, the sun dropped lower, presaging night shadows came creeping, and a gentle hush, a deepening red, colored the land. Brady cast off the lines, stretched mightily, went into the shade made by the horse, and squatted there cowboy-like, sitting on his heels to manufacture a cigarette and wait for Luther to come abreast of him with the planter, and also halt.

He lit up and exhaled. Against the faraway backdrop of flint-purple hills rolled miles of prairie. For near half a century cattle had run free here, cattlemen had prospered, grown wealthy and feudal, had ruled as lords, written the law to suit their interests, and now with their sun fast sinking they were clanning together for a supreme great effort to hold this realm that was larger than most European nations.

Buff smoked in deep thought. He knew, much better than most, how range men fought; he had been a part of their ruthlessness in former times; he had no illusions now, as he watched Luther come up, halt, kick black soil from his boots, throw forward a rueful grin, and stamp onward past the planter to halt nearby. He knew as surely as he knew anything that Colton Miller who had formerly grazed 10,000 critters over this selfsame land was not reconciled to seeing plows plunged into his free-graze land.

"There's got to be an easier way to serve the Lord than doing this," said Luther, sinking down in the shade, grinning and fishing around in a pocket for his tobacco sack. "Did I ever tell you what old John Slaughter told me one time when I rode up on him in his melon patch down by Tombstone?"

"No."

"He told me that once a man grows things out of the earth he's forever changed. He's never again satisfied just to graze animals over the top of it."

Buff put aside his hat and dragged a sleeve over his forehead. "I'd say Slaughter ought to know about that. I'd also say that for every old cowman who believes like that, there are a hundred who don't."

Luther gazed over their worked-up land. Dark

earth lay in cultivated squares, unfenced and surrounded by the grassland range. "Eighty acres of barley," he mused, "and thirty acres of this here corn." He smiled whimsically. "I used to watch clodhoppers planting corn like we've been doing and think a man had to want something pretty bad to hike all day behind one of these darned little seeders."

Buff, too, looked outward. "He wants to be an individual, I reckon. He wants something more than just loping into town with the boys and getting buzz-headed in some saloon. I guess he just wants to be himself, instead of always being part of something else."

Luther lit up, swiveled his eyes to let them linger upon his partner, and said: "You're feeling plumb solemn this evening."

Buff nodded. "For a fact I sure am," he murmured, gazing far out. "Why hasn't Miller sent his crew against us?"

"He doesn't have to rush things for my benefit."

"But you know dog-gone well he's going to do it, Lute."

"Yes."

"Then . . . why the delay? What's he waiting for?"

Luther made a slow and sweeping gesture with one arm. "When the barley's beginning to head out," he said. "When our corn's up and maybe three, four feet tall." He let the arm drop and said no more. He no longer wore his rueful small smile; his pale eyes were stonily fixed upon their plantings and his wide mouth was a drawn-out, humorless line low among his features. "He doesn't have to fight us off, Buff. He can't burn the soddy and there won't be any grass worth having this year anyway, so he can afford to wait."

Buff looked around. "You've been thinkin', too," he said.

Luther's shoulders rose and fell. "You got to do something while you're hopping clods behind that dog-gone seeder."

Buff nodded. "That's a fact," he agreed, then returned again to his thoughtful reverie. After a time he spoke again. "How'll he do it, Lute?"

"Easy. You've done the same thing, Buff. He'll make up a herd . . . drift it over here where the critters can scent up the corn and heading barley. One morning we'll get up . . . and there'll be nothing here but trampled stalks."

Buff nodded, evidently finding this reasoning in accord with his own thinking. "And the nearest forest is 'way off in those mountains," he said, meaning that to split rails for fencing would be a prodigious labor.

"I got another idea," said Luther. "Awful lot of moles and pesky little digging critters in our land, Buff."

Brady agreed with this. He had no idea what

14

Luther was coming to, but he knew his partner well enough to wait.

"Next time we go into Lincoln we'd better buy a few pounds of strychnine."

Luther looked up. His gaze touched Buff's steady regard and moved on.

"You soak a sack or two of seed barley in water and you toss a pound or so of this strychnine into the water. Makes the seed barley swell up, absorb the strychnine, and when anything eats the barley . . . it dies."

Buff's brows drew gradually down into a frown. For a while he struggled with his thoughts before speaking. "Hell, I got no fight against Miller's cattle, Lute. If we could get Miller to eat some of the stuff. . . ."

But Luther was wagging his head, thinly smiling. "Naw, I told you how it's done. I didn't say we were going to do it." Luther pushed out his cigarette against the earth. "If you and me buy a couple of pounds of strychnine at the store in Lincoln, Colton Miller'll know about it before we even get home with the stuff. I don't think we'll have to make any poisoned bait at all. It's sort of like holding a cocked gun under a poker table across from a feller. He knows the thing is there although he can't see it, and he can't prove you might use it on him."

Buff considered this a silent moment, then arose, swiped at the dust on his trousers, and said:

"Let's go fix some supper. I got to think about this. Normally I don't like to bluff, Lute."

Luther also arose. "With a few pounds of strychnine in hand, who can say we're bluffing? Colton Miller won't be able to say so, Buff."

They unhitched, led their team back beyond a green land swell where a small log barn and soddy house stood, and there prepared for night-time.

Around them the silence deepened, shadows broadened, thickened, took on bold substance, and gradually came to dominate this lonely, far, and troubled country.

Beyond 8:00 p.m. with the lantern swinging from its overhead nail, their meal finished and tobacco smoke hanging heavily in the still air of their sod house, Buff sat quietly at the cleared table, cleaning his six-gun. From near the wood stove Luther watched this operation a while, then said: "They don't much use pistols in this kind of fighting. You have to get too close to your victim."

Buff grunted without looking up. "Packing a carbine with you everywhere would be all right, if a man had three hands. When he hasn't, a pistol on the hip helps a little."

Luther hefted the graniteware coffee pot. It swished at least two cups' worth. "Want some coffee?" he asked.

Still without looking up from his work, Buff said: "No thanks." A moment later he put the cleaned weapon upon the table and sat gazing at it. "I thought, bein' a clodhopper would take a man out of the ranks of folks who have to use these things." He sighed. "Just goes to show you how wrong a feller can be without knowing it."

"My pa told me once," said Luther from over by the stove, "that when a man makes a big change in his life, he has to spend the rest of his days defending what he's done."

Buff got up and hefted his six-gun. "He was right, plumb right." He holstered the weapon, hung the shell belt from a peg in the earthen wall, and said over his shoulder: "What makes this seem foolish to me is that there's so much country out here. Enough for the cowmen and squatters both." He turned away from the wall. "What's the sense in killing someone, or getting killed, over something as endless as land?"

"No sense," concurred his partner, hanging a limp towel upon a stove rail. "When you convince Miller of that, let me know."

Buff moved toward his wall bunk, dropped down, and kicked off his boots. He sat, briefly wiggling his toes, then sighed, leaned back, and, propping up his head with both arms, let his body turn loose upon the bunk's straw mattress. "Maybe we should have joined the others when they wanted us to."

Luther turned down the lamp. "Maybe. I'll tell you one thing. If Miller doesn't ease off with his night riding and burning, all the squatters will have to unite for the common good."

"Bunch of foreigners and tomfools," growled Buff, unable even yet to overcome the range man's prejudice against homesteaders, despite the fact that he was himself one of them now. "Reminds me of a band of sheep."

Luther finished undressing. He got between his blankets and blew outward a loud sigh. "I have an idea," he said quietly, "that Miller feels about the same way toward them. But not us."

"What do you mean . . . not us?"

"When riders turn clodhopper, cowmen reserve a special kind of hatred for them. In their eyes we're traitors. They can hate the others . . . but not us. They'll despise us." Luther yawned widely. "When he gets ready to tackle us, believe me, Buff, he'll do his damnedest to make real gory examples of us, because we were his kind of people once."

Buff Brady turned up on his side. He said dourly: "You're sure a cheerful cuss."

Luther made no reply to this. The night pulsed on. Overhead a thin moon rode serenely across the high, arched vault of heaven.

II

The spring days passed quietly for Luther and Buff Brady. They went to Lincoln, got supplies, including two pounds of strychnine that they made a point of exhibiting carelessly. They saw the first warm spring rain bring forth their barley and corn crops.

They also built a network of pole corrals, for while they had no cattle at all yet, and only had four horses, this corral building reaffirmed in each of them the goal they had in mind. It seemed to put them closer to this goal.

While they worked, they discussed the rumors each had heard in the town of Lincoln. Some squatters farther north had banded together to fight cowmen. Closer, a family neither of them had heard about before had been burned out two days after moving into their new log house. Farther west, a man they did not know, but had heard of—an older man named Graham—had been shot and killed while milking his cow. Northeast of them, closer to Lincoln, a herd of wicked-horned cattle had been driven through a homesteader's planted fields.

What remained foremost in each of their minds, but something they did not speak of often between themselves, was a threat Colton Miller had made. It was one of those hearsay things a man heard, and wished not to credit, but still could not forget. Miller, so a fearful neighbor had told them in town, had said he meant to destroy Brady and Hart utterly, level their soddy with dynamite, bury Luther and Buff in their own furrows, then erect two immense white crosses. He wanted to make examples of them, the neighbor had fearfully whispered, so that every clodhopper on Miller's free graze would have to see those two white crosses every time he came and went between Lincoln and his homestead. The crosses were to be twenty feet tall and made of peeled logs, large enough to be seen for five miles in every direction in this flat plains country.

"That," said Buff, the day they finished the corrals and were leaning there, critically considering their work, "is the kind of talk that makes bad trouble."

Luther squinted at the lowering sun; it was late afternoon. "It puts a man under the gun," he opined. "If a feller sits back and waits, he'll likely get picked off from cover or in the dark. If he takes the bull by the horns and carries the war to Miller . . . then he's startin' the war himself. Like I just said, he's under the gun. He's likely to be damned if he doesn't do anything, and damned if he does do something."

Buff slapped a corral rail and turned to lean his back upon it. "I don't like waiting," he said.

Luther, less fiery, turned also to lean there in thoughtful pensiveness. "And I don't like forcing things," he said.

"All right, what do we do, then? Stand like we're doing right now . . . a couple of targets?"

Luther swung his head back and forth and replied mildly to Buff's indignant demand. "We're lucky. There's no brush on the ranch. The stone fences we've been putting up we can stay away from. If Miller's big talk means anything, he's going to have to ride up face to face when . . . and if . . . he really means to brace us."

"Don't you think he'll brace us?"

Luther had no illusions here. "He'll brace us, all right, but like I said . . . we're under the gun. We've got to leave the first move up to him."

"You just said you didn't like doing that."

"I don't like it. Don't like it at all. But I see it as the lesser of two evils, Buff. Remember, Miller's powerful and he's rich. If we jump him, he'll have the law on us within hours."

"He'll have the law on us, anyway," Brady growled. "The first excuse he can get."

"Sure, but we've got to keep the support of the other squatters. Without that we're as good as dead."

"For all the good those damned people are, we're more'n likely good as dead anyway."

"They may not be much with guns," agreed Luther, "but there are a lot of them. They've got votes, they've got numbers, and they've got legal rights. If we're outlawed by Miller . . . which we'll be the minute we pick a fight with him . . . a lot of them are going to half believe we aren't their kind of folks after all. Then where'll we be?"

Buff scowled, scratched his nose, hitched up his Levi's, and spat aside. "It doesn't make me feel real good knowing the kind of folks we got as allies," he said, still in the grim and growling mood. "By golly, Lute, I'd rather rely on ten good riders than a hundred of these sodbusters."

Luther smiled with his lips. "A hundred of us sod busters," he murmured, then broke off to twist from the waist as the sound of a ridden horse came to him across the dying day.

For a long moment the partners listened without moving or speaking, then Buff said: "One man. If Miller sent him, he's got more guts than brains."

Luther relaxed in the twilight. "You're slipping," he admonished. "Listen to that horse. No top hand ever willingly rode a poky old hide like that one sounds to be."

They did not speak between them again until the oncoming rider came fully into view, then Buff said quietly from the corner of his mouth: "One of the Buells." As the big old horse slowed, then halted, and his youthful rider peered gravely down at them, Buff said in recognition: "Good evening, Charley. Kind of late to be pokin' around the countryside, isn't it?"

Charley Buell gradually relaxed atop his team horse. He slouched a little in the saddle, and, although obviously relieved to be in the company of Luther and Buff, his solemn expression did not alter. He was perhaps eighteen years of age, tall, angular, and boyishly awkward-looking.

" 'Evening," he said, then paused to look beyond where dusk mantled the new corrals. "Wish we had a set-up like that. You fellers just finish it?"

Luther nodded. Neither of the partners spoke. They were waiting; they did not often visit with their squatter neighbors, and in turn were pretty much left alone. Charley Buell, son of Chester Buell, their closest homesteading neighbor, had not made this long ride in the late day for pleasure.

"Care to get down and set for a spell?" asked Luther, drawing the lad out.

"No, thanks," said Charley, bringing his attention back to the two men leaning upon the corral. "Got to be gettin' back. Pa says it's not a real good idea to be ridin' around alone in the dark."

Luther nodded. At his side Buff fidgeted; he shifted his weight; he looked pointedly at the boy; finally he sighed, the sound full of resignation.

"Pa sent me over to ask if you fellers would care to come over for supper tonight."

Luther's regard of the boy sharpened. Chester Buell was not generally a socializing man. If he extended this invitation, he had a reason for it.

"Anything wrong?" he asked the boy.

Charley shook his head. "Ma said you fellers must be good and sick of your own cookin' by now."

Buff rubbed his jaw; he gazed at Luther. "That's a fact," he said. Then to the boy: "You want to head on back or wait for us to clean up and get saddled?"

Charley said hastily: "Oh, I'll wait."

Buff nudged Luther. "We'll be back in a jiffy," he threw at Charley, and headed toward the house with Luther at his side. When they were in the soddy, he frowned slightly, saying to Luther: "You get a free chance at a woman-cooked supper and you hesitate. You getting soft in the skull, Lute?"

"Just wondering," mildly replied his partner.

"Do your wonderin' while we're ridin'," grumbled Buff, digging out clean clothing.

The three of them rode northwestward through the deepening evening, Luther and Buff having to restrain their mounts in order not to lose Charley Buell in the darkness, for, while cowboys turned homesteaders now and then, they retained their horsemen's ways and rode only the best saddle stock.

The homestead of the Buell family was a long hour's slow-lope distance beyond Buff's homestead. Because Buff's land lay westerly from Luther's 160, it took the three of them—with

Charley's thick-legged team horse slowing them all the way—nearly two hours to ride into the Buell yard. By that time full night was down, the sky was awash with yeasty stars, and a raffish old uneven moon, fat and pumpkin-orange, hung in the overhead heavens.

They were offsaddling in the sod barn when a large and bearded man appeared with a lantern held high in the doorway. He called forth a greeting, got one back, and forced an amiability that struck into the night with an insincerity neither Luther nor Buff missed.

"Sage hen and flour dumplings," he said. "Hot coffee and wild plum pie."

Luther turned away from the tie stall where his horse was nuzzling a manger of wild red-top hay. "Sounds better'n anything I've heard about in months," he said, moving up closer to study the bearded man's expression. "That's one thing about marriage a man can't argue against . . . home cooking."

Chester Buell's lips were mechanically smiling, but his eyes were not. He lowered the lantern as Buff also came forward, turned, and without another word led off toward the soddy. Luther and Buff exchanged a silent glance, and trudged through dark dust behind their host.

The Buell soddy, because old Chester had a wife, a son, and a ten-year-old daughter, was larger, roomier than most soddies. Instead of one large room half below ground, it had four rooms. Two bedrooms—one with a plank partition—a kitchen, and the combination parlor and dining room. Chester's boy Charley disappeared at once into the partitioned bedroom. His father, after greetings were exchanged between his wife Sarah and his two visitors, silently poured three stout drinks of whiskey, gave both Luther and Buff a glass without meeting their eyes, then swept up his beard, flung back his head, and tossed off his own drink. Immediately his nose assumed a fine pinkish color. A secondary aftereffect, more gradual but equally identifiable, was a general lessening of Buell's stiltedness and preoccupation. He became, in fact, more like the taciturn, somber, and direct man that he was by nature.

While little Anne worked with her mother in the background, and before Charley had returned freshly scrubbed and attired, Chester conspiratorially led Luther and Buff to a far corner and told them there would be seven people at supper, not six. He allowed this to sink in, shifting his glance from one partner to the other, then drew in a lungful of fresh breath and said: "Graham's daughter."

It took a moment for this to mean anything. Luther squinted in concentration. Finally, with his face clearing, he said: "Wasn't that the feller west of here who got dry-gulched while milking his cow?"

"The same," stated Chester Buell. "His place is three miles on west from here. The girl was his only kin. We took her in until she can sell out and go back East."

Buff, thinking of little Anne, said: "Too bad. This is a hard country on kids." His eyes kindled; he shot looks at both Chester Buell and Luther. "What's been done to find her pa's murderer?"

Chester ran the back of one hand under his beard; he fluffed it outward in an unconscious gesture. "What can be done?" he countered. "There were no tracks save those of an unshod horse. No boot tracks, no shell cartridge, no witnesses. John was sitting there milking one minute . . . the next minute he had a hole in his chest you could run your fist through."

Luther's eyes drew out narrowly speculative. "Buffalo gun," he murmured. "Did you see the hole, Chester?"

"I saw it."

"Look like a Forty-Five-Seventy slug or bigger?"

Chester Buell shrugged. "I don't know anything about guns."

Luther turned aside. "Who carries a buffalo gun that we know?" he asked Buff.

Then, his attention caught and powerfully held by the same vision that kept Buff from replying, Luther let off a slow rush of breath. They stood like that, one slightly ahead of the other, simply staring. Neither speaking nor moving in this silent moment until Chester Buell cleared his throat and started forward across the room, saying: "Boys, this is Jessie Graham. Jessie, the tall feller there is Luther Hart. The other feller is Buff Brady. They are my neighbors to the southeast."

Jessie Graham was ten years past being the little girl Buff had anticipated, and to see her now it was hard to believe she had ever been a little girl. She had curves where other women Buff Brady had seen in his lifetime didn't even have places. She had a face dominated by large, wide-spaced, direct, smoke-gray eyes, and a full mouth with the faintest lilt at its outer corners. Her hair was the color of spun copper and her expression, when she acknowledged the introductions, was both grave and frankly interested.

"I think we can eat now," said Sarah Buell from far back. "Chester, see what's keeping Charley. Annie, up on your bench. Boys . . . Luther! Buff!"

III

The meal was as excellent as the partners knew it would be, and afterward the subject that had prompted their invitation in the first place was brought up. Luther, who had great difficulty keeping his eyes off the lovely Jessie Graham, fell completely under her spell when she began describing the cattle she had to sell.

Buff, whose recovery was quicker, said they did not have enough money to buy the Graham cattle and still operate for another year as they had planned to do.

Jessie Graham bent a long smoky gaze upon Buff, saying: "I understand, Mister Brady. But I thought, if you'd like the herd and would pay me a little now, I could wait a year or two for the balance."

Chester Buell had obviously already discussed this with Jessie, for he now said: "Three years would be better. You'd get three calf crops that way. The critters would pay for themselves."

Luther broke his long silence here, asking Jessie a question: "How many head did your pa have, miss?"

"Sixty cows and two bulls. The cows are calving now." Jessie paused, made a small motion with one hand, and added in a rueful tone: "At least that's how many there were when I left the homestead three days ago."

"Branded?" asked Buff.

Jessie nodded at him. "The cows are, and so are the two bulls . . . but the calves aren't marked."

Buff considered this; he finished his coffee and sat back. "We'll buy 'em on three-year terms if you'll sell 'em that way . . . but subject to a count so that we'll have to pay for only what we actually get." He looked around level-eyed at Luther. Luther was looking at Jessie Graham. Buff's lips twitched in either amusement or annoyance.

"They are yours," Jessie said simply. "But I don't think you ought to wait too long to go after them."

Chester rumbled agreement with this. He offered to go with the partners the very next day and help drive the herd back. Buff demurred; two cowboys would have no trouble with sixty or seventy head of gentle-raised cattle.

"The milk cow doesn't drive well," said Jessie to this.

Luther started where he sat. "Milk cow?"

"Why, yes," she said, turning her full gaze on Luther. "We raised her from a calf, you see, and she'd rather follow people than be driven."

Luther swallowed. He turned toward Buff. "I never milked a cow in my life," he said. "I've trailed ten thousand head but I never got down under one and. . . ."

"I'll take her off your hands," said Chester Buell, faintly smiling behind his whiskers at Luther's consternation. "With my brood I always got use for more fresh milk and cream."

Both Luther and Buff looked relieved. Said Buff: "Miss, just how do we find the Graham place?"

Jessie considered this a moment, then faced

Chester. "Could you loan me a horse tomorrow?" she asked, and, when Chester nodded affirmatively, she said to Buff: "If you'll come by here in the morning, I'll be glad to show you the way."

"We'll be here," said Luther swiftly, getting to his feet. "Is seven o'clock too early, miss?"

Jessie and the others also arose. She was very sturdily handsome there by the supper table with warm lamplight touching her. She smiled at Luther, her first smile of the evening. "It won't be too early," she told him. "I'll be waiting."

They left after that. Chester followed them out to his sod barn and stood thoughtfully aside while they saddled up and got astride. As they were moving past, voicing their thanks for his hospitality, he said: "Guess I'll have to go to Lincoln and fetch back her friend."

"What friend?" asked Luther, reining down.

"She invited a girlhood friend of hers to come visit from Ohio. That was before her pa was killed. The friend's arrivin' on the stage tomorrow about noon."

"Oh. Well, good night, Chester, and thanks again."

They loped out of Buell's yard side-by-side with darkness forming swiftly behind them so that only the sounds of their passing remained behind. They did not rein down to a slower gait for two miles, then Luther eased off, saying: "Good thing we got those corrals finished." He looked around at Buff, who was thoughtfully frowning. "What's bothering you?"

Buff did not immediately reply. He shrugged finally, and groped for his tobacco sack. While drifting along on swaying reins and making his cigarette, he said: "Didn't figure we'd go out to supper and acquire us a herd of cattle, all in one evening, is all." He lit up, blew outward, and shrugged again as his voice firmed up. "Still that's all right. Maybe it'll strap us a mite for a while, but we got to get our feet wet sometime, don't we?"

Luther inclined his head very solemnly. "I never saw anyone before in my life I wanted to be in debt to . . . but her." He twisted from the waist. "She fair took my breath away."

"So I noticed," said Buff dryly. "So did everyone else, too. Unless Miss Jessie's plumb blind she saw it, also."

Luther spoke defensively now: "Well, you weren't exactly indifferent, you know."

"Yeah."

"I never before in my whole life saw such a girl. Never. She's the prettiest thing God ever made."

Buff squinted ahead, straining to see his partner's face. He began to scowl. He held up the cigarette to study its glowing tip, obviously framing careful words, but in the end he said nothing, which was the wisest thing to do under these circumstances.

They corralled their horses at home, forked out some hay, and went into their soddy. While Buff coaxed light from their solitary overhead lantern, Luther kicked off his boots, shucked his gun belt, and tossed his hat upon their oilcloth-covered table. He went to his bunk and sank down, saying: "She's going to leave the country, Buff." He said this with all the desolation a sudden, anguished realization could bring forth into words.

Buff stood directly beneath the lantern gazing ahead. He did not move for a full sixty seconds, then, moving toward his own bunk, he murmured under his breath: "Good Lord . . . !"

Luther was stirring before sunup. He had breakfast ready before Buff had scrubbed the sleep from his eyes at their outside wash rack. "Hurry up," he said as Buff sat down dourly to eat. "You're goin' to mule around here until you make us plumb late."

Buff glanced up, protesting. "Say, it's only a little herd of scrub cows," he said around a mouthful of food. "A couple hours isn't going to make them much older, Lute."

"Not the cows!" exclaimed Luther breathlessly. "You don't want Jessie to have to stand around in the sun while we're takin' our time, do you?"

Buff gulped down his coffee, and stood up. He shot Luther a brief, indignant look, and scooped up his hat and shell belt. He crushed the former onto his head and looked down to buckle the sagging weight of shells and holstered six-gun around his waist. "Girls aren't like apples," he growled. "Sunshine don't spoil 'em."

Luther was holding the door open, his impatience mounting with each passing minute. "You know dog-gone well it's not mannerly to keep folks waiting."

As Buff passed out into the cool, gray pre-dawn, he said: "It isn't mannerly to nag folks into gulpin' down their food, either." He was moving toward the corral. "For all you know, she isn't even out of bed yet. Besides, I could get the damned colic from havin' to gobble down my breakfast like that."

"Shut up and come on," commanded Luther, half trotting ahead of him toward the corral.

They left the yard in a swirling lope, Luther pushing swiftly ahead, Buff trailing disgustedly, muttering unkind and grumpy imprecations. Finally, in called-out protest, he said: "Slow down, you damned fool! You want to ruin that horse just so's you'll have a few minutes longer to look at a pretty girl?"

"Pretty!" exclaimed Luther, slowing, letting Buff come up. "You know darned well you never, in all your life, saw a girl so genuinely beautiful."

Buff's groan was loud and lingering. He looked the way he felt, totally incapable of describing how he felt, but wishing mightily that he could try.

Still all he said was: "Lute, for a fact, I never saw you like this before. You're as giddy as a green-broke colt. Your thoughts're springing around worse'n a schoolgirl's. Listen a minute. Sure, Miss Jessie's a picture . . . a real beautiful picture. . . ." He broke off, considered his partner's features a moment, then slowly wagged his head, saying: "Hell, and I always figured I was the hot-headed one and you were the level-headed one in this pardnership." He shook out his reins, resignation in his expression. "All right, lead out . . . but use a little judgment too, will you? These horses got a lot of country to cover before nightfall, and I don't cherish the idea of *walkin'* behind those cows on the way back."

Nothing more was said between them until, with a faint pinkish brightness firming up the length of the eastern horizon, they came in sight of the Buell place.

"There's a lantern burning," said Luther in a tone of triumph. "She's up already."

Buff saw the light but said nothing.

They entered the yard, swung down, and went forward. Around them the world was softly brightening. It was considerably cooler now than it would be in another few hours. Somewhere, beyond sight, a milk cow bawled; there came a tremulous reply, and the old cow, having located her calf, lowed contentedly. An old dog, gray around the eyes and nearly toothless, did not

35

awaken to the presence of moving shadows approaching the soddy until Luther was ten feet from him. Then, to make up for his dereliction, the dog sprang stiffly up and tongued his loudest. Buff told him to shut up, which he did not do, but instead retreated a safe distance, hackles stiff, and continued his racket.

Jessie herself appeared at the door. She was wearing a white blouse and split riding skirt. Her red-copper hair was drawn severely back and caught tightly at the nape of her neck. There a small green ribbon held it firmly in place. She saw Luther first and nodded. Luther stopped on the down step leading into the soddy and stood like stone until Buff bumped him—deliberately —and shouldered past saying: "Good mornin', miss. I think we're a mite early."

"No," murmured Jessie, looking away from Luther. "Would you like some coffee before we go?"

Buff cut across Luther's murmured assent to this by saying firmly: "No thanks, miss. I figure we'd best make time while it's still cool out."

"I'll get my jacket," said Jessie, and left the doorway.

Buff turned toward Luther and growled: "Come on. Let's find Chester's saddle horse and get it rigged out for her."

Ten minutes later they were riding westward, the three of them, with the new day brightening up around them. Buff took only a desultory part in the conversation that ensued as they made their plodding way across the empty plain. He did a little soul-searching though, and this did nothing to improve his disposition, either. He had never before felt the least jealously where Luther was concerned, but now he did. From the edge of his eye he appraised Jessie Graham critically. It didn't help any to see that she sat her saddle well, that under fresh sunlight she was just as lovely as she had appeared the night before in soft lamplight, that she was unqualifiedly as truly beautiful as Luther had said she was.

He could find nothing about her to criticize, and this added to his moroseness. Finally, although he knew it was his reticence that made this possible, he could not avoid seeing that Jessie preferred Luther to him. Yet Buff Brady was an inherently honest and fair man. If he had not been so, he and Luther Hart would have dissolved their close relationship years before because Luther was by nature the same kind of a man. So, Buff told himself, he should be glad that Luther had fallen in love. What kept him from being really glad was the awareness he had that Jessie Graham was not going to be around much longer, and, after she left, the prospect of sharing their soddy with a lethargic, sad, and listless Luther Hart was not very heartening. Additionally he felt that even the memory of Jessie was an intrusion on the singleness of purpose that had originally driven them to become homesteaders.

With full daylight settled upon the land so that even the faintest night shadows were no longer visible, Buff told himself that life was going to evolve whether he approved or not, and that life was not, in fact, either good or bad, but only a place *for* good and bad. He must then reconcile himself to some things because he could not alter them, and try to make something good come out of them.

His reverie was shattered when Jessie said suddenly: "There are some of the cattle."

Buff looked outward. Dark red shapes were grazing in the middle distance. He made a rough count. "Forty head," he said, speaking for the first time in over an hour. "The others must be close by."

IV

They rode until the sun was directly overhead, making a careful sweep of the prairie around the Graham place, but found only eleven head more of Jessie Graham's cattle. Finally, heeding the time and guessing ahead to the lateness of the hour when they would ultimately arrive back at the corrals with their drive, Buff said: "I think we'd best let it go for today. If the other critters were close by, we'd be able to see them."

"Yes," agreed Jessie, her face grave, her eyes unhappy. She looked at Buff, the knowledge of what they both thought passed between them. They would find no more Graham cattle. Either Miller's riders had stampeded them, or other homesteaders had butchered them. In either event, Buff and Luther would be unable to recover them.

"Fifty-one head," she said, then paused to look at the gathered cattle before adding: "And no calves at all."

Luther, swinging the drive and lining it out, counted bagged-up cows. When he was back again with Buff and Jessie, he told them that at least fifteen of the cows had had calves, and at least twelve of them had been suckling calves no later than two days previously. Buff nodded; he had also noticed this. To Jessie he said: "Who are your closest neighbors, miss?"

The lovely girl pointed with an upraised arm. "That is Colton Miller's deeded range," she said. "All the land west and north of our homestead." She twisted to indicate the southerly flow of prairie. "That land belongs to a new family by the name of Jorgenson. They've only been out here three months. I think they came from Minnesota. My father and I met them just once."

Luther looked longest to the west. He said nothing aloud but his thoughts were plain enough from the expression he wore. Buff, noting this, said to Luther: "Forget it. You'd never make it stick. If Miller got the critters . . . and I'd give you big odds he did . . . he'd have the brands re-worked by now and the calves mammied up on other cows."

Luther held his silence. He said no more until they were angling southerly below the Buell place. Here, he drew up, looking fully at Jessie Graham. "Miss, if you ride northeast a little, you'll come to the Buell place. It shouldn't take you more'n an hour to be back there." He fidgeted with his reins and cleared his throat. "Miss, when are you leaving the country?"

Buff, casting one long and understanding look at both of them, kept urging the cattle along, leaving his partner and Jessie Graham alone. The girl, both hands lying upon her saddle horn, considered the unruly mane of the horse she sat on.

"I think in three or four days," she told him solemnly. "A friend of mine is arriving in Lincoln today. I invited her out to visit . . . us . . . before my father was killed." Smoke-gray eyes lifted, met Luther's strong gaze, and did not drop away. "I'll go back with her."

"Do you have kin in the East?" Luther asked.

"No, but I have friends there. I'll go to work." Jessie lifted the reins preparatory to moving out.

"Miss . . . ?"

"Yes?"

Luther forced out the words, speaking rapidly. "You could get work in Lincoln. It's a nice little town, and that way you wouldn't have to leave Colorado at all."

She smiled at him with her mouth, but her eyes retained their somberness. "I liked Colorado when we first came here. I even liked the hard work and the loneliness, Luther, but so much has happened. So many things have changed." She stopped speaking. He could see the struggle that was going on behind her eyes, and sought vainly for words that would ameliorate the pain somewhat. She raised the reins then, before he spoke, saying to him simply: "I won't regret leaving Colorado. But I will regret leaving it alone."

She rode away from him and did not look back.

He looped up his reins, twisted up a cigarette, lit it, and savagely cursed Colton Miller for what he had done to her. Then he booted his horse out and overtook Buff a long two miles from the corrals.

Dusk was settling down, the way it always has in Colorado, gently, benignly, fragrantly, and by the time they were close enough to make out their claim, its deepening shadows hid from sight anything that might otherwise have brought them both straight in their saddles, such as the armed body of mounted men sitting stone-like atop their horses watching the first of the driven Durhams head toward the corral, impelled forward by a scent of water.

"Count 'em at the gate!" called Buff, angling up to head the last of the cattle. "Don't want to lose any in the shadows."

They came together moments later to swing out and down, slam the corral gate, and lean there, gazing upon their little herd. For a space of moments neither spoke, then Luther turned, saying a little tiredly: "We're in the cow business a year or two ahead of what we figured."

Buff also turned, but he did not speak at all. He started to, his lips were parted for words to pass out, but his body began to straighten up, to stiffen, to brace ahead. Over his partner's shoulders he saw for the first time that hard knot of dim shapes down by their soddy. He breathed out in a sighing way. Luther, sighting Buff's suddenly changed stance and expression, turned slowly. As he did this, the foremost rider over by their soddy urged out his animal. He rode ahead at a flat-footed walk, moonlight or star shine touching faintly, wickedly upon the blue-steel sheen of a naked revolver lying over his saddle swells. This man came on alone, he said nothing, and hat shadow obscured his face until he reined up twenty feet from the partners.

"Drop the guns," this rider ordered in a thin and toneless voice. When he had been obeyed, he urged his mount up closer and leaned from the saddle. "I didn't believe it," he said. "Not even when Miller showed me the bill of sale."

Luther recognized Sheriff Tom Dowling of Lincoln County, wherein lay the village of Lincoln. Buff also recognized the lawman. The three of them had exchanged drinks; they had upon rare occasions played poker together, and had also stopped to speak on the streets of Lincoln.

"I'd have thought you fellers would have had better sense than to bring 'em directly here," said the lawman, his expression mirroring more disappointment than grimness, more disillusionment than resentment.

"What are you talking about?" asked Luther.

Dowling jutted his jaw toward the corral. "Miller's cattle," he said. "That's what I'm talking about."

Buff brushed fingers over Luther's sleeve. Ignoring the sheriff, he said: "Brother, that was as neat a trap as two tomfools ever rode into, and that's a damned fact."

Luther, understanding this to be an implication that Jessie Graham had deliberately brought them to this, swung upon Tom Dowling. "Those cattle belonged to John Graham. We bought them from his daughter this afternoon."

"You got a bill of sale, I suppose," said Dowling, his square-jawed, hard-eyed face withholding judgment pending Luther's reply to this.

"Naw," spoke up Buff in deep disgust. "We got no bill of sale. We made a verbal agreement with Jessie Graham is all. She took us over there, showed us the critters, and helped us drive 'em back here."

"Is that so," said Dowling, his expression settling into bitterness and disbelief. "Then where is she now? You fellers come in here alone. I know . . . because me and my posse watched you corral them critters."

"She cut off to head for the Buell place," said Luther, who then added: "How come you to be waiting here for us?"

"Miller sent a rider into town. He was with some of his boys and saw you two slip up, cut out those critters, and start driving them south."

Luther turned this over briefly in his mind, then he exclaimed: "Now I understand why you said you thought we had more sense than to bring 'em here! Well, dammit all, Sheriff, we *do* have more sense than that. If we'd rustled those critters, you could've sat here all night . . . believe me, you'd never have seen us show up here."

Sheriff Tom Dowling eased back in the saddle. He holstered his handgun and stretched his full six-foot length without speaking. His regard of the two men on foot before him was unwavering. Finally he began to wag his head. "I don't know what this is all about," he said, "an' I can't say as how I really care very much. Miller's sworn out a warrant against you. I got it here in my pocket."

Buff started to speak. Sheriff Dowling held up a broad hand. "It's a long way back to town," he said. "Neither me nor the boys I brought along have had any supper. We're a mite short-tempered because of that, so don't start bellerin' Miller's a big cowman and you two're just victimized squatters. We've all heard this so much lately we're plumb sick to death of it." Dowling motioned with his upraised hand. "Now just walk over there easy-like, get aboard those two horses, and let's all go back to town nice and peaceful like." He dropped the hand, let it rest significantly upon his gracefully curving pistol butt, and continued to stare downward. Finally, almost wearily, he inclined his head. "Now!" he said. "Not tomorrow. Get moving!"

Buff led the way, and Luther followed. They stepped across their animals as the posse men came forward at a signal from Sheriff Dowling, forming up silently around their prisoners. Because many of the riders knew Luther and Buff, there was little said, and generally the posse men avoided meeting the glances of their captives.

A mile onward with only the hoof falls around them of mounted men to break the hush, Buff looked over at Luther. "It just happened too pat," he said. "Miller was out there somewhere watching. He deliberately let us drive those critters away." Buff looked glum. "He even had it timed so that he could send to town, have a posse made up, and out here waitin' for us when we got home."

Luther said nothing; he knew what Buff was implying because his partner had already said it aloud once—that Jessie had made it possible for Colton Miller to frame them.

"Well?" Buff demanded.

"Well, what?" replied Luther testily.

"You know cussed well what I'm gettin' at."

"I know you're makin' a mighty big jump at a far-fetched notion," growled Luther. "You always were handy at pre-judging folks, Buff. Give her a chance, will you?"

"Yeah," muttered Buff. "The same kind of a chance she gave us."

Neither of them spoke again until the posse was plodding wearily into Lincoln's dark roadway. People stopped along the plank walks to look, to point at the dark shadows of prisoners, and to speak quickly, questioningly among themselves.

Sheriff Dowling drew down at the hitch rail before his office; he did not immediately dismount, but bent a baleful look at his prisoners, then sighed loudly. He might have spoken but Buff, stung by the sigh and the dour look, said grumpily: "Go to hell."

They were taken inside and locked together in a strap-steel cage that sat against the back wall of the office, aligned with two additional ready-made cages of identical structure. Sheriff Dowling dismissed the posse men, closed the office door, flung down his hat, and dropped into a chair.

"Hey," complained Luther, "I'm hungry."

"So am I," said Dowling, still staring at them through the bars. "What's more, I'm tired." Dowling drummed upon his desk with one hand. Finally he said: "I sent for Graham's daughter . . . if that's any consolation to you."

Buff cocked his head. "Real thoughtful of you," he said sarcastically. "And what about Miller?"

"What about him?"

"Isn't he coming, too?"

"Why should he?" asked Dowling. "He swore out the warrant. I served it. Now you two get arraigned before Judge Spicer in the morning and that's all there is to it."

Luther was studying the sheriff's expression. He had a sinking feeling, for Dowling's pronouncement had had a strong sound of finality to it.

"What do you mean . . . that's all there is to it?"

"You ever been jailed before?" asked the lawman.

"No."

"Well, first you're arrested. Second, you're arraigned. Third, the judge weighs the evidence, and fourth, he sentences you."

Luther found a stool and dropped down upon it. He kept his gaze upon Dowling's iron-jawed face. "Just like that?" he asked ultimately.

Dowling got up and stretched, then he said—"Just like that."—the finality more noticeable than ever. "I'll go get us some supper."

Luther said nothing until Dowling departed, closing and carefully locking the front door behind him. Then he faced Buff, saying: "I didn't think, on the way in here, it was this serious."

"Didn't you now," grumbled his angry partner.

"Buff, we got to get out of here. This is too well thought out to risk the trial in the morning."

Buff thumbed back his hat and turned to make a cigarette. He said nothing until the smoke was curling up and around his hat brim, then he fixed Luther with a sardonic gaze. "Got any ideas about that?" he asked, nodding toward the wide straps of hammered steel that surrounded them.

Luther did not reply. He got up, paced the width of their cage, then returned to the stool. Buff watched him from one of the two bunks in the cell, his cool gaze missing no change in his partner's face. "It finally soaked in, didn't it?" he said to Luther, then sat up, punched out his cigarette, and swung his feet to the floor.

"Miller has a bill of sale for evidence. Miller and half his crew probably saw us drive the critters off. Sheriff Tom and his posse saw us bring the critters to the ranch and corral 'em. That's all evidence against us." Buff squinted at Luther. "What kind of evidence have *we* got?"

"Jessie's word."

Buff rolled his head despairingly. "Why don't you get some sense?" he said.

Luther raised his head for Buff to see in his face an expression he had only once or twice before seen since they had teamed up as partners: cold and calculating fury.

"I said leave her out of it, Buff."

"All right. All right."

"I promise you one thing," Luther said next. "Trial or no trial, Jessie Graham or no Jessie Graham . . . Colton Miller is going to wish he'd never engineered this."

"That," said Buff stoutly, "is the kind of talk I've been waiting to hear from you . . . pardner."

V

Tom Dowling returned with two trays. After pushing them beneath the strap-steel door, he took down the lantern to trim a smoking wick, and said casually: "Graham's daughter and old Chester Buell just drove in. There's another girl with 'em . . . don't know her, though." He finished with the wick, examined it critically, then lowered the lamp mantle and re-hung the light from its overhead hanger. In the same conversational voice he said: "That's pretty fair stew, isn't it?"

Buff looked up from his plate. "If you like mutton," he said.

Dowling crossed to the cell and leaned there. "I thought all clodhoppers liked sheep meat."

"You sure got a big mouth," growled Buff.

Dowling smiled. He watched the partners eat for a while, then he said: "That sure smelled like a put-up job to me . . . waitin' until you boys were movin' those cattle before swearing out a warrant for you."

Luther's head came up slowly. He regarded Dowling quizzically. "Then why did you go along with it?"

"That's my job. I get warrants to serve and I serve 'em." Dowling shifted his stance. "I'm only a sheriff. Sheriff's got no business judging things. That's Lem Spicer's department."

"You could put in a word for us, though, couldn't you?"

Dowling shrugged. "Sure, I could say I've known you a year or so, that you two are law-abiding, that you don't make trouble or get too drunk in town." Another shrug. "What good would that do? All Miller'd have to say is that he can prove you're rustlers. Judge Spicer has to make his decision on the known facts."

Buff now put his tray aside, began to make a cigarette, and, as his fingers worked, he studied Tom Dowling's face. "How many times you got to get hit in the head with a hammer before you yell *ouch?*"

"What does that mean?"

Buff smoked a moment before saying: "Miller's burned out several homesteaders. His men have been identified stampeding Miller cattle through homesteaders' fields and crops. There have been killings, too, like this John Graham. Does everyone in this damned country have to be buried, Tom, before you go after the right man?"

Dowling's expression altered from relaxed affability to harassed annoyance. "Listen, Brady," he said sharply, "everything around here gets blamed on Miller by you clodhoppers. What you people don't blame on him, he blames on you. I just told you . . . the law deals in facts. Not hearsay or wild accusations . . . facts. No one can prove Miller or his boys have done any of the things you accuse him of."

Buff nodded. "That's what I mean. The facts are there . . . if you're not too busy to see them. Or maybe it's not a case of being busy . . . maybe it's a case of being paid to look the other way."

Dowling's rugged countenance turned darkly red; his eyes sparkled with fire points of wrath. "Good thing these here steel straps are between us," he told Buff.

Brady smiled enigmatically. "Maybe it is at that," he said. "Seems like I stung you where it hurts, Tom."

"Save that smile for Judge Spicer," said Dowling, beginning to turn away. "I got a feeling

51

you're going to be needing it on your way to prison tomorrow."

Dowling had completed his turn when the office door opened and Jessie Graham came through, followed by iron-eyed Chester Buell, and a girl with hair the color of spun gold. The three of them stopped uncertainly, watching Sheriff Dowling.

Said Buell: "We'd like to see your prisoners."

Dowling, his eyes unblinkingly upon the blonde girl, made a careless wave with one hand. "Help yourself." He stepped aside as the three of them swept forward, stopped against the cell, and finally, with a visible effort, yanked his stare away from the girl and crossed to his desk to sink down there and begin shuffling through an untidy heap of papers.

"This is Evelyn Wyant," said Jessie, introducing the lovely blonde girl.

Buff and Luther stared. The Wyant girl was something out of an artist's imagination. She was slightly shorter than Jessie, and her coloring was quite different, also. She had violet eyes and a full mouth whose center slightly protruded. Her skin, normally cream-textured, was faintly reddening now under the dual stare of Buff and Luther. She smiled uneasily and nodded.

Jessie, her smoky stare warming in the face of Luther's obvious admiration for Evelyn Wyant, said with enough edge to her voice to jar Luther's attention away from Evelyn: "I brought you a bill of sale for the cattle."

Luther and Buff arose to cross the cell and stop against the bars. Luther held out his hand without speaking. Jessie handed through a folded bit of paper. Buff took it from Luther and began reading it. He said: "Hey, Tom, here's evidence that we didn't steal those critters."

Dowling came up, took the offered paper, and also read it. He sighed, gazed at Jessie, and said: "Colton Miller's got one just like it, ma'am, and it's signed by your pa."

"That can't be!" exclaimed Jessie. "It's got to be a forgery. My father wouldn't have sold those cattle. We scrimped too hard and too long to get them."

Dowling handed the paper back through the bars to Luther, who began reading it. He said to Jessie: "Ma'am; I'm only the sheriff. Judge Spicer'll have to decide who has the legal bill of sale."

Dowling shot a sideways look at Evelyn Wyant and returned to his desk, turned his back upon them all, and resumed working with the papers he had left off in order to examine the bill of sale.

Chester Buell spoke now for the first time, his voice rough-sounding: "I sent Charley to pass the word around you fellers are being persecuted. Half the homesteaders in Lincoln County'll be at your hearing tomorrow."

Buell's militant words brought Dowling around

in his chair. He considered the bearded settler for a time, as though he meant to speak, but in the end he simply wagged his head and went back to work.

Buell's fierce stare lingered on the prisoners. He cleared his throat; he glanced at the girls, and away again. They both watched him, saying nothing but clearly awaiting his next words. Luther and Buff, seeing this interplay, wondered.

"You got something else to tell us?" asked Luther of Chester Buell.

"Yes. But I don't like having to do it, boys."

"That's all right," said Luther. "It can't make the fix we're in any worse."

Jessie looked Luther fully in the face. "Yes, it can," she said, and then faced Buell. "You said you'd do it."

Buell's flinty glare touched briefly upon Sheriff Dowling's broad back before it swung to Buff and Luther and remained there. "Your soddy has been dynamited," he said in a strained voice. "There's nothing left but a hole in the ground where it used to be. Your corrals have been torn down, too." Into the great silence that came now to fill Tom Dowling's office, Buell added roughly: "I'm sorry, boys."

Tom Dowling's chair squeaked as the sheriff slowly turned toward the cell to stare at Chester Buell. That was the only sound in the room. "Were you over there, Buell? Did you see that this happened for a fact?"

"I saw it, Sheriff, and I saw the shod horse tracks of riders, too."

"But you saw no riders."

"No. We heard the blast clear over to our place. That's what made us go over to see what caused it."

Sheriff Dowling gazed past where Luther and Buff were standing stone-like, gazing at the bearded homesteader. Luther's unmoving eyes darkened even as Dowling watched, but otherwise his face remained smoothly blank. Buff's lips were tightly locked, his jaw muscles bulged, and his normally ruddy complexion paled. After a time he went back to the bunk behind him, sat down upon the edge of it, and began automatically to make a cigarette. When he had it going, he fixed his stare upon Chester Buell.

"Look like quite a bunch of riders, did it?" he asked with deceptive mildness.

"Yes," answered the homesteader. "Charley, who reads signs better'n I do, said it looked like maybe ten cowboys to him."

"Wait a minute," protested Dowling, arising and moving forward. "Ten men maybe," he said sharply to Buell. "But not necessarily ten *cowboys*."

Buell, his eyes angry and his bearded jaw out-thrust, stood there, wide-legged, thick and adamant, in appearance strongly reminiscent of some ancient, Biblical patriarch. "I said cowboys," he told Sheriff Dowling, "and that's what I meant."

"You got any proof?" demanded the lawman.

"Plenty of it. And it'll still be out there if you're a mind to go look, Sheriff. Ten sets of boot tracks. High-heeled boot-tracks, Sheriff. No homesteader ever worked his ground in high-heeled boots, only professional range men wear that kind of footgear."

Dowling stood, frowningly silent. He said nothing. After a time he returned to his desk, scooped up his hat, crushed it on, and faced around again.

"Visitin' time is over," he growled. "I got work to do. You folks'll have to clear out now."

"Where are you going?" asked Luther.

"Out to look at those tracks . . . if it's any of your damned business." Dowling made a gesture. "Buell, you 'n' the girls'll have to go now."

Chester Buell nodded. Luther thought he detected a growing paleness in the old home-steader's face as he moved closer, saying to Jessie and Evelyn: "All right. Tell them good bye, girls."

Without warning, Jessie put both arms through the cage, caught Luther by the upper arms, and drew him to her. She found his mouth with her lips and pressed a kiss against him. He was too stunned to kiss her back, or even to raise his arms.

Beside him, Buff had also been caught in the same way by Evelyn Wyant, drawn up close, and kissed squarely upon his mouth. Buff was too startled to do more than reach out and steady himself.

From behind old Chester Buell, Sheriff Dowling's eyes sprang wide. He could not see through Buell and therefore had no way of knowing that both Jessie and her childhood girlfriend from Ohio had each lowered one hand, brought forth from their clothing loaded pistols, reached around, and pushed these weapons into the rear waistband of Buff's and Luther's trousers before breaking away to turn toward him, their faces scarlet. Dowling, too, felt himself coloring; it was very unlady-like for girls to kiss men in public. The sheriff groped behind him for the latch, lifted it, swung the door partially open, and with averted glance said: "All right, you can see them tomorrow at the trial."

Chester Buell walked woodenly past Dowling looking neither right nor left. His paleness was now very pronounced. Behind him the girls left Dowling's office without a backward glance or another word.

The sheriff stood in the doorway, gazing steadily outward. His thoughts were troubled, and they were mixed. He sighed. "There ought to be a law," he began, then broke off to turn and gaze toward the cell. "The Lord sure must love you clodhoppers," he said. "He sure gave you folks the prettiest women He ever made."

"You a bachelor?" asked Luther very mildly.

"Yeah. But I got more'n a lousy hole in the ground to offer a girl as pretty as either of those two. I got a steady-payin' job, too." Dowling shook his head dolefully. "They didn't even see me."

"I didn't ask if you were a bachelor because I figured you were wife hunting, Tom. I asked it because I wouldn't want your wife to worry when you didn't show up for breakfast in the morning."

Luther brought forth the loaded six-gun from behind him. He cocked it.

Buff, off slightly to one side, also trained his weapon upon the sheriff's middle. When he cocked it, a small but very ominous sound *clicked* in the hush.

"Come on back into the room," said Luther, "and bar the door behind you."

Sheriff Dowling looked fixedly at the guns. He moved into the room, closed and barred the door without looking around, then his face turned gradually very red and he began to swear with eloquence and feeling.

"Drop your gun belt."

Dowling obeyed, his fluent profanity dropping into the room's atmosphere like steel balls striking glass.

When he at last straightened up, he said: "Now, listen. You'll be outlawed for this. Don't be a brace of tomfools. Miller'll have every reason under the sun to hunt you down and kill you. Don't give him that right."

"Come over here and unlock this cell," said Luther, ignoring Dowling's plea completely.

The sheriff caught up some keys from his desk and moved to obey. As he bent forward, he exclaimed: "I never would've believed it of 'em, being so pretty and all! Consarn it, anyway." He straightened up, flinging the cell door wide and moving back. "Boys, if you walk out of here, you're as good as dead. I'm warning you now."

Buff pushed his six-gun inside his waistband and stopped less than three feet from the sheriff. His testy stare was clearly war-like. "I'll say it again, Sheriff. I think you're being paid to Shanghai squatters. I think you're a lousy sheriff. An' I also think you won't even make an effort to help a squatter." He reached up to tap the larger man's chest with a rigid finger. "Since you won't enforce law and order, me and Lute will." Buff's finger went higher; it wagged in Dowling's face. "All right, we've been forced into outlawry. Well, get ready to do a heap of riding, Tom, because up until today you didn't know what real trouble was." He dropped his hand, and stepped back. "One more thing. Did you see those girls hand us any guns?"

"See them? I. . . ."

"Just the facts, Tom," said Luther quickly. "You know how it is. The law only deals in facts."

Dowling scowled. "No, I didn't see 'em give you them damned guns."

"Good. Remember that. If you make any trouble for old Chester or either of those girls. . . ."

"You'll do what?" snarled Dowling, glaring at Luther.

"I'll kill you," answered Luther, his voice quiet, almost soothing in its lack of inflection.

Dowling drew up a little. He studied Luther a moment, then he said: "I believe you would, at that."

Buff pushed the sheriff forward. "Into that cell."

They locked him in and left. Nighttime was their ally. They rode out of Lincoln without arousing even a ripple of interest; they appeared to be simply two range men heading home after a night at the bars.

VI

It was with the small hours of dark morning that they came across the prairie to the site of their soddy and corrals. There, in a great pall of silence and ruin, they found everything exactly as Chester Buell had said it was.

Gazing upon the wreckage of their soddy, Luther said from the saddle: "It must have taken a heap of dynamite to do that much damage."

Buff, alternating between looking grimly at their shattered corrals and the great hole that had once been their home, agreed. But he added something to it, too. "The thorn is still in Miller's hide, though. We still own the land, and that's really what he wants."

Luther crossed his hands on the saddle horn. "Be kind of hard keeping him from grazing it, though," he opined dryly, "when we're on the dodge."

"Nope," contradicted Buff. "That's where you're wrong, pardner. Me, I've been through this before. Let me tell you something, bein' outlawed has it compensations."

"Such as?"

"For one thing, we don't have to worry about staying within the law. Miller does. For another thing, when a man's home and office is in his hat, he isn't bound to return to anything. He has no ties. He can move in the dark like an Indian." Buff shortened his reins, cocked an eye at the sinking moon, and said: "Come on, I'll show you what I mean."

They rode west with predawn coolness coming into the night around them. They dropped south around the Buell place, still westering, and Buff looped his reins, letting his horse pick its own gait.

"She's the prettiest thing I ever saw," he said suddenly with reference to nothing they had been discussing. "And she kissed me." He squinted over at Luther. "I liked to fainted when she reached through those bars, Lute."

"Yeah."

"Her hair smelled like new-mown hay. Did you see how it shone?"

"Like red copper," murmured Luther.

"Red copper, hell, like gold. Like pure gold."

Buff roused himself to throw a look at his partner. Luther was easing along loosely in the saddle. Buff cleared his mind of these soft and pleasurable thoughts to say: "And he's got the critters, too."

Luther's brows climbed upward. "Huh?" he asked.

"Miller, he's got our cows."

"You sure jump from one thing to another."

Buff grimaced. "Whatever I say from here on, you can figure it's about one thing or another. Evelyn or Colton Miller. Got no room upstairs for anything else at present."

They passed along under the cobalt heavens until the land began dimly to form into frozen undulations. They passed the Graham homestead and rode onto Miller's deeded land. With a vague paleness forming off in the east they came across dozing bunches of cattle. The light was too poor to make out brands, but this did not bother Buff Brady at all. He eased around behind a large slumbering herd, roused it with little effort, then flagged northward with his arm. Luther moved out to push the cattle along, not certain what Buff had in mind, but an inkling of the idea.

They were still herding along Colton Miller's beef when dawn came, sending its brilliance against them and also against the nearing swells and knobs that prefaced higher country farther north. They stopped twice, once at a water hole to let the cattle tank up, and again, shortly before high noon, when standing mountains loomed darkly ahead. They had covered, according to Luther's estimate, seven miles.

After pushing the cattle high among the tree-shaded parks where stirrup-high grass stood greenly inviting, they retraced their way back to the lower country and there made a camp.

Buff was tired but satisfied. He had deliberately chosen the flinty trails and talus pathways. He smiled now as he lay smoking in the shade, watching their off-saddled horses grazing. "Even after they find them," he told Luther, speaking of the cattle, "they'll have one helluva time driving them back. One thing about cow critters, you can do just about anything with them, except drive them over stony country when they're tender-footed."

Luther snared a fat sage hen. They cooked her over a black-oak fire that sent forth no smoke. They bathed and drank at a brawling creek, and they slept away the afternoon. At dusk they were astride again, and this time Luther led out.

He had in mind something quite different from harassing Colton Miller. He meant to give him a fright Miller would not soon forget. When they were crossing the plain again with dying daylight fading out into long shadows, Buff said a trifle uneasily: "There's only two of us, remember. Miller's got at least ten men in his crew and this is all open country down here . . . in case you don't know it, Lute, you're headin' straight for his headquarters ranch."

Luther smiled. "Did I make a lot of tomfool talk last night when you were ramrodding things?"

Buff sank into silence. He remained that way as long as he could, but when they came at last within sight of Miller's lamplit buildings, he growled: "You're takin' chances, Lute. They got fresh horses down there. We been ridin' these same animals pretty hard lately."

"They'll get a little rest now," said Luther, reining to a halt and swinging out and down. "Fetch along your carbine, Buff."

Brady mumbled under his breath but he obeyed. They passed through deepening dusk, making a wide circle and stopping finally near a corral full of saddle horses.

"Open the gate," said Luther, "then stand there so the critters don't run out until I come back."

"Where are you going?"

"Miller's pretty handy with the torch. I'm going

to see how well he likes it when he gets burned out a little."

Buff licked his lips. There came softly down the night the sound of a rider singing somewhere among the lighted buildings to the music of a guitar.

"You'll likely get us killed," he grumbled.

Luther checked his carbine. He looked fully at Buff. "I'm sort of getting the hang of this outlaw business," he said. "I think I'm going to like it."

"If you live long enough. Listen, at the first lick of flame they'll come boilin' out of that bunkhouse like a stirred-up nest of hornets."

Luther said: "I sure hope so. Be awful ridin' this far for nothing." He moved off.

Buff eased the corral gate open and stood there blocking the gap he had made. He lost sight of Luther almost at once, and, as moments passed, uneasiness came to plague him. It was one thing to push Miller's cattle into the mountains; it was something altogether different to come down into Miller's very yard and. . . . A moving shadow scattered his thoughts. Buff dropped down to try and skyline the oncoming silhouette. It was not Luther, he was sure of that; the man was too broad and short. A cigarette's red glow marked this stranger's approach. Faintly, too, came the tinkle of spur rowels. Buff very carefully put his carbine aside in the dust, drew forth his handgun, and waited.

The rider was humming softly. He had no notion of anything at all until Buff rose up nearly under his feet and cocked the gun he held. The cowboy's breath went out in a long whoosh; he stopped dead still, staring.

"Turn around," ordered Buff.

"Wait a minute," said the rider swiftly, "I got no fight with you fellers."

"What fellers?" demanded Buff. "You don't see but one man, do you?"

"No, but I know who you are."

"Who?"

"One of them two squatters who stoled Miller's beef." The cowboy was quite young; Buff could make that out even in the darkness. His voice was rising, too, in fear and anticipation. "Listen, mister, I had no hand in the dynamitin'. Honest, I wasn't even. . . ."

"Turn around."

"Mister . . . listen a minute. You can't just up an' shoot a man in the back for nothing."

"I'm not going to dry-gulch you. Now, damn it, turn around."

The cowboy obeyed, but his feet dragged and his shoulders twitched.

Buff's handgun arched overhead. It struck the rider across the head, hard. He sagged forward making a very slight rustling sound as he went forward into the dust.

Buff dragged him clear of the gate. He was

breathing hard from the effort and did not immediately see the abrupt leap of flame, then, straightening around and upward again, he heard the quick, light slam of running feet and Luther came up.

Luther stopped, peering downward. "Who's that?" he demanded.

Buff, sighting the flames, holstered his six-gun, scooped up his carbine, and started sprinting for their horses. Over his shoulder he said: "How should I know? Some darned fool who had to come nosin' around the corral." He might have said more, but at that moment the corralled horses discovered Buff no longer barred their way out of the closure. Their high squeals and hammering hoofs reverberated through the night. A moment later someone back at Miller's bunkhouse let off a loud cry of alarm.

Buff clawed up into his saddle, wheeled away, and led out in a belly-down run. Luther was only seconds behind him.

They rushed swiftly over the plain until in the diminishing distance a fire's red glow seemed no more than a faint brightness low upon the horizon. They did not rein up until Luther called forward. After that they jogged, letting their animals catch a second wind.

Luther said: "That ought to hold the old devil for a while." He was referring to Colton Miller.

Buff agreed, adding simply that it was one thing to start a war, but quite another thing not to be overwhelmed by an irate foe. "Five to one odds aren't exactly my idea of a gambler's dream," he said tartly.

Luther's spirits would not be dampened. "I figure the secret of success in this fight is to keep Miller off balance. Keep him busy guessin' where we're going to hit him next."

"On the defensive," said Buff succinctly. "Agreed." He bent a thoughtful look on his partner, partially smiling. "You'd have made a pretty good outlaw, Lute."

They passed from Miller's range over the land of Jessie Graham and beyond that to the worked-up earth of Chester Buell. Here, Luther studied the moon, then said: "Now'd be as good a time as any to find out who our friends really are, I reckon. Let's go roust up old Chester and see about getting some breakfast."

Buff, too, gauged the descending moon. "Kind of early for breakfast, isn't it?" he queried. Then, remembering something suddenly, he straightened in the saddle, adjusted his hat, squared his shoulders, and said: "On second thought I am sort of hungry."

He was thinking again of Evelyn Wyant and her kiss.

They came upon the Buell buildings from the south, sat for a time in darkness, studying the stillness, the square, low outlines, and the great depth of hush.

"Wouldn't surprise me," said Buff, "if Sheriff Tom had a man hidden around here somewhere."

"Maybe four or five men," said Luther, urging his horse ahead.

"Where you going?" said Buff. " 'Pears to me if you feel that way you'd be a mite prudent."

Luther shrugged. "I'm hungry," he replied simply. "Besides, I've got an idea."

Buff kneed out his horse, saying with a groan: "Not another one. You're goin' to get us killed yet."

VII

They left their animals saddled, but with loosened *cinchas* and with bridles hanging from saddle horns in Buell's barn. It had taken only moments to fork two mangers full of red-top hay. They then went forward in true outlaw-fashion, carbines cradled, eyes sharply watchful in the night's soft gloom, to make a large circling study of each foot of ground around the soddy, and out beyond it as far as a sentry for Sheriff Dowling might be waiting. They found nothing, smelled no tobacco, skylined no drowsing, saddled horse, or cut any sign of another human being.

As they approached the darkened house, Buff

brushed fingers lightly across Luther's sleeve. Under his breath he warned of Buell's ancient watchdog. They spent more time scouting up the dog's bed, found him blissfully sleeping there, and went noiselessly far around to the soddy's front entrance. There, Buff rapped sharply with his gun butt.

He rapped again, louder his second time.

The door opened a little, a shotgun barrel came out to stop inches from Buff's middle. Buell's voice, hoarse from sleep, demanded to know who was out there. Buff identified himself. The shotgun was withdrawn, the door swung wider, and both escapees passed inside.

Chester Buell had a robe about his nightdress. He also had his flat-heeled homesteader's boots on, and his hair stood awry and disheveled. He put aside the shotgun wordlessly, groped for a table lamp, lit it, turned the wick far down so that only a very dim brightness filled the room, then he motioned toward two stools.

"Sit down. I'll fetch some coffee."

Luther and Buff sat, both maneuvering their stools so they could watch the door. At the stove Chester poked in the fire box, muttered to himself as he pushed in some cow chips, then spoke louder.

"Dowling was by this morning with a posse. He was madder than a wet hen, too."

"What'd he say about the guns?"

Buell turned long enough to bend a quizzical look upon his youthful visitors. "Very little. I got the impression he didn't want to discuss that."

Buff winked at Luther but both of them turned blank expressions to Chester Buell. The older man completed his work at the stove and padded forward with two cups of black coffee. "You're hungry, too, I take it," he said, and without awaiting an answer rummaged in a floor-to-ceiling cooler cupboard, brought forth a great haunch of cold roast antelope meat, and set it upon the table.

"Eat up," he said, pushing knives forward. "Then take what's left in your saddlebags. I don't think you're going to get too many chances to come visitin' after this."

They ate, noisily and without speaking, until their hunger was cared for, then Luther sipped his coffee, watching Buell and obviously considering some private thought. After a time he said: "Miller been around?"

"Yes, he was here, too. Someone rustled a big bunch of his critters. But his men didn't discover it until too late in the day to do anything about it." Buell grimaced. "He said he thought I did it."

Buff looked. "You . . . ?"

Buell nodded, but it was Luther who spoke next, wagging his head: "Miller doesn't think any such a thing."

Buell regarded him from his bearded, dour face.

71

With heavy sarcasm he said: "I sure got the impression he thought that, Luther."

"Chester," explained Luther over the rim of his coffee cup, "Miller has got rid of Graham. He thinks he's gotten rid of Buff and me. Except for you that gives him a clean sweep of his former free graze."

Luther said no more. He finished his coffee, set the cup aside, and began making a cigarette. Buell and Buff Brady watched him, then Buff said softly: "Sure, why didn't I think of that?"

"Of what?" said Buell, switching his attention from the taller man to the shorter, darker one.

"It's the land Miller's after. You're all that's left between his deeded land and the old free-graze land. He's engineering another frame-up, Chester, only this time it's going to be you."

"How?"

"Like with us," interjected Luther, smoking now and looking thoughtful. "He'll find the cattle. We didn't drive them too far for him to recover 'em. And when he finds 'em, he's going to produce witnesses that saw you drive them into the mountains." Luther's cigarette went out. He paused to relight it. "Tom Dowling'll come out here with a posse like he did with us. He'll have a warrant for your arrest and he'll herd you off to jail."

When Luther stopped speaking, an ominous silence filled the soddy. Chester Buell reached forward, tilted the pot, and refilled his own coffee cup. He set the pot back down and stared at his cup. His bearded face was screwed down into harshness; his pale eyes burned with a fierce fire.

"I won't go," he said finally, raising his glare to Luther. "Dowling can kill me right here . . . I won't be taken to jail and Shanghaied into prison."

Buell drank off his coffee in two great gulps and leaned upon the table, big, knotty fists clenched. He looked from Luther to Buff and back to Luther again, his eyes defiant, his lips compressed and his shaggy face adamant.

For a time none of them spoke, then, from a far doorway, a husky voice said: "No, it can't come to that. The land isn't worth it."

Jessie Graham moved forward so that soft light fell upon her robed figure, her swept-back red-copper hair and her enormous gray eyes filled now with frank concern.

"Neither the land nor the cattle."

Luther, watching her, was mute. So was Buff. Old Chester, with nothing irrelevant to distract him, shot her only a brief glance, then returned to staring flinty-eyed at the table top.

"It's not the land or the cattle," he rumbled. "It's a man's dignity, his God-given rights, his independence. My folks've been fighting to preserve these things a hundred years now.

Damned if I'll be the first of my line to let those things go by default."

Because Chester, a very devout man, never swore, his grim, although mild curses lent an uncompromising hardness to his words now that seemed to fill the soddy with his determination.

"Maybe," said Luther to the lovely girl, his voice unconsciously softening, "you'd best go back to bed, Jessie."

She swept forward and stopped close by the table where they sat, grim, beard-stubbled men with carbines leaning close at hand, sweat-stained and smelling strongly of horses, their weathered faces showing darkly shadowed in the faint orange lamp glow.

"Give him the cattle, Chester. Give him the land. He's rich and he's powerful." She stopped, drew back a breath, then pushed on. "When my father was murdered . . . I was the only one left behind. Think of Annie and Charley. Think of Sarah. What will happen to them if Miller's gunmen kill you, too?"

Chester Buell's face, as much as they could see of it through whiskers, looked pale and tortured. He sat like stone, saying nothing, his fisted knuckles white with straining.

Luther said: "Maybe she's right, Chester. Maybe you'd better go hitch your wagon up right now, load your family, and head out of the country."

Buell's hot, hard eyes rose to cling unblinkingly

to Luther's face as the younger man continued speaking.

"With Buff and me, it's different. Miller's already ruined us. Besides . . . well . . . we're younger. We got no families."

"No!"

Buff shot Buell an imploring look. "Chester, you don't stand a chance and with us on the dodge we won't be able to help you."

"No!"

The three of them read in Chester Buell's face the blind-stubborn resolve of a man who could not and would not abandon a cherished principle. Buff sighed; he swung his gaze to Luther; he raised up his shoulder points and let them fatalistically fall.

Jessie would have implored Chester again, but Luther silenced her with a gesture. He pushed out his cigarette and leaned both elbows upon the table. His voice, when he spoke now, was crisp; he was no longer pleading; he was planning.

"All right, then I want you to do as I say, Chester. I want you to round up ten homesteaders who own riding boots."

Jessie and Chester looked hard at Luther. Even Buff's eyebrows climbed. "High-heeled boots?" Jessie asked.

"Yes."

She inclined her head. "All right, and what else?"

"You know Miller's range, Chester. Take those

ten men where Miller's cattle are grazing. Split them up into several small bands, have them make a gather, and drive it north into the mountains. Do it at night, though, otherwise you're going to be seen."

Buff's face was clearing, brightening with understanding. "Yeah," he breathed softly, approvingly. "I'm beginning to see what you got in mind, Lute."

"I'm not!" Chester exclaimed bluntly. "Maybe you'd best explain."

"Sure," answered Luther. "Miller's got ten riders. He'll know where they are during daylight, and they'll know where each other is as well. At night this won't be true. He's so busy planning ways to blame squatters for rustling his livestock, Chester, that, when he finds range men's boot tracks, it's going to give him a jolt. He'll think some of his own men are using his private war against squatters to rustle from him."

"But what is the point of this?" asked Jessie.

Luther smiled up at her; he arose, took up his carbine, and said: "I've got a plan, too. It doesn't involve getting squatters blamed. It has to do with keeping Miller off balance until I can work out another idea I've got."

"Such as?" asked Buff, standing now.

Luther removed his neckerchief and methodically began wrapping the cold meat in it. He did not reply, so Buff looked at Chester Buell and

Jessie, shrugged. He followed Luther to the door, touched his hat to Jessie, and passed through into the night.

Luther paused a moment to gaze at Jessie and Chester in the doorway. To the bearded home-steader he said: "Can you do it, get ten men with high-heeled boots I mean?"

"Yes, I think so."

"And have them ready to ride by tomorrow night?"

"I'm sure of it."

Luther nodded at Buell. "Good. Then do it. But be very careful. I don't think Miller'll be watching you, but I've got a feeling Tom Dowling will."

Jessie, seeing the sardonic look in Luther's gaze, exclaimed: "Why won't Miller be watching?"

"We burned him out a little tonight. He'll be busy with other things tomorrow."

Luther turned away with a nod of his head and hastened to catch up with Buff near the barn.

In the doorway Jessie and Chester stood rooted. "Burned Miller out . . . ?" said Buell in a rising, incredulous way. Jessie said nothing. She lingered in the doorway, holding her robe closely about her until two dark silhouettes passed out of the barn and faded beyond sight into the yonder night.

When the faint sound of loping horses diminished to only an occasional *clatter,* Jessie faced around. Chester was tugging at his beard, his brow creased and his eyes narrowed in thought.

"I trust them," she said simply. "I think they can do what no one else has been able to accomplish."

Chester turned inward and closed the door behind them. "Yes," he said to her quietly, "but they are much like Miller himself. Blood is going to be spilled, girl. These men know only one way to fight."

"With guns," said Jessie, gliding around the table to stop and watch old Chester seat himself, stretch forth one hand, and let it lie lightly, gnarled and scarred, in faint lamp glow.

"Yes, girl, with guns."

"You don't approve?"

Chester hung fire over his answer. His eyes dulled and his lips compressed. He was clearly at odds with himself, and, when he eventually spoke, his voice was softly muffled and doubting. "I'm against killing, girl."

"Yes," rejoined Jessie a trifle sharply. "So am I. So was my father. I think normally that Luther and Buff Brady are, too. Chester, what has it gotten us all to be this way?"

Buell nodded listlessly. "I know, Jessie, I know," he murmured, then straightened up in his chair. His big fist drew up, curled and club-like. His voice firmed up. "All right, we'll do it. The Lord knows it's against my beliefs. But He must also know by now that on this frontier a man must fight for what is his." Chester arose; he towered over Jessie. "Amen," he rumbled. "Go to bed, girl. You and Miss Evelyn can help my Sarah around the place tomorrow. I'll be riding out before sunup."

VIII

By steady riding, Luther and Buff were back in the far away foothills by sunup. They located a camp east of where they had left Miller's Durhams and gave their animals a needed rest. They went afoot then, higher along the stone-flanked ridges and waited. Not until late forenoon did they see the dun dust banner of approaching horsemen.

With audible satisfaction Luther said to Buff: "It looks like half his crew."

Buff smiled thinly. "The other half'll be cleaning up that burned-out bunkhouse." His smile broadened. "Colton Miller'll be madder'n a man with two left feet this morning."

There were, indeed, five cowboys in the oncoming party. They slowed to a walk near the foothills, gazing upward. Several of them made arm gestures. They were clearly annoyed and this heightened their watchers' droll amusement.

After a brief halt and palaver, the Miller riders

pushed on, slower now because the land here was rising. The tracks they were following were clear enough.

Luther made a cigarette, lit it, exhaled pleasurably. "We've seen enough," he said to Buff. "Let's go hunt up Tom Dowling now."

Buff stiffened. "What!"

Luther arose, dusted off his trousers, and started down toward their camp. "The sheriff," he said. "Let's go see what he's up to."

Buff got up but did not at once follow along. "Are you figuring on another of your long chances?" he demanded.

"Not exactly, pardner. In fact, Dowling isn't going to see us at all . . . I hope. But he's going to smell something fishy."

"Like what?"

But Luther kept on walking, saying only: "Don't be so chary, Buff. I got it all planned out now."

At their camp he began saddling up. His expression indicated that he was deeply reflective. When he finally settled across the saddle, he turned to watch Buff toe in and spring up.

"I'll make you a little bet," he said. "I'll give odds old Miller's got a reward on both of us by now."

"Yeah," agreed his partner. "And I'll make *you* a bet, too. Miller's gunhands'll be hunting us like we are a couple of calf-killing wolves so they can collect that reward."

"No bet," said Luther. "But you got to hand it to Miller. He's pretty good at engineering things."

"Too good."

Luther turned in the saddle. "I think you're going to find out we're just as good. You wait and see."

"I've got no choice," mumbled Buff. "And if you turn out wrong, pardner . . . rest in peace."

They passed down from the foothills with an immaculate sky as background to a burnished sun, swept northerly over empty prairie until the town of Lincoln was dead ahead on the hot horizon, then slowed to a walk and rode as far as the east-west stage road. There, they halted in the miserly shade of a scrub-oak thicket, got down, and studied the countryside.

"This is kind of close to trouble," said Buff, scowlingly raking the land around about. "We could bump into anybody out here."

"Let's hope the first one along is a clodhopper," said Luther, and later, when a faded old ranch wagon appeared, he said to Buff: "I reckon when a man has had as much bad luck as we've had lately, why things've just got to improve."

Buff considered the oncoming vehicle. "So it's a squatter," he said. "What good's that going to do us?"

Luther did not speak until he'd had a close look at the gaunt and grizzled settler high on the wagon seat. "Doesn't look much like an angel in disguise, does he?" he queried, moving out of the shade so the settler could see him and draw down to an uneasy halt.

"Thinks we're hold-ups or cowmen," muttered Buff. "Watch out for a riot gun. These danged sod-busters are hell for shotguns."

Luther approached the stationary, watchful man in the wagon. He spoke his name and also mentioned Chester Buell. Gradually the settler's rangy frame relaxed; his prominent jaw began masticating again upon a cud of chewing tobacco. "Heard about you fellers," he said, eyeing Buff as he also strolled up. "Busted out of jail and got dynamited by Colton Miller. Reckon by now you wish you'd stayed with the cowmen."

"No," corrected Luther, "we're not sorry we turned settler. But we sort of resent being stomped on."

The rugged older man's faded eyes shone appreciatively at this statement. "Amen," he murmured, gazing steadily from Buff to Luther. "What can I do for you?"

"It depends. Do you know Sheriff Dowling in Lincoln?"

"Yup."

"Know him very well?"

The settler's thoughtful eyes crinkled a little in quiet, pensive irony. "Just come right out an' say it," he replied. "What's on your mind?"

"We want someone to pass word around town so Dowling'll hear it."

"What kind of word?"

"That it isn't squatters who're rustling Miller's beef, that it's Miller's own riders who are doing that."

The settler ceased chewing; he stared a full thirty seconds at Luther without saying a word. Then he expectorated over the side of the wagon and nodded. "All right, I'll do it. I take it you boys got something up your sleeves."

"We have."

"Anything else?"

"Yes. Sort of let it out that the rustlers are driving the cattle into the hills north of Miller's spread where they're trying to make up a good-sized gather before drifting them up into Wyoming to sell them."

The settler put down his lines, rubbed his jaw, and considered. "A feller could get into trouble if any of this was traced back to him," he told Luther, then he shrugged. "Well, reckon I can take the chance . . . seein' as how you boys're takin' even worse chances." He picked up his lines again, flicked them lightly so that his team leaned into their collars. "All right, it'll be done." He nodded as he went on past. "Wish you both luck, an' by the way, tell Chester hullo for me . . . my name's Will Butler. I'm from Ohio, too."

Buff remained silent until the settler's wagon was growing small, then he pushed back his hat and wagged his head. "I see part of your plan," he told Luther. "You figure to get Dowling out into the country lookin' for rustlin' cowboys . . . of which there are none . . . but why do you want him out of town? We das'n't ride into Lincoln. You know that, don't you?"

"I don't particularly want Dowling out of town. It's not that. I want him in the foothills with a posse so when the big trouble comes we'll have the law handy."

"I expect you know you just put Buell's high-heeled clodhoppers in real peril, don't you?"

"Yes, but that's where you and I're going to come in." Luther went back to his horse and got astride. "I figure these settlers'd faint if they knew a bunch of posse men would be out looking for rustlers. I don't think even old Chester would have gone along with us if he'd known the danger. So. . . ."

"So you engineered him into it, anyway."

"I had to."

Buff grunted up and settled across his horse. "All right. What next? You told Chester not to ride out until tonight. Dowling'll be out lookin' for rustlers by noon with his posse. There's a heap of time between now and then."

"Now," said Luther, heading back the way they had come, "we make a short visit to Chester, and after that we head for Miller's range again."

As they loped along, Buff said: "I don't suppose

you'd care to tell me exactly what this is all about, would you?"

"Sure . . . ," said Luther, then broke off to add sharply, his tone flattening with apprehension, "riders ahead, Buff. Two horsemen."

They cut swiftly outward in a westerly way making for a small hump of land. There, they watched the riders swinging ahead, and after a time Buff screwed up his face. "Sure aren't cowboys," he observed. "Ride like . . . Good Lord, Lute, that there is Miss Jessie and Miss Evelyn."

Luther said nothing. He, too, was puzzled. The girls were heading straight for Lincoln. Buff's former suspicion came briefly to bother Luther, then faded out as swiftly as it had appeared. He kneed his horse forward, saying: "Come on, this may be the break we need."

Buff had no inkling what Luther meant by that, but he jumped his mount out and settled into a sweeping run that carried him far enough forward with Luther to block the way of the two girls. They saw two cowboys loom up suddenly cutting them off, and, as though with one hand upon both sets of reins, both girls yanked back. Dust flew from beneath their startled mounts.

Luther went forward at a walk. He touched his hat without smiling, curiosity bright in his stare. "Out kind of early," he said by way of greeting.

Jessie Graham's color slowly returned. "You gave us a scare!" she exclaimed. Then, annoyance darkening her eyes, she demanded: "What are you doing down here by Lincoln . . . jumping out at folks?"

"I was going to ask you the same thing, miss. Lincoln's quite a piece from Buell's place."

"We came down to get Evelyn's things. She left them at the stage station."

Luther smiled. "You're dog-goned pretty when you're scairt," he said strongly admiring the girl.

"I am *not* frightened," Jessie shot irritably back at him. "I was simply a little startled."

Buff eased up closer to Evelyn Wyant. He said nothing at all, simply looked, admired, and smiled. This had an effect upon the blonde girl that was more disconcerting than words might have been; she looked once into Buff's face, colored redly, and did not look directly at him again.

"I want you to tell Chester something for us," said Luther to Jessie. "Tell him, when he rides out tonight, to go *south*. Do you understand that?"

"Certainly, go south. Has something happened to change your plan?"

Luther shook his head. "No, the plan is working so far. Just tell Chester to take his riders south on Miller's range. Everything else remains the same. He's to gather up some Miller cattle and push 'em along as though they're being rustled. Tell him also to have his men dismount now and then in their high-heeled boots."

"How far should he drive Miller's cattle?"

"Five, six miles."

"Then leave them and head home?"

"Yes. But tell him to warn his men not to dismount in their high-heeled boots until they are again in their own yards. Leave no tracks a posse can trace them by."

"All right, Luther."

"And one final thing. After they abandon the cattle, tell Chester to have his riders split up, ride off separately so they can't be traced as a group."

"I understand."

Buff cleared his throat now. "One thing more," he said. "About those guns you brought us. . . ."

"Yes?" said Jessie, looking around at him.

"Well, not the guns exactly, miss. The way you gave them to us was more what I was aimin' at."

Suddenly Evelyn Wyant said: "Come on, Jessie, we've got to get my things and hurry back."

Both girls eased past, broke over into a lope, and pushed rapidly away from Luther and Buff, who sat in the bright sunlight watching them.

"For gosh sakes," protested Buff. "You'd think a rattlesnake buzzed in her lap the way she said that . . . and ran off."

Luther, thinking of something else, said: "Come on, we've got plenty of time now that we won't have to stop by old Chester's place."

They rode at a steady, mile-consuming jog until the abandoned buildings of the Graham homestead came into view. Here, Luther halted long enough to water his horse, wait for Buff to do so as well, then he led out for the heat-hazed distances between the Graham place and those friendly far foothills. He rode slowly now, broodingly, and did not speak until Buff called his attention to fresh tracks of driven cattle.

"They got 'em back," he said simply, and shrugged. "They served their purpose, although when we ran them off, we didn't know how much they'd help us."

"How did you happen to think of it?" asked Buff.

"When I dismounted at that first camp we made, and saw our boot tracks, I got the idea of tryin' to make Miller think his own men were rustling from him."

"And . . . do you figure that squatter with the wagon will spread the word so the sheriff hears it?"

"I'm confident he will." Luther yawned. "I'm also confident of two other things. One, the sheriff'll come a-helling out here to catch rustlers. Two, he'll send word to Colton Miller what he's doing and why he's doing it."

Buff chuckled. "I'd like to see Miller's face when he first hears the law thinks his own riders and not us squatters are stealing from him."

IX

"This," said Luther, allowing his tired body to soften against the earth with the sun standing directly overhead, "is about the wearyingest job I've ever taken on." He closed his eyes. "Let me know if you see riders."

They were close enough to the foothills again, but well east of their former camp to go undetected except by determined searchers, and Luther expected no such riders until mid-afternoon at the earliest.

Behind them their horses grazed in the heavy stand of foothill forage grass that luxuriated this far from Miller's normal grazing grounds. The heat here was pine-scented but nearly motionless, breathless, because of the nearby mountains. Ahead, farther than human eyes could see, lay nothing but flat to rolling prairie, still green with the richness of spring, but beginning to fade out a little here and there, where hardpan lay inches below the soil-surface, making a pastel shading found nowhere except on the endless plains.

Buff, his back braced against a shaggy old bull pine, struggled valiantly to remain awake. In the end he lost the battle and dozed fitfully, opening his eyes from time to time for a squinted look around. In those waking moments he reflected upon Evelyn Wyant's attitude when they had met earlier. This being something less than encouraging, Buff squirmed, he scowled, and finally, tortured into full wakefulness, he roused Luther by saying: "I reckon I don't look real presentable, do I?"

Luther, peering from swollen eyes, did not understand the implication at all.

"I'm talkin' about the way she run off," explained Buff.

Gradual understanding came to Luther's face, then exasperation came, too. "For gosh sakes," he groaned, "if you got to worry about Miss Evelyn, can't you do it without talking?"

Buff bent a dark look downward. "If it wasn't for your danged planning, I'd be able to clean up an' shave. She'd. . . ."

"*I* didn't get us arrested," said Luther swiftly, half rising up. "*I* didn't dynamite our soddy or tear down our corrals. If you got to blame somebody for makin' you look uglier than usual . . . blame Miller."

Buff's dark look did not lessen, but he inclined his head at this. "Miller," he muttered. "Yeah, you're right. And that makes another score I got to settle with him."

Luther turned up on one side, pulled his hat so that it covered his one exposed ear, and growled: "Can't you think without talking?"

Buff's mouth snapped closed. He was wide

awake now and irritable. He settled lower against the old pine tree and turned to blocking in squares of country, searching each square minutely for some sign of movement. There was, for the time being, nothing but shimmering heat waves to see. He made a cigarette, smoked it nearly down, still gazing outward, then froze hard with his stare upon the easterly flow of land.

"Luther!"

His pardner came awake in response to some half-heard urgency in Buff's tone. He sat up rubbing his eyes.

Buff said: "Coming in from the direction of town yonder. Looks like maybe a dozen riders."

Luther got up, squinted outward in the indicated direction, then turned toward their grazing animals. "Time to go," he said.

"Yeah," agreed Buff, also getting to his feet. "Up into the hills where they can't find us."

"No," explained Luther, moving toward their beasts. "Out toward the Miller place."

Buff considered his partner's retreating back a moment, then scooped up his own bridle and trailed along. To himself he said aloud: "No sense in asking." He caught his animal, led it back to where the blanket and saddle lay, and went to work rigging up. Over the saddle seat he kept a baleful watch on the distant riders coming steadily onward, but angling northerly now, as though they meant to strike the mountains. Luther spoke from behind him.

"They aim to get up into the hills and maybe lay an ambush." Luther smiled mirthlessly. Buff did not see this but he heard the words that went with it as he turned his horse once, then sprang up. "Dowling's being real clever. Figures to make sure he's got part of his men in position in front, while he leads the rest of 'em out on Miller's range to intercept the rustlers and trail 'em up where his ambushers can get in their licks at them."

"Somehow," said Buff sardonically as they struck out westerly, keeping well beyond the sight of the posse men, "I just can't get too concerned about what that sheriff's up to. What I'd like to know right now is what *you're* up to."

"That's easy," answered Luther airily. "We're going down where those gun hawks of Miller's will see us."

"What?"

"Sure. How else we going to get them to chase us?"

"What the hell do they have to chase us for?"

Luther studied the sinking sun while he answered. "Two reasons. For one thing, we want 'em to concentrate on us so they won't stumble onto Chester's clodhoppers. The other reason is because, in the dark, all they'll know is that somewhere ahead of them are riders who don't act like squatters at all."

"They'll find that out easy enough," said Buff stoutly. "No clodhopper ever rode like a cowboy . . . when he's scairt."

"Right," said Luther, slowing to look behind them. "So, when they don't catch us in the dark and go back to report, they'll tell Miller it could've been cowboys they were after."

"And Miller'll think of us right off?"

Luther shrugged. "Maybe. He probably will. But he'll also wonder if maybe the word Tom Dowling sent him wasn't true . . . and that, instead of us, his gun hands could have stumbled onto some of his own men out rustling."

"All he's got to do is count heads," said Buff.

"He won't have the time for that."

"And why not?"

Luther yawned again. "You'll see. I'm getting dry from all this palavering." He turned another long gaze toward the rear, then led out southward away from all foothill protection.

Luther's move was a bold maneuver. Dowling's riders could easily make out two horsemen loping southward out on the prairie. But even Buff, with his misgivings, silently conceded that the sheriff would think they were a pair of Miller riders heading for the home ranch. Still, he shook his head, never, not even in his earlier outlaw years, had he taken the chances he was now. So far everything had worked out well enough, but that didn't mean too much, either, for every man had just so much luck to use up in his lifetime, Buff was convinced, and no matter how charmed his life had been up to the time when the last of that luck was used up, nothing could save him, neither boldness nor shrewd planning, when his number came up.

He rode along studying Luther from the edge of his vision. It was too early yet to tell whether his partner possessed more shrewdness than their enemies possessed; it was also too early to assess their chances of success. One thing, however, continued strongly in Buff Brady's thoughts—he had shared experiences too long with his partner not to believe fully in his courage and steadfastness. This cheered him now, as the sun sank steadily beyond the earth's farthest curve, permitting evening's long shadows to spread and thicken around them.

Behind them somewhere, Sheriff Dowling's men were probably dividing into two parties, one to lie in wait in the foothills, the other group to head for the Miller ranch. Ahead of them, vastly more dangerous to the partners, were the aroused riders of Colton Miller—and Miller himself.

Luther kept his strong silence, concentrating on the land they were passing over, until full dusk was down, then he reined to a halt and peered ahead where distantly the Miller ranch buildings showed faintly dark against the slightly lighter skyline. "By now," he told Buff, "Chester's men will be heading out."

"Yeah," Buff agreed, "but what bothers me is whether or not Miller's hands are at the ranch. If one or two of them were to stumble onto Chester drivin' off Miller's cattle. . . ."

"It won't matter," interrupted Luther. "No rider in his right senses would tackle that many armed men."

"I know that," said Buff tartly. "But he'd sure hightail it for the home ranch and stir up a nest of trouble."

Luther slumped in the saddle, clearly thinking of something different. He said, a trifle shortly: "There's danger, Buff. We can't expect everything to be safe from here on."

Buff said no more. Instead, he followed out the direction of his partner's gaze and also studied the far buildings, dimming as darkness settled deeper, more strongly upon the land.

Finally Luther said in an almost resigned tone: "Let's go."

They pushed ahead at a slow gait, neither saying it aloud but both acutely conscious of the need now for conserving the strength of their mounts.

Behind them and westerly, dying day, lingering until now in the far-away mountain crevices, suddenly winked out. There arose from cooling earth a faint fragrance, a vague scent of dust and growing things and dryness. Overhead the first star shine came weakly, in a diluted way, to lessen somewhat the darkness's obscurity. As yet no moon had appeared.

"Smoke," said Buff softly, when they were less than a mile from Colton Miller's home ranch. "Suppertime."

To this Luther made no reply at all, but he began angling a little to the west.

"How do you figure to flush them out?" Buff asked.

"Let them hear us," came back the brusque reply.

Nothing more was said until, sitting motionlessly less than 100 yards from Miller's lighted buildings, Luther began with great deliberation to manufacture a cigarette. He lit it behind the shielding oval of his hat brim, took a deep inhalation, and faced around. "If the going gets rough," he told Buff, "and we have to split up, I'll meet you at the place near that brawling creek in the hills where we camped after we first drove off Miller's cattle."

"All right."

Luther grinned a little crookedly into Buff's eyes. "Sure never figured homesteading was going to be like this, did you?"

"Nope," said Buff, matching his partner's mood. "But then . . . a feller's got to take chances now and then, I reckon." He also smiled. "The only thing I wish right now is that we had two fresh horses."

"We've got the night. Maybe that'll substitute for 'em." Luther punched his cigarette out on the saddle horn and tossed it aside. "Let's go," he said, and eased forward, kneeing his mount into a continuation of its former slow-paced walk.

Somewhere in the darkness ahead a horse whinnied. Farther out, southward, came the distant bawl of a cow. From the buildings ahead orange lamp glow lay low upon the ground in diffused orange puddles. Past the sheds, barns, and other outbuildings, stood the large log house of cowman Colton Miller himself, the big, paunchy, childless, and unmarried ruler of 6,000 acres of unfenced land, a man with a reputation for hardness, stubbornness, and aggressiveness, who had never made any secret of the fact that he despised homesteaders above all other forms of life. A man to whom wealth was power.

In the minds of both Luther Hart and Buff Brady was a solid awareness that Miller would have them both killed without a chance, if he could force them to earth long enough to accomplish this. But desperate men, and uncompromising ones, too, with nothing left to lose but the lives they were now putting upon the altar of chance, born and reared in the environment of a harsh frontier, were less prone to value lives highly— even their own lives—than men whose back-grounds were different. Finally, even with Buff's misgivings, they neither of them ever for a moment doubted but that in a stand-up shoot-out fight, they were the equal of Colton Miller or the hirelings he would set against them.

Men who came to maturity with guns in their hands, on their persons, part of their daily lives, were altogether different from other men—the ones, for example, who came to settle the West with no knowledge of gunmanship—and fate had decreed that Luther Hart and Buff Brady were better than average gunmen. This, above all else, was now fully in their favor.

X

Luther was slightly ahead when they came to the very edge of Miller's yard and halted a second time. Ahead of him men were moving in a relaxed fashion through the night, most were smoking, a few were talking, but mostly, well-fed and replete, they simply headed outward toward whatever substitute for a bunkhouse they had contrived the night before.

Buff counted the shadows he could distinguish in this shadowy gloom. "Six, seven, eight," he said aloud, then paused. "Nine. That's all. There's a man shy."

Luther dismounted, sought and found a sharp-edged piece of stone, got back astride, and threw it straight at the nearest men. Ahead, someone let off a quick curse and called fiercely into the night: "Who flung that danged rock?"

Luther called out in a quiet and muffled way. "Is that you, Ed? We got the critters."

To this statement, which made no clear sense to any of the Miller riders, there came back not only no answer, but a sudden freezing among them.

"There he is," said someone in a rising tone.

"Two of 'em." There was a sharp gasp, then: "It's *them* two!"

Luther and Buff whirled now and put the gut-hooks to their horses. They were plunging erratically through deep darkness when behind them came a loud shout followed by a gunshot. Then more shouts as Miller's riders went rushing forward toward the horse corral.

Luther flagged Buff down to a slow lope. "Don't get too far ahead or they'll never find us," he said.

"Suits me," quipped Buff, keeping a close watch over his shoulder.

They heard the abrupt rumble of charging horses moments later and, keeping this sound directly behind them, urged their horses onward.

After a half hour of this steady riding with brief halts to gauge the distance behind them of their pursuers, Luther called to Buff: "Head north! Lead 'em away from the ranch!"

It was a dangerous business and required expert horsemanship to conserve, or expend, the horse strength under them in such a way as to allow for short periods of rest, alternated with spurts of sudden speed, but both Luther and Buff were equal to the occasion, and, as Buff had observed, they had good reason to use every wile they possessed.

After an hour of this kind of riding, evidently at someone's order, Miller's hired hands began firing their guns. They had nothing but sound to aim for, but with their numbers that might have eventually been enough. As it was, Buff's old owlhoot-trail experience came into play here. He rode twisted in the saddle, harkening; when Miller's men halted to listen, Buff would raise his arm. He and Luther would then also cease all movement. In this way Miller's riders were balked in their effort to place the distance and direction of the men they were chasing from the telltale sounds of their ridden mounts.

They were by this time a long way from the Miller ranch and perilously close to the foothills. Luther drew in close to say: "Head farther west. We're getting too close to Dowling's boys."

Buff required no urging to comply with this. He swung nearly southwest. Luther, because he had not mentioned something else he had in mind, did not protest to this; he simply pushed on, weighing their chances and feeling that they were better than he had initially thought they would be. He gave full credit for this to Buff's outlaw canniness.

A mile farther on Luther came in close a second time, saying: "Now let's lose them."

Buff was beginning to nod his head when dead ahead loomed a rider, then a second horseman, and a third and fourth mounted man. Buff said something in sharp warning but Luther had already spied the oncoming figures. He wheeled low and dug in the spurs; he had seen bared carbines in the late but quickening moon glow.

"It's the law!" he bellowed with unnecessary loudness, adding in an equally thunderous voice: "Ride for it! They might have Miller with 'em!"

This was purest improvisation on Luther's part but circumstances were with him. Dowling and his posse men, having already heard gunshots and now encountering fleeing horsemen, threw outward a red-tongued and ragged volley. It was wide of the mark because Luther and Buff were rushing fully southward now, back in the direction of the Miller ranch, but the oncoming pursuit, not yet aware of this, had not swerved. Bullets cut around them and a horse pin-wheeled, flinging its screaming rider head over heels.

"They're makin' a stand!" boomed a bull-bass from far back where Miller's men were oncoming. "Get down! Dismount! They can skyline you!"

Dowling's riders would have followed Buff and Luther, but a quick, wild volley from ahead of them off in the east threw them into confusion. Over the grisly curses of someone who had been

101

stung by a bullet came the unmistakable voice of the sheriff. "We got 'em!" he cried fiercely. "Fight forward on foot! Come on!"

Luther and Buff drew down to a halt a long half mile south of the flashing weapons. Luther dismounted to lead his winded animal in a large, cooling-out circle. "Nice fight," he remarked as he came abreast of Buff, using a calm and quiet tone that was pure affectation.

"Real nice," Buff shot back, excited and unable to conceal this fact. "Now tell me you engineered it to happen like this."

"Why do you figure I told you to ride north when we first had 'em chasing us? Only I didn't expect it to be as good as this. I figured a flurry might happen, during which we could get back to the ranch."

"Back to the ranch!"

Luther stopped cooling-out his animal. "Sure, I want Colton Miller."

"I think there are easier ways to get him than like this!"

Luther shrugged. He said no more but concentrated on watching the battle northward where full night and the nearby foothills made gunshots sound louder, and also flushed up each red-flaring tongue of muzzle blast.

Occasionally a man would cry out, either in anger or anguish. Otherwise, the fight was being prosecuted with the savage determination of brave and bull-headed men. Finally though, as Luther now remarked, Dowling's hopelessly outnumbered posse men had to give way. When they began firing less, and their shots came from farther back as if they were retreating toward their horses, Luther got astride and called for Buff to come along. They still had some work to do.

They passed down the darkness side-by-side, in a hurry, but for the time being unable and unwilling to punish their animals further. Behind them the fight still raged. Miller's cowhands, conscious they now had the whip hand, pressed in upon the posse men, maintaining a steady firing.

Suddenly, when Luther and Buff were still well within hearing, the firing stopped altogether. They glanced at one another, wondering what this presaged, then came two widely spaced single blasts, each one a little farther easterly than the former shots had been.

Luther relaxed. "Headin' back for Lincoln," he said. "I guess the sheriff had his belly full of one-sided battles for now."

They continued southward, and after a quarter mile more Buff spoke: "He isn't the kind to give up. He'll get half the men in town if necessary, but Dowling'll be back."

"What interests me right now," said Luther, straining for sounds to the rear, "is how much time we'll have at the ranch before the crew returns all orrey-eyed and feathered-up for war like a herd of bronco Injuns."

"Plenty of time," said Buff, affecting Luther's earlier airiness of attitude. "The way you cut the mustard, pardner, we're ridin' along with one foot in the grave an' the other on a banana peel every second anyway."

"You got some better plan for dealin' with Miller?"

"Sure, just lie quiet until he comes along . . . then pot-shoot him if he's with his crew, and, if he isn't, get him down off his horse and make him draw against one of us." Buff paused, then said: "It'd sure be easier on horseflesh anyway, to do it my way."

Luther rode another 100 yards before saying anything in reply, then he nodded. "No imagination. That's what's wrong with you, Buff. No imagination. Now me. I want to bust Colton Miller down to his true size, then make him crawl a ways."

"Humph!"

"Then make him pay for as much damage as can be paid for with his cash. Y'know, once when I was a little kid, an old horse trader told me . . . 'Don't cuss your enemies, boy. Get your hands into their pockets about up to the elbows. They'll forget a cussin' out in time, but no man ever forgets bein' outsmarted in the pocketbook.' "

Buff jutted his chin forward. "All right," he said, dropping his voice. "There's Miller's house. Go ahead and try it your way. Only since the place doesn't have a blessed light showin', I don't think you're goin' to prove nothing after all, and that suits me, because about now his crew is boilin' down this way like a herd of devils after a crippled saint."

Buff was proven correct; there was no one at Colton Miller's residence. In fact, although they made only a cursory examination, there did not appear to be anyone at the headquarters ranch at all. Luther, undismayed by this and again recognizing opportunity, went into the blacksmith shed, kindled a small fire against the wall, then just as boldly fired the cook shack as well. He and Buff next rode on southward and stopped a mile farther out. There, each of them twisted up a cigarette in the saddle, sat there impassively and silently smoking, while against the northward horizon two furious tongues of spark-laden flame twisted higher and higher into the night sky.

"You know," said Buff conversationally, studying the flames with a connoisseur's critical attention, "I'm beginning to like this business . . . even if you do take chances no one in his right mind would take." He took up the reins, waggled them against his horse's neck, and reined around southward again. "In fact, I got a notion not to go back to plantin' corn and barley any more a-tall.

Think I'll just hire out to the squatters to rough up and burn out big-time cow outfits."

"You'd last about as long as a rooster in a snake pit, too," said Luther dryly, eyeing the eastern sky. "Dawn'll be here directly and we das'n't go back into the hills. Reckon we'd better go see what Chester's been doing."

They cut diagonally over the prairie with a view to intercepting Buell and his settlers shod in cowboy boots, but never found them. They did find, after the sky began to brighten, where a good-size herd of cattle had been driven due south. For a time they traced out this wide blaze upon the vague and lightening earth, then halted where a number of men had dismounted. Luther looked from the boot tracks up to Buff and nodded.

"They make pretty dependable allies, after all," he said.

Buff agreed, then added a tart observation of his own: "They sure didn't waste any time getting the job done and getting back home, though."

"Before sundown you were about half ready to blame me for leading them into trouble. Now you sound disgusted because they brought this off neat as a pin. Just what does it take to satisfy you, anyway?"

"Never mind that," Buff shot right back, swiveling his head to study the countryside around them. "Every time I mention what'd satisfy me, you get disagreeable. I think it's because she's got blonde hair and you're jealous."

Luther grinned, studied his partner's beard stubble, and chuckled aloud. "I wish she could see you now," he said, turning easterly and riding on.

"You're no beauty, either. Now where the hell are we going? You know . . . when this is all over, I'll be so bowlegged from forkin' this consarned saddle I'll have to sleep cross-legged to keep from kickin' myself out of bed."

"We're going out a ways where we can see anyone comin' before they can see us . . . then we're goin' to eat the last of that antelope roast Chester gave us."

"Sleep is what I need most," said Buff. "Anyway, my belly thinks my throat's been cut, it's been so long without food."

Neither of them spoke again until Luther, finally satisfied that they were, at least for several hours, quite safe, dismounted stiffly, flexed his legs, then began untying the grease-soaked neckerchief that lay aft of his saddle cantle. Buff then asked what Luther had planned for them after they'd rested.

"Go see Tom Dowling."

Buff dismounted. "Like before, send him word?"

"No. This time we ride right up to him."

Buff squinted as he turned away from his horse.

107

He considered his partner's tired, lined, but undismayed countenance over an interval of silence, then he said: "The riding's got you, or the sun, or the lack of sleep. I knew it would sooner or later." He dropped down upon his haunches, regarded the unappetizing mess Luther's unwrapping of the meat disclosed. "That's one helluva last supper," he said, and reached forward for the slice of meat Luther was holding toward him.

XI

Luther's bravado was wearing exceedingly thin now. He could not conceal his weariness, and moments after finishing his portion of the antelope roast he fell sound asleep sitting, cross-legged, upon the ground. He jerked awake only when he began to fall forward. Buff, observing now the range man's code, affected not to notice; he was busily wiping grease from his fingers, eyes averted, when this occurred.

They both smoked, sunlight warming their bodies, adding to the drowsiness that already plagued them, and for a time, in unspoken agreement, they did stretch out fully upon the ground and slumber.

It was a short rest, however, for the soft nicker of a horse brought them both whirling upright, guns palmed and hearts pounding, to face in the direction their animals were grazing. Solidly pacing toward them and close enough to be easily recognized rode the Buells, Chester with his great, gray-shot beard and gangling young Charley, mouth hanging wide at sight of Buff and Luther, not only at the speed with which they had come up off the ground with readied guns, but also at sight of their faces, their soiled, rumpled clothing, and their rattlesnake-red and deadly eyes.

Chester halted and said nothing as the partners holstered their weapons. He continued to gaze at them impassively for a time afterward, then raised his shaggy head to turn a long, searching look outward.

After that he stiffly dismounted, handed his reins to Charley, told the boy solemnly not to get down, then strode forward to halt where Luther and Buff stood waiting.

"I didn't expect to find you," Chester said in his rumbling, grave tone. "I suppose I'm entitled to some good fortune."

Luther, sensing trouble, motioned toward the ground and let himself down cross-legged again. Aside, to Buell's son, he called gently: "Keep an eye peeled Charley." Then he fastened his gaze upon the older man. "What's happened, Chester?"

Buff remained standing, but with thumbs hooked in his shell belt and his squinted, speculative stare fully upon the bearded settler.

"We did like you said. We got high-heeled boots and rounded up some of Miller's animals and drove them off."

"We saw the tracks," said Luther. "You did a good job of it, too."

"Yes, we left the cattle about three miles south of where we are sitting now." Chester raised his head, fixed Luther with a bitter look, then said: "All for nothing."

"What do you mean?"

"Miller was waiting at the Buford place when Lester Buford came back." Chester paused. "Miller didn't suspect a thing, I'm certain of that, but Lester Buford is not a strong man."

"You mean," said Buff doubtingly, "that this Buford told Miller where he'd been?"

"That's exactly what he did."

"When was this?" asked Luther.

"About midnight, I'd judge, maybe an hour or such beyond midnight."

"Then," said Buff roughly, unable to keep the scorn and cold wrath from his voice, "how come you to get away?"

"Miller rode to Lincoln for Sheriff Dowling. At least that's what Buford told me when he came charging up to my place." Buell's weary eyes shifted from each man back to the ground directly in front of him. "Buford's conscience gnawed him afterward . . . he rode to warn as many of us as he could." In a compassionate tone, Buell then said: "It was the right thing to do, men. You mustn't blame Lester Buford too much. You see, he's new out here. I expect it was my fault for taking him along."

"So now you're on the dodge," said Luther, then glanced up at Charley. "But why take the boy along? Who'll watch over your womenfolks?"

"They've gone into town to take rooms at the boarding house there. I insisted upon it." Buell's gaze hardened. "I know Colton Miller, too. He'll dynamite my place and he'll send men to shoot my milk cow and my team." The bearded old settler clenched his fists until cords stood out in his arms. "Just this once . . . ," he flared, his eyes burning savagely, "just this once in my lifetime I wish I could handle firearms as well as the cowmen can."

Luther looked away from Buell's troubled face, from the older man's slumped shoulders and despairing, bitter mouth. To Buff he said: "That's why we couldn't find Miller." Then he swung back to Buell. "What was he doing at this Buford's place in the middle of the night?"

"It seems," said Buell grimly, "that Miller is a better judge of men than I am. He was over there secretly to offer Buford a bribe to locate you two, posing as your friend, and tell Miller and his gunmen where they could catch you."

Buff blurted wrathfully at Luther: "I told you we should've blown him in two."

Luther arose stiffly, saying in reply, his voice very gentle-sounding: "It's not too late, Buff. I reckon I've got to admit we aren't going to lick him a little at a time like I'd hoped."

Chester Buell sat motionlessly unheeding, his gaze still upon the earth in front of him. Luther bent, caught his arm, and tugged. Buell came upright. "Charley and I'll keep on riding south," he told Luther now, every vestige of the fire he'd once shown in tone and look entirely quenched. "We can get down to the Dead Man's Pass country and hole up there for a while."

"Fat lot of good that'll do," rejoined Buff bitterly. Then, catching Luther's reproving scowl, Buff turned aside to go stamping out where their horses dozed. He commenced tightening both cinches, swearing blisteringly to himself. By the time he was finished, Luther had helped Chester Buell back into the saddle. As the settler and his boy resumed their southward way, Luther joined Buff where their horses stood. For a long while neither of them said anything, then Luther, in his softest voice, spoke without looking around at Buff: "I reckon that's a boot that fits both feet."

"What?" demanded Buff gruffly.

"That scarin' the truth out of folks," said Luther. "Get astride, we're goin' to catch us one or two Miller cowhands and sweat a few facts about Miller out of them, his burning and shooting and dynamiting."

Buff obeyed, still grim-visaged. As they plodded northward again, he snarled: "If anyone's laid a hand on Miz Buell, little Annie, Jessie, or Evelyn, he's as good as dead right now . . . and that's a damned fact!"

Luther had nothing to say. They passed along slowly, to all outward appearances simply a brace of cowhands going somewhere in a leisurely way, until, still a goodly distance off, yet close enough to see the last smudge rising over Colton Miller's ranch from the two burning sheds, Luther halted, straining ahead.

"You see anything?" asked Buff, his earlier anger still audible when he spoke.

"A pair of riders," answered Luther. "Looks like they're heading east from Miller's place."

Buff eventually made out the small specks. They were quite distant and appeared to be scarcely moving. "If they're coming from Miller's," he said, "that's good enough for me."

They began to angle now, in such a way as to keep south of the horsemen, but holding slightly northward, too, in order ultimately to intercept their prey. Once, shortly before the sun hung briefly suspended directly overhead, they sighted a hurrying band of other horsemen, these, though, were pushing rapidly along toward the Miller place. They were too far off to pose a threat right then.

It took several hours of steady plodding to get

even an idea where the men they were following were going. At first Luther had considered it likely they were heading for Lincoln. Subsequently, when the horsemen made no upland sweep but held to their easterly course, it became evident this was not their intention. Gradually, then, it dawned on both the partners that Miller's two hired hands were making straight for the Buell place.

"Now that," said Buff with bleak satisfaction, "is what I'd hoped to see."

Again Luther, eyes narrowed against sun smash, kept silent. At length he halted. The men far ahead were turning into Buell's yard. They were dismounting. One man stayed back with the horses, standing between them as any experienced gunman did when he could, protecting not only his exposed partner in this fashion but also protecting himself both front and rear. The other man strode up to the soddy. He rolled one gloved fist across the door and stood, hip-shot, waiting.

"Let's go," said Luther. "They're from Miller all right, and they don't aim to make any arrests, either."

It was possible to get only a little closer without being seen by the sentry standing between the horses. In every direction the prairie was clean-swept, treeless, and brilliantly sun-lighted. But Buff Brady's canniness was once more their saving grace; he led southward in a wide, circling lope, until Buell's barn was between Miller's gun hands and the partners. He then began the long ride upland, toward the Buell soddy. In this fashion, while they would eventually be heard, they would not be seen.

It was Luther who, moved to caution when no more than 1,000 yards separated them from the unseen gunmen, hissed at Buff to draw down to a walk. This Buff did, unshipping his booted carbine as he walked his horse onward. Nearing the barn now, they heard the two men over by the soddy talking back and forth. One kept insisting someone had to be on the homestead. The other one, equally as insistent, said Buell had gotten word like some of the others had also been warned off, and had fled. To this the man by the horses swore, saying loudly enough for both Luther and Buff to hear: "All right. Come, get the dynamite then, and we'll wreck the place." This second man emerged finally from between the horses, rummaged in the off saddlebag of a saddle, brought forth four taped-together sticks of powder with the fuses already interwoven and ready to be ignited, and stood there waiting for his companion to return from the soddy.

Behind the barn Buff and Luther stood by their horses' heads, ready to pinch down hard if either of the animals attempted to nicker. Luther nudged Buff.

"Watch my horse," he said, and went forward a

few feet to kneel, then go flat upon the earth, pushing his face carefully around the barn's log mudsill. His chin was pressed into dust but his view of the yonder yard was excellent. He began immediately to draw back and slowly arise. "One's coming this way," he whispered to Buff.

"Sure," whispered Buff, "one blows up the soddy while the other one fires the barn." Buff released the reins of both horses, brought forward his carbine, and cocked it. "Get 'em," he said commandingly to Luther. "Now! While they're both in sight." He dropped flat, inched forward until he could twist with ease to fire toward the house, and, although this fully exposed his upper body, Luther, moving out into plain sight, standing clear of all protection, his carbine held in two hands across his body, amply covered Buff.

The oncoming gunman did not at first see Luther. There is doubt that he ever saw Buff on the ground at all. He was a hawk-faced, lean, and whipcord-thin man, and, as he moved onward toward the barn now, an ornately carved ivory-butted six-gun rode professionally low and lashed hard at his thigh. The partners saw instantly that this man was not the kind you ever gave a second chance; killer was written into his every move-ment. It was stamped across his predatory features, in his moving eyes that suddenly sprang wide. The gunman jerked upright in a sudden halt. He was staring unbelievingly straight at Luther and Luther's belt-high cocked carbine.

Back by the horses the second man was moving off toward the soddy. He had the taped dynamite sticks in his right hand, a normal enough condition for a right-handed man, but under these circumstances a very grave error, for this gunman could not draw his belt gun without dropping the dynamite. He could easily enough do this, of course, but in a shoot-out speed was paramount. The brief fraction of a second that would be wasted when this man opened his fingers to drop the dynamite sticks, then began the sweep toward his holstered pistol, would be his last moment of life, for he could not, no matter how fast he was, hope to prevail against two cocked and readied carbines.

His fate was sealed the moment he walked clear of the horses. Behind him his startled partner had uttered no sound of warning at all. The man with the dynamite had laid his life on the line without the least inkling this was so, until a totally unfamiliar voice came to hit him in the back with a cold, deadly command.

"Hold it . . . you over there by the house. Freeze. Don't make a single move or you're dead."

The four men were statue-like in their shallow-breathing silence. Luther moved his carbine barrel inches to cover the farthest man's back. "Drop the dynamite," he ordered. "Good. Now put your hands atop your head."

The hawk-faced man, burning eyes seeing Luther's averted weapon and glance looking away, chose this second to make his play. He was fast, too, probably one of the fastest men either of the partners had ever seen. But he was struck in the chest by Buff's upward-angling slug at about the same time Luther's carbine exploded no more than fifty feet distant. He was knocked over backward by impact, dead before he struck the ground. What Buff and Luther never in their long lives forgot was that this man actually got off one shot before he went down, drew and fired his pistol in that 100th part of a second before Buff's slug struck, knocking him off balance so that the bullet plowed up dirt ten feet short of where Luther stood.

The remaining gunman, having estimated his chances, realized he could not hope to turn around, locate his foe, draw and fire, too, against readied guns. He stood, humped-shouldered and wide-legged, praying that in the excitement he would not be shot down, also. He was not.

Buff got upright, moving widely around Luther. When he was well around the surviving Miller rider, he called to him.

"You care to make the same try, mister?"

"No," stated the gunman, realizing from Buff's voice that he was bracketed between the partners. "No, I quit."

"Toss out your gun," commanded Luther. When

this had been done, he said: "Now put your hands down and turn around."

The gunman obeyed. Luther stared at his fear-shadowed eyes and bloodless lips. A tiny muscle twitched in the gunman's right cheek under the eye.

"I think we ought to kill him," he said aside to Buff. "What do you think?"

Buff levered his carbine; the smoothly functioning mechanism meshed loudly. "You want first shot?" said Buff. "Go ahead. I'll bet you I can get two slugs into him before he hits the ground."

"I'm unarmed," said the gunman. "You fellers ain't nesters. You wouldn't down a man like this. You fellers been riders, too."

"Yeah," snarled Buff, "but we weren't the kind of riders you an' your dead friend were. We didn't go around dynamiting folks' soddies or burning their barns or shooting them in cold blood while they squatted under a milk cow."

The gunman licked his lips. He risked turning his head just far enough to sight Buff's dark and glowering countenance. The shock of what he saw in Buff's face made him brace forward.

"I said I give up," he said weakly. "Anyway, 'twasn't me shot that old sodbuster when he was milkin'. It was Booth there, that feller you boys killed."

Luther lowered his carbine, and leaned upon it. "I suppose you didn't aim to blow up Buell's soddy, either," he said dourly. "You just always ride around with dynamite sticks in your saddle-bags."

The gunman, seeing Luther's relaxed stance, was encouraged. He softened a little in his stance, too. "I'll tell you how it was," he said.

Buff muttered disgustedly as Luther spoke now, saying to their captive: "All right, move over here into the shade. We'd kind of like to hear how it was."

XII

Their prisoner's name was Arthur Cooley. The hawk-faced gunman they had downed was a hired gunslinger named Booth Hardin.

"He was from down south somewhere," said Cooley, gazing dispassionately at the dead man.

"New Mexico," muttered Buff, also considering the still and unnaturally flattened form. "I've heard of him." He gazed around at Cooley. "Miller didn't get him cheap. His kind demand pretty big pay."

Cooley watched Luther's fingers work up a cigarette. "Miller pays good," he said. "He's got to. This is sort of risky work."

Luther lit up and exhaled. "Booth Hardin killed John Graham," he said. "Is that right?"

"Plumb right, mister."

"How do you know he did? Did he tell you?"

"I was with him when he done it. We lay back out a ways. It was just comin' daybreak. The old nester come out with his bucket. Booth sighted on him. . . ." Cooley shrugged, avoiding their eyes. "He was usin' a buffalo gun. It liked to cut that old sodbuster in two."

"What was your part in that killing?"

"Nothing. I was there in case Booth needed support. He didn't need it. We afterward rode back to the ranch."

"How much did Miller pay Booth for that killing?"

"Three hundred dollars. He give me fifty."

"Did he pay you both at the same time?"

"Yes, in the parlor of his house. Me fifty, Booth three hundred, like I just told you."

Luther glanced briefly at Buff. The darker and shorter man was looking coldly down at Arthur Cooley, lips drawn flatly in distaste. Luther continued with his questioning. "How much did Miller pay you for dynamiting our soddy and tearing down our corrals?"

"Twenty dollars apiece."

"You and Booth?"

"Yes, we pretty near' always went out together." Cooley looked at Luther. He avoided seeing Buff as much as he could. "What you fellers aim to do with me?"

"That," stated Buff, breaking into the conversation briefly, "depends on you."

"What you want me to do?" asked Cooley, shooting a quick glance at Buff, then turning toward Luther again.

"Tell Sheriff Dowling everything you've just told us," said Luther. "And the other things you know about Miller."

Cooley nodded listlessly. "I figured you'd want that. If I testify against him in a court o' law, he'll likely get convicted. Of his hired hands me 'n' Booth were the only ones he sent out to do his real night ridin' and . . . other things." Cooley studied his hands before saying more. "He'll pay someone to kill me. I reckon you fellers know that, don't you?"

"He'll try, maybe," agreed Luther, "but Tom Dowling keeps a tight jail."

Cooley continued sitting there, looking downward. After a time he said: "You reckon he'll give me a break for testifyin' against Miller?"

Luther shrugged, got to his feet, and gestured for Buff to fetch their horses. "Let's go ask him," he said. "Stand up, Cooley."

The prisoner stood. He turned slowly to gaze out over the seemingly endless prairie. "You'll never get to Lincoln in broad daylight," he said. "You fellers roiled Miller real bad burnin' out the bunkhouse, then, last night, torching the cook shack and the shoeing shed. He's put five hundred dollars on each o' you . . . dead. When Booth and me left this mornin' to come over here, he was sendin' the regular riders out in pairs to hunt you down." Cooley began wagging his head. "You try 'n' make it to Lincoln now, and you'll likely get all three of us killed."

Buff came up with the horses. He jerked a thumb at the prisoner. "Get aboard," he growled.

As Cooley moved to obey, he looked over his shoulder at Luther. "He'll have me killed just for bein' with you two. You can guess why, can't you?"

Luther nodded but said nothing until Cooley was astride and Buff handed forth the reins to Luther's own animal. Then, to Buff, he said: "We could lie over until after sundown. I think Cooley's right. Miller'll want him dead even worse than he wants us dead. He'll know why we're keepin' Cooley alive. Cooley's the only living proof now of the things Miller's done to the squatters. Booth Hardin is dead. . . ."

Buff sat his saddle in thought. From his facial expression it was obvious he did not care a whit whether Cooley lived or died, but in his eyes lay the knowledge that Luther's logic was sound. After a time he said: "I'll stay with Cooley. Take him 'way over east of Lincoln, but southward where Miller's riders got no reason to go. You head for town and get hold of the sheriff. Bring him with you when you start out and I'll find a way to keep watch for the both of you."

Buff gazed down where Luther stood. He

pursed his lips when Luther nodded, having accepted Buff's plan, then said quietly to Luther: "If you don't show up by midnight, Lute, I'll know you never made it to town, that Miller got you." He jerked his head sideways at the prisoner. "I'll kill him, leave his carcass for the buzzards, and go get Colton Miller."

Luther stepped up, settled across his saddle, and said: "No, deliver him alive to Dowling. Killing Cooley destroys the evidence against Miller. Killing Miller makes his money and his land an estate. We don't want that, Buff. What we want is for Miller to be alive when the settlers get judgments against him. We want to be around to see him squirm when he has to pay for the damage he's done to these clodhoppers. That's what we started out to make him do. Let's not change now."

Again Luther's logic received Buff's accord, but this time it was very grudgingly given. He mumbled something under his breath while glaring at Cooley, but when Luther gathered his reins preparatory to riding off, Buff's steady gaze cleared.

"You recollect that old German homesteader who used to live east of us?" he called quietly to Luther.

"Yes, what about him?"

"Recollect that kickin' old mule he had?"

"Yes."

Buff's eyes crinkled into a worried, small smile. "He used to tell everyone when they walked around that danged mule to look a little out. You remember?"

Luther smiled. "I remember," he said.

"Well, that's what I'm tellin' you now, Lute. Look a little out."

They exchanged a steady look, a comradely grin, then Luther rode clear of Buell's barn, head up, eyes raking the countryside, and moments later he emerged beyond the barn loping north-easterly.

Buff sat there, watching him go. He did not move as long as Luther was in sight, but eventually he took up his reins, saying from the corner of his mouth without deigning to look around at the captive gunman: "Come on, mister. We got a lot of ground to cover between now an' midnight."

As Buff and his prisoner passed overland, bright, early afternoon sunlight burned against them. Cooley kept his head moving from side to side. Buff only infrequently made an identical circuit with his eyes. Of the two he was the least disturbed by being exposed upon the plain in the light of day.

They had covered perhaps two miles when Cooley said: "You got any tobacco?"

Buff passed across his sack and papers without speaking. When he got them back, he also made a cigarette, ignored the match Cooley patiently held for him, lit his own smoke, and sought to pierce the northern distance for some sign of either horsemen or the town of Lincoln. Another mile farther along Cooley spied Lincoln's southern-most environs and spoke out. Buff looked, saw, and nodded, all without speaking.

Cooley tried one final time to draw the dark man out into conversation, and this time Buff turned an icy stare upon him saying: "Mister, you close your mouth. You keep it closed until I tell you to open it. An' while you got it closed, you better do a little prayin' because if anything happens to my pardner . . . I don't care what anyone says . . . you're goin' to die. Now shut up and just keep ridin' along."

They passed well east and far south of Lincoln. Buff was passably familiar with this range. Here, the land was not entirely flat. There were occasional land swells that stood forth rib-like; usually they were gravelly and nothing grew upon them. It was from one of these slight eminences that Buff figured to keep watch until sundown, and after that he hoped to utilize them as cover if need be. Beyond that, he had no plan. His chore was to guard and keep alive a man he would have preferred seeing dead. He would do it scrupulously, too—but only as long as he was convinced it was advantageous to keep Arthur Cooley alive. He had not been speaking idly or in pointless wrath when he had told Cooley he would kill him if anything happened to Luther. Unlike Luther, Buff never had had, and did not now have, any great or high regard of their settler neighbors. Whether they were recompensed by Colton Miller or not meant less than nothing to him. He was alive to only one thing—his partner's survival. If Luther did not survive, first Arthur Cooley would die, then Colton Miller would die, and afterward anyone else who had a hand in Luther's killing could also expect to be tracked down and killed. Buff Brady was a fair, honest, unimaginative, and uncompromising man. He was not at all complex. He was exactly the kind of a man Cooley understood, so when Buff said for the captured gunman not to open his mouth again, Cooley did not open it. A whole herd of stampeding cattle could have come at them over the plain and Arthur Cooley would not have said a word. He had, in his lifetime, known many men as deadly as his captor; he therefore knew upon what a slender thread his continued existence depended. He made up his mind completely and without reservation to do exactly as Buff Brady told him to do.

As he rode along now with Brady, Arthur Cooley, for the first time since hiring out to Colton Miller to harass, shoot, burn out, and dynamite homesteaders, had a very strong suspicion that Miller's wealth, his big crew of riders, and his ruthless determination were not going to be enough. If this proved true, Cooley told himself, then he'd better begin thinking of ways to save his own skin. That was what occupied him as he rode through the dying day totally silent, keeping Buff in view from the corner of his eye.

XIII

Luther, after he left Buff and their prisoner, rode tiredly for town. It was dangerous, he knew, to head for Lincoln in broad daylight. It was compounding the peril to ride directly there without taking any of the precautions a hunted man ordinarily would have observed. On the other hand, both he and Buff had used their saddle stock severely these last trying days and sooner or later the animals would give out under this consistent abuse. He was therefore left with no real choice at all.

He rode, though, with his remaining strength concentrated toward caution, and it was fortunate that he did so, too, for long before Lincoln hove to on the flat-spreading horizon, he sighted two riders loping together from the north. They saw him about the same time he saw them. They slowed to a walk, seemed to speak briefly together, then continued on toward him.

Luther could not hope to outrun their fresher animals. Because the land was flat here, he could not hope either to go long unrecognized. As he pushed steadily onward, he considered and discarded a number of ruses. The one he ultimately accepted was actually the only one he could have used. When the oncoming horsemen were roughly a quarter mile ahead, he threw up his arm in a gesture of casual greeting, as though he recognized them, and at the same moment booted his horse over into a run, passing swiftly over the ground straight for the two men. They, in turn, waved back and slowed in preparation of his arrival. They did not see, in fact could not see, that when he lowered his arm he drew his handgun, cocked it, and held it low behind the tossing mane of his mount. They had no inkling he was not another of Miller's riders until a mushrooming red burst of flame, followed by a loud gunshot, speared directly at them. They then frantically sought to swerve away, drawing their own weapons as they did so.

Luther's second shot dumped one of the horses. Its rider cartwheeled through the air to land with spread-eagled impact. He was knocked breathless and lay writhing.

The second rider was speeding clear, fighting his frightened horse's head with one hand and throwing unaimed shots with the other hand. Luther drove straight at this man. When his six-gun was emptied, he drew forth his carbine and kept on firing.

Miller's rider then holstered his gun, turned his full attention to escaping, and fled with his spurred boot heels drumming frantically against his mount's ribs, urging the horse to its maximum efforts. In this fashion he rushed far beyond carbine range without once slackening speed.

Luther, favoring his mount, made no effort at additional pursuit. He watched the cowboy fade out far ahead in the direction of the Miller ranch, then rode slowly back where the writhing, downed rider was fighting for breath. He dismounted and dispassionately beat the injured horseman upon the back until he could breathe normally again, then he yanked him to his feet, plucked away the cowboy's gun belt, and propelled him forward with a hard shove.

"Walk," he commanded. "Your wind'll come back."

He rode along behind the staggering rider, keeping vigil for either the return of the other cowboy, or additional horsemen. When, sometime later, the uncomfortable horseman could speak without gasping, Luther asked him where the balance of Miller's men were. What he was told astonished him.

"Couple of 'em are in jail in Lincoln. Me 'n' my pardner was on our way back to tell Miller when we run onto you. We thought you was. . . ."

"Who put them in jail?" interrupted Luther.

"Well, dammit all, the sheriff put 'em in jail,"

snarled the rider, probing his ribs gingerly as he trudged bitterly along. "Ain't no one else got the authority to do such a thing, have they?"

"Why?"

"Because of the fight in the dark . . . that's why. Couple of Dowling's town posse men got winged in that fracas an' he's mad enough to chew nails and spit rust." The rider turned slightly to glare over his shoulder at Luther. "You worked that pretty neat, mister. By the time each side figured out who the others were, you 'n' your slippery pardner was plumb gone, four men'd been wounded, and Dowling was fit to be tied. When four o' us rode into Lincoln this mornin', there he was, all loaded for bear. He upped and arrested two of us and told me 'n' my pardner to get out of Lincoln and stay out."

"Sounds like he's mad at Miller," said Luther.

The cowboy took a tentative deep breath and expelled it slowly. "No broke ribs," he said with relief. "What'd you say?"

"I said it sounds like Miller and Dowling aren't spittin' through the same knothole any more."

"You ought to know about that," retorted the rider, wrinkling his forehead. "You worked it so's nobody dares trust anybody else around this danged country any more."

"How unkind of me," replied Luther sarcastically. "By the way, do you know a man named Booth Hardin?"

"I know him," growled the walking man.

"He had heart stoppage a couple hours back. He's dead."

The cowboy halted in his tracks, turned, and screwed up his face. "You kill him, mister?" he asked, taking a closer look at Luther.

"I had a hand in it, yes, but those things happen pretty fast. I think it was my pardner's bullet that stretched Hardin out."

"Was he alone?"

"No. But we didn't have to kill Cooley. He didn't have any fight left in him after he saw Hardin get killed." Luther bobbed his head. "Keep walking, cowboy."

The rider's attitude toward Luther changed abruptly, his replies were civil, even respectful, and he volunteered information willfully. They were nearly in sight of Lincoln's outskirts when the cowboy halted a second time, saying: "Listen, mister, don't make me go into that danged town with you."

"Why not? Dowling'll just put you in jail. Right now, I think that might be a good place to. . . ."

"Miller's got two new hired gun slicks waitin' there for you or your pardner to show up," blurted the rider.

"I see," said Luther. "Is that why you went to Lincoln this morning?"

"Yes, me 'n' them other fellers was to ride together as far as town, then split up and circle around north and south on our way back to the ranch. I had an envelope of money for them two gunfighters from Miller." The cowboy paused, appeared to balance a thought in his mind, then he shrugged, saying: "It ain't only you. Them fellers are to provoke a fight with any squatters they can. Miller is to pay them a hundred dollars a head for every one they down."

Luther scratched his head, tugged his hat forward again, and gazed up where Lincoln showed sturdily against an azure sky and land turning brown. After a time he said: "Do you know both those gunmen by sight?"

"Yes, when I delivered the envelope, they was standin' there in the hotel parlor side-by-side."

Luther gestured. "Start walkin', cowboy," he ordered. "You're going to point them out to me."

The hired rider protested. Luther said no more on the subject. Each time the cowboy offered to stop and plead, he simply flagged him onward. In this fashion they came finally, with afternoon dying around them, to the edge of Lincoln's ramshackle, tin-and-tarpaper environs. By then the cowboy was resigned to Luther's determination. He was also being diverted from his apprehension by two oversize blisters, one on each heel, that pained him every time he took a forward step. He minced along unhappily, shooting hard and searching glances ahead, where Lincoln's solitary, wide main thoroughfare ran past the stores, saloons, livery barns, and more saloons that made up the bulk of Lincoln's mercantile establishments and business district. At the extreme north section of town stood one of the few painted buildings in Lincoln. It was the Federal Eagle Hotel, Lincoln's most venerated establishment.

"I'm warnin' you," said the cowboy in a final plea to Luther. "They've seen pictures of you. They're just waitin' for you to poke your head up where they can blow it off."

Luther dismounted, tied his horse to the hitch rail of a saloon, and made a methodical study of Lincoln's dusty roadway. To his prisoner he said casually: "I don't mind dying. I just don't want to die alone is all."

This brought forth fresh and vehement protestations. "I never harmed you," spoke the cowboy, his words running all together in anxiety. "I only hired out to Miller a couple months back. I been strictly a range rider, mister. You can prove it by. . . ."

"Shut up," said Luther, his eyes fixed on the far figure of a lounging man in a handsome frock coat and black string tie. "See that skinny feller up near the hotel, smoking a cigar?"

The cowboy looked, swallowed, and nodded. "I see him. That's one of 'em. The other one'll be close by."

Luther turned thoughtful. He leaned in the

shade of an overhang watching people stroll by on both sides of the roadway. There was also a little trickle of late buggy traffic, and an occasional horseman trotted past. Beyond these commonplace things there was no indication that death lurked in this warm, early summer, late afternoon. On the east side of the roadway Sheriff Dowling's office was sandwiched between a saddler's place of business and a general store. There was a drooping, recently ridden saddle horse tied before the sheriff's office.

"Dowling's in town," said Luther thoughtfully, not specifically addressing the cowboy and not even looking over at him, eyes restlessly moving between the solitary visible gunfighter at the far end of the roadway. "Tell you what we'll do," he said, speaking conspiratorially now and swinging to hold the cowboy's glance. "You'll cross the roadway and keep going north until you're even with that gun slick up there. Then you'll tell him you just saw me down here tying my horse, and you'll tell him to fetch his pardner and come along, that you'll lead them to me."

The cowboy framed a final plea with his lips. His eyes were imploring and his ruddy cheeks had paled to a sick-gray, putty-like color. Luther stopped the words before he uttered them with a curt one-handed gesture.

"Stay on the boardwalk," he ordered. "I'm going to keep my gun on you all the way up there. If you try to duck into a dogtrot or a store, I'll sure enough get a piece of you before you get out of sight. Now go on."

"Hell," squeaked the rider, face contorting. "I ain't even got my gun. Listen . . . please . . . they'll get me sure when the shootin' starts. I couldn't get clear if I had wings."

Luther's mild gaze remained adamantly unwavering. In the same quiet way he repeated again his final order: "Go on."

The cowboy's eyes were desperate. They also began to show anger as he pushed out of the shade into the sunlight. "You're goin' to have a murder on your conscience," he fumed. "You're sendin' an innocent man to. . . ."

"Wish I had a fiddle," said Luther callously. "I'd play something real sad for you." He dropped a hand to rest on his holstered six-gun. "Pardner," he said, his voice turning brisk now, "you wanted to work for Colton Miller. You could've quit any time, but your kind likes being top dog around a herd of defenseless homesteaders. Well, get going. Don't turn yellow now just because you've run into a little of the same kind of trouble you've been willing to dish out to squatters."

When the cowboy did not immediately move, Luther took two swift forward steps, caught him by the shirt front, and flung him off the plank walk. "If you start walking, you may live through it. If you don't, you're going to get shot right here."

The cowboy started walking.

Moments passed. Nothing was visibly changed in Lincoln's roadway. People continued to drift past. Some boys with a raffish old tick hound scurried past, eagerly talking. A man with a great paunch beneath a greasy, once-white apron came from a café part way down the roadway and flung a bucket of water into the roadway to keep down the dust in front of his place.

Where Luther stood in the quiet and concealing shade, he could see the cowboy pass Dowling's office. He thought the rider hesitated just the smallest part of a stride as he passed the sheriff's open door, but he did not offer to duck inside or stop. Luther relaxed. He hitched at his shell belt, bringing his holstered gun into position. He did not remove his eyes from the cowboy's shoulders until someone coming from the sheriff's office cut across his view. Even then, though, he spared the intruder only the briefest of looks. The man was a cattleman. He saw that much, but there was nothing familiar about him.

Now the cowboy was slowing, dragging his feet, coming to a reluctant halt beside the thin man in the handsome frock coat and string tie. They were speaking. Luther drew back a big breath and let it out slowly. He ducked into a very narrow dogtrot separating two buildings, hurried into the yonder alleyway, and there turned north, quickening his pace.

XIV

Against a listless afternoon of peace and quiet was now played out a grim little one-act drama. Luther swung into another dogtrot farther north and emerged upon the far plank walk in time to see Miller's rider, his eyes glassily set and his jaw tightly locked, stump past across the roadway. Trailing after him were two men similarly dressed, except that one, being thinner, looked more funereal than his companion. None of the trio glanced in Luther's direction at all. When they were well past, Luther hastened across the roadway, sprang into Sheriff Dowling's office, and held up his left hand, palm outward, as the dust-streaked and harassed-appearing man at the desk glanced up—then sprang to his feet with a loud curse.

"Hold it!" exclaimed Luther swiftly. "Save all that for later, Sheriff. Right now come out here on the walkway."

Sheriff Dowling stood swaying like a great tree in a high wind, glaring bleakly at Luther. He made no move around his desk. Luther said again: "Come out here where you can see down the roadway. Hurry, damn it, this is important."

Dowling finally moved. Keeping a baleful, ominously silent glare upon Luther, he crossed the office in two large steps, shouldered past onto the plank walk, and squinted.

"Those two men walking south there behind that rider of Miller's are hired gunmen. They get one hundred dollars for every squatter they bait into a gunfight and kill. You see that young feller ahead of them, there?"

"Yes. He was in town earlier today."

"He brought those two gunmen a wad of cash from Miller. That's why he was in town."

Without another word Sheriff Dowling struck out after the three men. Luther paused only a second, then he hastened to catch up with Dowling. Without taking his eyes off their prey, he said from the edge of his mouth: "We've got John Graham's murderer, too, and another of Miller's hired gun hands who was there with the killer, saw the whole thing, and will testify against Miller in court."

Dowling, steadily lengthening his stride, said nothing. He was swiftly closing the distance now and reached down as a precaution to loosen the six-gun at his hip. Then he spoke. "I owe you something for that jail break, Hart. You and your hot-tempered pardner. I also owe you something for engineering me into believing Miller's riders were rustling from him, and for maneuvering me 'n' my posse into a Mexican stand-off with Miller's cowhands."

"Later," said Luther, beginning to slow.

"Look, he's going to lead them across the road."

Sheriff Dowling squinted; he also slowed. Finally he deliberately drew his six-gun and said to Luther: "I only know one way to handle that kind. Draw first, then call out, an', if they don't raise their hands, shoot 'em. You ready?"

"As ready as I'll ever be," replied Luther, also drawing his gun and swinging it to bear upon the men crossing through roadway dust behind their sweating guide.

"You fellers!" called Sheriff Dowling, his voice striking harshly into the drowsy late afternoon. "Keep your hands away from those guns and turn around slowly."

The gunmen did not stop at once, but the cowboy did, halting so jarringly that one of the gunfighters caromed into him and the other one missed colliding by only the smallest of margins and some nimble footwork. This latter man ripped out a curse.

"Easy," warned the lawman. "You're both covered. Turn around now."

For the second time that day Luther saw one man attempt to buck greater odds than any man could hope to prevail against. It was the thin gunfighter; he crouched, spun about, and sprang sideways all at the same time. His right hand was a blur of movement. Two cocked, already bared guns fired pointblank. The thin man jerked half around; he flung up both arms as though to retain his balance, or perhaps to find something to support him. Then his knees sprang outward; he bent over at the belt line and slid out his length in the roadway's soiled dust.

"Now you," said Tom Dowling, his eyes wickedly glowing. "Make your play."

"Not me, Sheriff!" called forth the heavier of the two gunfighters. "I don't like to bluff with busted flushes. You can come get my gun if you want."

Dowling jerked his head at Luther. "Go get it," he ordered. "Herd him and Miller's cowhand ahead o' you back to the office."

Lincoln's boardwalks, emptied miraculously before the initial gunshot echo had entirely faded away, now began to fill up again just as miraculously. People stood, they stared, they whispered back and forth, but none of them said anything in a loud voice or said anything at all to the sheriff as he passed by with Luther and his prisoners.

At the doorway into his office Tom Dowling paused to glance back. "Clancy!" he called to a burly man with a black cigar jutting through a splendidly upcurling moustache. "Drag that body over to doc's embalmin' shed." Dowling closed the door after him, leaned upon it, and said with a glare at both men: "Damned if I know which of you deserves being locked up the most." He then motioned for the gunman to turn around, and to Luther he said: "Look him over. Those fellers got a habit of packin' hide-out guns on 'em some-where."

It was true. Luther found a .41 caliber under-and-over Derringer concealed in the gunfighter's clothing. He handed it to Dowling as the sheriff unlocked one of the empty strap-steel cages, reached forward to catch the gunman by the shoulder, and push him roughly inside, motioning the cowhand toward another empty cell. He then locked the cell doors, tossed the keys upon his desk, and turned a glowering scowl upon Luther.

"I reckon you know you liked to got some pretty good men salivated the other night, engineerin' that fake fight with your rumors of Miller's hired hands stealin' cattle from him."

"*My* rumors," said Luther with exaggerated innocence. "Sheriff, I haven't talked to you since the. . . ."

"Never mind remindin' me of that," snapped Dowling. "I'll settle with you an' that gun-happy friend of yours later. What was that you said about knowing who killed John Graham?"

"Get your horse. I'll take you to him. Buff's keeping him alive east of town. Miller's crew is out manhunting. Buff and I didn't want to get shot up, and we didn't want our prize witness against Miller killed, either."

"East of town where?" demanded the sheriff suspiciously. "If you fellers think you can trick me twice durin' the. . . ."

"This is no trick. Now, come on."

Dowling went, but he did not look happy.

As they got astride and rode at a gallop side-by-side through Lincoln, townspeople watched their passing with considerable interest and wild speculation. One prim merchant noted that it was no longer possible to tell who was a friend of law and order and who was not, seeing that the chief law enforcer himself was now riding openly with a homesteader everyone had said up until this very afternoon was an outlaw.

From among the crowd standing by this man came the chewing-tobacco-moistened words of a gangling, raw-boned settler whose faded eyes followed Luther and Tom Dowling as they hastened past. "Hell," this man, named Will Butler, said drawlingly: "I'd a sight rather associate with some of these so-called outlaws than with a lot of some other so-called respectable folks." Several men in the crowd tittered. The merchant glared, turned about, and stalked into his store.

Dusk was fast falling now. Out on the prairie, land shadows thickened around the hastening hoofs of Luther's and Tom Dowling's mounts. A coolness came gradually to fill the atmosphere with evening's first fresh fragrance. For an hour the two riders rocketed along side-by-side, making no attempt to speak. Not until the fading light compelled them to slacken pace did the sheriff say in his rumbling voice: "You two sure stirred up a heap of confusion, Luther. Judge Spicer was madder'n a bull at fly time."

"What about your friend, Miller?"

"*My* friend!" exclaimed the lawman. "He never was no friend of mine and you danged well know that, too."

"I don't know any such a thing," contradicted Luther. "We tried to get you to. . . ."

Dowling interrupted with a loud groan. "You simpleton," he rumbled. "I told you an' told you . . . the law don't go by rumor or hearsay or guesswork, it goes strictly by fact. Fact and fact alone. Not a cussed one of you homesteaders ever came forward with anything but loose talk. Not a danged one of you!"

"All right," said Luther curtly. "Now we've got some facts. We've also got some witnesses, too. But if you don't stir out of your tracks and arrest Miller, he'll fly the coop."

"He won't fly anywhere," growled Dowling. "I sent a couple of special deputies out to his ranch to bring him in for questioning. By the time we get back, he'll be there waitin' for us." Dowling turned a hard glare upon Luther. "You an' your hot-headed friend'll be there, too. I'm going to sift through this mess once an' for all . . . and, believe me, Luther . . . somebody's goin' to sweat bullets for a few years up at the penitentiary before all the smoke clears away. You can put *that* in your pipe and smoke it, too."

144

Luther sighed. "That's the first really sensible thing I ever heard you say," he told the sheriff, then looked quickly away from the older man's rising wrath, saying: "We'll be running into Buff pretty quick now, so don't get rattled and go for your gun."

Sheriff Dowling made an inarticulate sound deep in his throat.

They rode with the descending darkness dripping its steadily increasing gloom over them. They by-passed several gravelly little land swells where nothing grew, and were beginning to angle slightly northward around still another low rise, when a voice came out of the murk dead ahead to halt them.

" 'That you, Lute?"

"It's me. I've got Tom Dowling here, too."

"Thought I recognized that fat silhouette," said Buff dryly, walking his horse forward into their vision. At his side, expressionlessly watching the big lawman, was Arthur Cooley.

Dowling and Buff Brady exchanged a long, bristling look, then Luther explained who the prisoner was. Dowling listened, still looking thunderous, and finally he said to the prisoner: "Is that all true?"

"It's true."

"You'll testify to that under oath in court?"

"If you'll keep Miller from hirin' someone to kill me, I will."

"Then come along," said the sheriff, turning his horse.

On the ride back Dowling exhaustively questioned Cooley. He did not cease probing until the lights of Lincoln were coming up to them across the plain. Then he turned toward Buff to say: "Y'know, for that damned jail break I ought to knock the lights outen you."

Buff looked at Dowling, then away. He scowled. He shot a sideways glance at Luther, who was watching him closely now. Then he surprised them all by saying: "I reckon you got the right at that. I'm sorry, Tom. I apologize."

Dowling, thrown completely off balance by this humility in a man neither he nor Luther, who had known Buff much longer, had ever seen before, looked nonplussed. He cleared his throat and rubbed his jaw and squinted to make certain Buff was not being sarcastic. Then he muttered: "Aw, hell, forget it. Buy me a drink when this is all over and we'll call it quits."

"I'll do that," said Buff in the same contrite tone. Then his voice firmed up into briskness again. "What about Miller?"

Dowling was beginning to bend his horse's neck toward the hitch rack in front of his combination office jail when Buff said this. He did not reply until he had dismounted, then he said: "Inside. He ought to be here now."

Colton Miller was inside. He was shaking with

wrath as Buff, Sheriff Dowling, Luther, and Arthur Cooley pushed in out of the night. At sight of Cooley, Miller's hot stare froze. He did not take his eyes off the hired gunman until the sheriff said gruffly to him: "Sit down!" Miller sat. Dowling said next: "You cooked your own goose, Miller. This here ex-rider of yours told me enough to just about get you hung."

"He's a liar!" shouted the cowman, gripping the edge of his chair. "He's blaming me to save his own skin. I didn't know him and his pardner were goin' to kill Graham. They rode off and I never. . . ."

"Who said anything about this man and his pardner killing John Graham?" barked the sheriff, stemming Miller's flood of words. "No one in this room said anything about that. No one here told you about it, so how come you knew . . . unless you ordered it done like this feller says?"

Miller gulped. He swung frantic glances at the woodenly staring and silent men who ringed him around. "I'll get the best lawyers in Colorado," he said, his voice beginning to rise again. "You'll never send me to prison. Not as long as I've got a cent to fight you with."

"That may not be very long," interrupted Luther. "As soon as Buff and I leave here, we're going to call a meeting of the homesteaders, Miller. We're going to have them file damage suits against you for everything you've done to them."

Miller's florid face paled. He stared up at Luther. After an interval of silence when only the big cowman's shattered breathing was heard, he said: "Listen a minute. I'll pay you for your soddy. I'll have your corrals rebuilt and give you some more cattle. Listen, I'll set you up in the cow business myself. I'll make it right with the others, too."

"How will you square it up with John Graham's daughter?" asked Luther, and turned toward Sheriff Dowling. "I need some fresh air. While we were fighting this man, I thought maybe we were up against a real *man*. He makes me sick to my stomach, Sheriff. I got to have some fresh air."

Tom Dowling nodded solemnly. "Help yourself," he said. "There's a big night out there, Luther. Just one thing. Judge Spicer'll want to talk to you and Buff at the trial."

"We'll be either here in town or out at our homesteads. We'll be handy, Sheriff. You just send word and we'll come a-ridin'."

Dowling accompanied both Luther and Buff out onto the plank walk. "I'm obliged," he said. "And if I was a mite rough on you boys, I apologize."

"I'll take mine in whiskey," said Buff, grinning. "Good night, Sheriff."

"Good night, boys."

Luther looked at Buff. They both turned north with the same thought in mind and hiked along the sidewalk in the direction of Lincoln's only boarding house. "We ought to clean up first," said Buff, all his doubts and tremulousness returning with a rush.

"Jessie won't care," said Luther solemnly. "But I can't answer for that Eastern dude-raised pretty little blonde." He paused, then added: "Tell you what, Buff. You go get cleaned up and I'll go along and see 'em both . . . sort of console 'em until you come along."

"You," said Buff stoutly, "can go to hell."

They continued on along the hollow boards, their boot steps making musical echoes, their shadows dancing through roadway dust, and their bone-weariness forgotten now in a kind of anticipation that left them both more fearful than either had ever been in the face of Colton Miller's deadly wrath, or under the guns of his hired assassins.

Man from Durango

I

The town of Winterset was a grid of blacks and grays. It had been steadily raining until the previous day and the one, wide, long roadway running north and south was an unrelieved length of black mud. Along Front Street were businesses. Among them a bank, a bakery next door to a saddle shop, three cafés, and in the center of the roadway, halfway from Front Street's two endings, was a barn-like old building that was, so the overhead sign said:

Winterset's Emporium
Bolt Goods, Groceries & Sweets
The Best Quality at Lowest Prices

There were also six saloons and two churches. Of the latter, one was Catholic and one was Baptist. The Catholics had come to Winterset first, but with the influx of Texans, Baptist Bible-backs had also come, for clearly in their view a need existed in Winterset to administer to the salvation of souls, and say what you like about Texans, they were as clan-like as peas in a pod, whether religious or otherwise.

A man called Durango rode into Winterset while some vague but discernible uneasiness lay over the town. He came from the south—down Mexico way—and he had a waterproof poncho covering most of him, including the ivory-butted gun lashed low to his right leg. He saw the two churches, one northerly and one southerly, facing each other from opposite ends of town, looking for all the world like stubborn old men, uncompromisingly adamant, blind, and bigoted.

In the Southwest, Catholic churches were common enough; the *padres* had pioneered this land in the name of a temporal trinity: glory, God, and gold. But outside of Texas one did not ordinarily encounter very many Baptist churches, unless of course there were a lot of Texans around, and this fact told Durango that Winterset had its share of Texans.

He had nothing in particular against Texans. He was in fact a native Texan himself, but there had been some unpleasantness a few years back and a Texas boy named Bent Ander had run south with the wild wind, down over the line into Mexico's Durango province, and stayed there ever since. Now he was back. Now he rode that quagmire roadway with a fish-belly sky overhead, swollen, leaden, and scarcely moving, and, as he passed onward toward the *Winterset Livery Stable—Amos Fallon, Prop,* he sighted an occasional face peering at him from a window, a doorway, or from behind a discreet curtain. Most of these faces were brooding, with fear tugging at their lips. But there was nobody in the roadway. Bad weather, he told himself wryly, and made a little wintry smile. Just bad weather was all.

He rode into the livery barn, got down, removed the poncho, and deftly tied it aft of the cantle. Then he turned to put a serene look upon the older man standing there, his breath steaming in the gray chill, his muddy eyes examining Durango and his bearded mouth a thin, silent line.

"How much for a week?" asked Durango.

"Two dollars."

The money came out of Durango's pocket. The liveryman took it, pocketed it, and automatically reached for the reins. He had offered no greeting and he now turned away without a word. Durango noticed this, kept his eye on the man until in the runway's rank gloom he was difficult to make out. Then the man from Durango passed out of the barn to lean against a yonder wall and assess this hushed and unfriendly place. He was still standing there when a little knot of horsemen, pygmies against that lowering dark sky, appeared to the north, coming steadily down on the town with steely mountainsides far out behind them. Durango paid them no attention at first, then he distantly heard a man's sharp cry of warning somewhere among the nearby buildings and this alerted him to the imminence of something, and he put his liquid dark gaze outward once more to study those moving riders.

There were six of them riding all in a bunch, and obviously they had a purpose in mind. It was very clear from the way they rode that these men were not range riders approaching Winterset for release of the long hungers that built up in range riders. Durango's brows drew inward and downward in a small frown. There was a strong feeling of trouble here, a mood of violence. He started to push off the wall.

"Better come in here," said a voice at Durango's elbow. "Better be quick about it, too."

Durango obeyed both suggestions, glimpsed the liveryman's bearded face as he whipped around moving deeply into shadows, then halted. "What's going on?" he asked.

For a breathless moment the liveryman said nothing; he kept a careful vigil of those oncoming horsemen, then he also glided back out of sight, his face and eyes reflecting worry and fear.

"It's the Clancy bunch," he said to the man from Durango. "Burt Clancy and his riders."

Durango was unimpressed by the name, but he was very impressed at the way his companion there in the darkness said it, as though Burt Clancy and the devil were one and the same.

He heard those riders passing recklessly down through town, showering mud and cursing at the poor footing for their mounts. He would have gone out to look at them, but as he moved, the liveryman snagged his arm, holding him back.

"No, don't go out there," husked the liveryman. "Leave 'em be."

Durango shook off those detaining fingers, passed forward as far as the edge of the doorway, and looked out. All six horsemen were alighting at a saloon hitch rack. They were mud-caked and beard-stubbled as though they had been in the saddle a long time. Their animals, though, were good ones and showed thoughtful care; even mud and sweat could not now conceal the quality of those animals.

"Good horses," murmured Durango.

Behind him the liveryman agreed quietly: "Sure. In their business you got to ride the best horses. Good horses are your life insurance."

Durango watched all six riders stomp up out of the mud and slam their way into the saloon. They scarcely cast looks around them at the town and this solid scorn sang out over the distance to touch Durango. He returned to the liveryman's side. "What's it all about?" he inquired. "What's going on here?"

"Trouble," muttered the liveryman, and started away.

Durango shot out an arm to catch hold of the liveryman and swing him back around. "I asked you a question," he said. "I expect an answer."

That worried, bearded face turned fearful, troubled. "I ain't a man to talk against others," he muttered. "You're a stranger here. Take my advice

157

. . . saddle up and ride out the rear door of my barn . . . and keep on riding."

Durango let his hand fall away. He said: "Mister, this is poor weather for riding. Besides, my horse needs a rest and so do I. Now suppose you tell me what's wrong with this town."

"Nothing's wrong with the town. Not exactly anyway. Our marshal got killed last night yonder in the Lone Star Saloon. The place them fellers just entered. We got no law now until the city council can get together and find us another feller who'll wear the star." The liveryman shot a sidling glance across the roadway. He seemed to be considering something, then he said: "It was a fair fight. That much I know, 'cause I was havin' a drink at the bar when it happened." He shook his head. "But it just happened to be fair. If our lawman'd come out of it alive, them others would've shot him anyway."

"Who are they?"

The liveryman squinted and put an indignant look upon the man from Durango. "The Clancys. What kind of a question is that, anyway? Everybody knows the Clancy bunch."

"Not quite everybody," stated Durango. "I've never heard of them."

"Then you got to be new in these parts."

"All right. I'll admit that. Now tell me who the hell the Clancy outfit is."

"Burt Clancy owns the Muleshoe cow outfit up

against the hills to the north. Two of them other fellers are his brothers, Nate and Aaron. The others are Muleshoe riders." The liveryman, speaking obviously against his will, jumped his gaze away from Durango and back again. "Now you know," he said.

"Not enough. Which one killed your lawman last night?"

"Aaron Clancy. He was that big, raw-boned feller."

"Why hasn't a mob of townsmen got together and run these Clancys off, if you folks don't like them?"

The liveryman squinted. He considered the stranger for a thoughtful long moment before saying, in an almost reverent tone: "Mister, don't nobody run a Clancy anywhere. Nobody!"

"That tough, huh?"

"Yes, sir, that tough."

Durango turned, glanced out into the empty roadway. At his side the liveryman also shot one swift glance outward, then he paced away quickly and became lost in the barn's gloom.

Durango waited in the barn for two full hours before the Muleshoe riders came banging out of the saloon across from where he sat watching them, got back astride, and went loping back the way they had come, flinging chunks of mud from beneath them in their headlong rush out of Winterset. Then Durango picked his way through roadway slime to the far plank walk, halted there to kick methodically that weighty and sticky gumbo from his boots, and pass on into the Lone Star Saloon.

The place was utterly without customers, which was extraordinary for weather such as now hung over Winterset. Only a white-faced barman stood watching as Durango crossed forward, each footfall making a solid echo in the stillness.

"Never saw anything like it before," said the man from Durango, placing both elbows upon the bar top. "A whole town treed by six cowboys."

The bartender blinked. His look at Durango sharpened. But all he said was: "What's your pleasure, stranger?"

"Rye whiskey."

When the drink came, Durango downed it neatly. "Hit me once more," he directed, and also downed that drink. He smiled at the barman and he insultingly said: "I saw the Baptist church. That means Texans. Must be a pretty scurvy lot of 'em hereabouts to let six men tree their town."

The bartender's gaze hardened at this. He leaned over the bar a little and spoke in a low and brittle voice: "Stranger, we lost a helluva good lawman right here in this saloon last night. One of them six killed him."

"So I heard," said Durango, still half smiling.

The barman drew up off the bar. Something moved in the depths of his considering eyes. He did not speak right away. Then he said: "Mister, talk like you're makin' ain't real healthy in Winterset. You're makin' light of the Clancys and the Texans both. If one don't get you, the other will . . . unless you ride on, which I'm advising you to do."

The man from Durango widened his slow, quiet smile. "No," he said, "I've got nothing to fear from the men of this town."

"And the Muleshoe, the Clancys?"

Durango leaned there, gazing ahead at the barman. His smile faded out little by little. He said: "What are the three Clancys worth to this town, dead?"

The barman drew back as though stung. He said not a word but very gradually a peculiar expression mantled his face. Then he turned and stiffly walked down the bar and busied himself there, head averted, face blank, and his hands very busy in a bucket of wash water.

Durango lingered for a time in the saloon, waiting to see the kind of men who lived in Winterset. But after an hour he was still alone with the abruptly unfriendly bartender. He left the bar to stroll north a way, then south, looking into store windows. He frequently saw people in the stores but encountered very few out in the roadway. Finally he took his saddlebags from the livery barn and went to the Winterset Hotel. There, he paid for a bath and a room, enjoyed the bath first, then afterward, with quick night descending, he drew up a chair to his upstairs window and, hooking both booted feet upon the sill, sat there in heavy darkness, looking out.

The town revived somewhat after supper. Riders came picking their way through the mud to tie up outside saloons or variety houses. These, Durango saw in that sooty gloom, were typical range riders, ordinary cowboys. He studied them casually and he also studied the townsmen, what of them he could see. It was curious to him that six men could frighten a town half to death. He had seen this identical situation develop down in Mexico, but there the towns had been invested by drunken *revolutionistas*, hundreds upon hundreds of *pronunciados* who had looted and murdered at will. Here, there were only six men. He had seen them and they had struck no awe in his heart.

He shrugged. Not that he cared at all. Within a few days, a week at the most, he would be on his way northward again. Winterset would be forgotten. If he ever recalled it in after years, it would be to remember that he'd actually seen a cowardly town, once.

He was tired. It had been a hard ride up out of Durango province. It was a bad time of the year for riding; springtime was always squally, alternately warm and cold, rainy, blustery. But he'd been in Mexico too long. He longed to ride in the dust of a cattle drive again, to lie around campfires listening to his own kind.

The things that form a man in his earliest life also sustain him. He cannot forget them; they exert a pull upon him, and, if he dares, he will one day return to them.

Durango stood up, yawned, kicked off his boots, and eased down upon the bed. It was good to be back. Even in a town like Winterset. Old recollections crowded around him in the dark solitude of that upstairs room, thoughts of other places and earlier times. He recalled with no effort how a shock-headed boy had acquired his first six-gun, how he had secretly swaggered in the seclusion of a plum thicket practicing drawing and firing at imaginary enemies.

He also recalled how, at eighteen, after four years of familiarizing himself with that gun, a giant of a bearded freighter from Santa Fé, liquored to the gills, had ridiculed him in the roadway dust on a glaring hot day before the whole watching populace of a little backwater Texas town near the border. He could remember that brutish shaggy face with no trouble at all. He recalled how the huge freighter had started for him, saying he'd disarm him and paddle him for presuming to carry a gun when he hadn't yet shaved. And the warning. He'd stood, stockstill and wide-legged, seeing in this juggernaut of a man all his imaginary enemies rolled into one.

And the second warning. Then the freighter's fury, his cursing, and finally his downward sweeping hand. There had been only that one pistol shot. The freighter fell dead and the kid from a backwater Texas town had fled over the line.

II

Winterset was stirring by the time Durango got downstairs at the hotel. Roadway traffic was brisk and noisy. He breakfasted at a café next to the hotel, then passed outside to let sunshine warm his ribs.

Roadway mud steamed, firming into a kind of black glue. The sky had changed entirely away from its former glowering, and far northerly where mountains sprang from the plain there were shafts of a sharp shining from rain-exposed rock croppings.

Even the town itself seemed clean-scrubbed and different. The fear that had gripped it the day before was much less in evidence this day. Durango, leaning idly upon an upright post, saw and sensed all these things. Then he moved idly out into the roadway bound diagonally for the livery barn. He let two ranch wagons pass, brands burned deeply into side-board wood, and a third incoming wagon, too, but this one's brand struck a chord within him so he threw an upward look at the driver as the vehicle ground past drawn by two jenny mules.

The driver was a girl. She was tall and blonde and had skin the color of churned butter. Durango stood still for that wagon to pass and nearly failed to note that deep-burned brand upon the tailgate that struck down into him: *Muleshoe.*

He trudged ahead to the far walkway and halted there, ostensibly to kick the gumbo off his boots, but actually to watch that Muleshoe wagon wheel in before the Winterset Emporium and halt. From down in the wagon box a lanky youth rose up, vaulted down, and made the team fast. Then he stood back, grinning, and the blonde girl climbed down. Durango saw how her tan skirt pulled taut across a firm thigh, how her powder-blue shirt swelled forward from the solid strain put upon it. Then the girl got on the plank walk beside that lanky, smiling youth, and swung her head to glance steadily up and across the roadway where Durango was standing. Durango was confused by her unwavering regard. He had not thought she had noticed him at all, and now something was coming out of her to reach that far distance and stir all his male instincts.

Durango continued his way to the livery barn. There, he encountered the same wispy, bearded man he'd initially spoken to. He smiled at him and asked about his horse, and all the time in the back of his mind was a warming recollection of that

Muleshoe girl. With her was a compounding curiosity. He finally said: "Something you didn't tell me yesterday about the Clancys and their Muleshoe outfit."

The liveryman pondered; he studied Durango's face; he grunted. "Lots I didn't tell you, stranger. Like I said then, I ain't much of a hand for talkin' about other folks."

"The girl," said Durango softly. "Who is she?"

"Oh." The liveryman turned pensive. "That's Burt Clancy's kid. Her ma died four years back. She does the cookin' at Muleshoe."

"She Burt Clancy's only kid?"

"Yup."

"She just drove into town with a Muleshoe supply wagon and there was a string bean of a boy with her."

The liveryman began shaking his head. "Ain't no relation at all . . . that boy. He's an orphan. Indians killed his folks 'bout ten years back and Burt took him in to raise."

"That was charitable," mused Durango.

The liveryman's expression turned sardonic. "I'd be that charitable, too, if I could find a chore boy who'd work for nothing but his keep."

"What's the girl's name?"

"Maryann. It's spelled like it was one word," answered the liveryman, and spelled it. "M-a-r-y-a-n-n. Not Mary Ann."

Durango gravely nodded. "I'll remember that.

Like it was all one name." He turned and slowly paced back outside where the sunlight was picking up heat as the morning advanced.

At the hitch rack, that Muleshoe wagon was being loaded with supplies. Durango stood watching, waiting for Maryann Clancy to reappear. But she did not do this; the boy came and went with armloads and an aproned clerk from the emporium also passed back and forth, but Maryann did not come out into the roadway at all. But Durango had spent a long time in Mexico; he had long ago learned how to wait; he could lean upon something as the Mexicans also do, and while away whole hours, even whole days, doing nothing at all but keeping a vigil and privately shuffling his secret thoughts. It was something a man learned in Mexico, and it was grounded in a kind of Indian fatalism.

Then the girl came forth and halted at the wagon side. She was frowning over a crumpled paper. Where that fresh sunlight struck down, her hair showed golden and her throat and bare lower arms were the same color. With all his attention closed upon her, Durango saw how her lips lay together, full and willful, how her dark eyelashes were lowered, intent, totally unaware for this moment of his constant scrutiny, and how also her strong and vibrant and blooming figure stood there indifferently and unconsciously as she concentrated on that supply list.

Then her glance rose quickly, and without any searching at all she went that full long distance to where he stood as though through some pre-arrangement they would look into one another's faces like this.

She didn't look away; she took his glance and held it, as direct as hers also was, as though she were challenging him some way, as though she were daring him to intrude on the drudgery of her days.

Her eyes were tawny brown with gold flecks in them and her hands holding that supply list were square and small and nut-brown. She was handsome, and he thought that she evidently knew this, because there was a definite pride in the way she stood still and straight, scorning to slouch as women usually did who wished to minimize a greater-than-average fullness of bosom. Her assurance, too, under his steady look told him she was proud, and in his hungry gaze this seemed a good thing, too. He pushed off the livery barn wall and started forward, struck the roadway, and paced over it oblivious to traffic.

A store clerk came forth with a bag of flour on one shoulder at this point, and behind him came the lanky Muleshoe chore boy, also laden. They deposited their burdens in the wagon. Maryann stepped off the plank walk, got beside the forewheel, stepped firmly on the hub, and sprang up. She stooped to unwind the lines from the brake handle and ignored Durango as though he not only did not now exist, but had never existed.

"Let's go," she said. The chore boy released those jenny mules, vaulted atop the wagon-bed load, and called back a cheery good bye to the aproned clerk. The mules hit their collars, chain tugs sang tautly, and Muleshoe's ranch wagon forged ahead through the drying roadway.

Durango halted beside the clerk, watching. "She going on south?" he asked.

"No," replied the clerk, and put a considering look upon Durango. "She'll make a sashay at the lower end of town, get turned about, then go north back up this way and on out of town."

Durango waited.

"Sure can handle a team, can't she?" said the clerk in a tone of admiration.

"Sure can," Durango agreed. "And she's pretty."

The clerk shot another glance at Durango. His easy smile began fading. "Her father's Burt Clancy."

"Yes, I know."

The clerk's gaze at Durango sharpened. He threw a look down where Maryann was bringing the wagon about with miles of prairie to maneuver in. He said: "Stranger, you got the look in your eye of a man admiring a handsome woman."

"Is that a fact?" said Durango, watching the wagon reënter Winterset, coming steadily northward toward him.

"Stranger, that there is Burt Clancy's daughter."

"You said that before. I heard you."

The clerk sighed and wiped his hands upon his apron, shot Durango a pitying look, turned, and went back into the store.

Maryann saw him; he was certain of that fact, long before she was close. His watching heightened a self-consciousness that he felt was quite foreign to her. Still, she tooled that laden wagon around the deepest chuck holes and through roadway traffic without once looking away from her onward course, and, when she was even with him, and he was sure she would not look at him, she did so, slowly turned her head and got a good, close look at him—and he at her.

"Hell," murmured Durango, "she's downright beautiful."

He watched her, continued to watch her until, just before she passed on by, he was sure he'd seen a break of interest in her eyes. Then she was gone and in her place was the boyish countenance of Muleshoe's chore boy perched atop the wagon's load, his raw-boned big frame cutting out Durango's view of Maryann entirely.

Durango returned to the present only gradually. He had never before in his lifetime had a woman's beauty or nearness cut down into him like this. He turned, paced along to the Lone Star Saloon, entered, and crossed to the bar to lean there, knee-sprung and suddenly moody. That same barman to whom he'd spoken the previous day came up, put his accusing and disapproving eyes upon Durango, and said: "What's your pleasure?"

Durango's moodiness was increasing, making him testy and raw-edged; it was an inexplicable thing, but it was there in him nevertheless, and he did something he'd never done before; he deliberately picked a fight.

"I don't like that expression you're wearing," he told the barman, and heard talk along the bar dwindle a little at his statement while men turned to see whose voice that was. "You're thinking what I said yesterday about killing the Clancys, bartender, and you're all full up with righteousness. You think I was making this yellow town of yours a proposition. I wasn't."

The barman's eyes dropped. He moved back from the bar as far as he could but did not take his hands off the edge of it. He cleared his throat.

"Rye whiskey, bartender, and fast."

He got his drink ahead of other waiting customers at the bar. Men's careful sly eyes were appraising him from beneath hat brims, from partially averted faces, from exaggeratedly disinterested backbar-mirrored looks.

"Leave the bottle."

The bartender left it.

Durango had his usual two straight shots and no more. He lingered, though, groping inward for an explanation to this new way he felt—as though he wanted to hit someone, or get drunk, or kiss a woman, or run a fast horse into the wind. He knew they were looking at him, assessing his worth and his danger potential, and that deepened the irritation, so he turned, hooked both elbows upon the bar, and tossed a contemptuous look out over the room and said ringingly: "First time in my life I ever saw a yellow town. I've seen cowardly men and horses and dogs, but never before a cowardly town. Six men ride in here and kill your town marshal and tree the lot of you . . . and here you sit playing poker or buying drinks or talking about whether it'll rain again or not . . . too yellow to go out and bring that man in here to stand trial."

From a card table near the door a swarthy man with a fierce dragoon moustache and a cigar jutting from a lipless mouth put his sulphur gaze on Durango. He did not, however, move, nor did the other men at his table. In fact, the other poker players acted as though Durango had not spoken. They continued to consider their card hands impassively. Then the dark man reached up to thumb back his gracefully upcurving black hat and gently lower the hand, and he said: "Stranger, in this country ain't no man tried for a fair fight." The smoky gaze held to Durango; cigar smoke rose up lazily past those boring eyes. "Now have your drink and shut up," this swarthy man said, and in those seven words sealed off all avenues for withdrawal or retreat for himself and Durango.

Something like a half-heard sigh rose up from the Lone Star's morning patrons, and here or there a man shuffled toward the door, or away from the bar on either side of Durango, or silently arose from the table where the swarthy man sat, and went well off to one side.

"Stand up," said Durango.

The swarthy man pushed back and got to his feet. He was compactly built and there was something familiar about him to Durango. He still smoked his cigar but his dark gaze was impersonal now, cold as ice and very lethal. He stood confidently waiting. He seemed an old hand at this, very assured, and easy in his mind as to the outcome.

From off to one side the barman said, grudging the fact that he was required to speak these words: "Not in here, boys. Outside if you will."

Durango was like ice. His every primeval instinct was sharpened. Tobacco smoke in the atmosphere came sharper to him. That dark and waiting stranger's face was clear as glass in each flaw and small detail. He said: "One man in Winterset isn't a coward. Mister, you want to turn and walk out that door?"

"No," said the swarthy man, standing like stone. "Do you?"

Durango shook his head. "I'll give you an edge," he said. "Go for it!"

That dark man's shoulders slumped, his hand blurred toward his hip. Durango was a 1,000th of a second behind him but the dark man's gun was only half clear when Durango's muzzle blast near burst the eardrums of all those white-faced spectators. The dark man was flung as though by a giant fist back upon the yonder wall, and he was half turned, also. His hat fell, and he lost the cigar. Through twisted lips he ground out: "God damn!" Then he locked his jaw hard against waves of spiraling pain and awkwardly squared himself around, still holding his gun loosely so that it pointed toward the floor, and stared over at Durango. "Go ahead," he finally croaked. "You got the right."

There was a spreading scarlet stain just below the shoulder of his gun arm.

Durango leathered his weapon. He jerked his head at the bartender. "Fetch him some rags and some hot water. Be quick about it."

The injured cowman groped forward and went down into his chair at the poker table. He pinched off the flow of blood with his free hand and, looking at Durango, said: "A double whiskey."

Durango poured it, and took it across to the table. He hesitated then, with his back to all those statue-like onlookers, and addressed them curtly: "Clear out, the lot of you."

They went, trouping one after the other until

only Durango, the wounded man, and the troubled bartender remained.

Durango sat down, handed his adversary the double shot, watched him drink it off neatly, and said: "Mister, what's your name? Too bad we had to meet this way, but it's good to know Winterset's got one resident who's not yellow."

"I don't live in Winterset," answered the swarthy man, putting up a hand to dash away the tears that double shot had caused. "And my name is Nate Clancy."

III

Durango's memory dumped an identifying profile downward. Durango had seen this man before, one day earlier when those six strangers had charged into a silent town and tied up outside this same saloon. He gazed at Nate Clancy, saying nothing, while the barman brought a bowl of water and some clean rags and went to work with a closed face and experienced hands to tend Nate Clancy's torn upper arm.

Clancy's steady, cold gaze clung to Durango. He said: "You like a little advice, stranger?"

Durango shook his head. "No thanks. Folks've been giving me nothing but advice since I rode into this town."

"I'll give it to you anyway . . . ," began Clancy.

But Durango cut across his forming words with a short sentence of his own as he rose up from the table: "When you're able, Clancy, get on your horse and leave Winterset." The barman and Nate Clancy both lifted their heads, both stared at Durango, and Durango, seeing himself already committed, added more to it: "And when you come back, don't be wearing a gun."

He stood a moment waiting, but Nate Clancy said nothing, only kept staring at him. The barman looked swiftly away and went on with his bandaging.

Durango left the saloon, stood a moment upon the outside plank walk, seeing how little bunches of men up and down the roadway were heatedly speaking together, and also how they ceased talking at his appearance and put their hooded looks on him, then he pushed on out into the road and struck out once more for the livery barn.

That bearded liveryman was there, his face saying plainly that he'd heard of the shooting. Durango said disgruntedly: "Fetch me a horse. I'm goin' to ride out and get some fresh air."

He waited while the liveryman scurried off on this task. When the horse was brought forth, Durango ran a thumb under the cinch for precaution, then toed in, and swung up.

"Maybe," suggested the liveryman, "you'd ought to take your own critter, mister, and keep on riding."

Durango looked down at that troubled face. He took up the reins. "Mister, what's your name?"

"Amos. Amos Fallon."

"Mister Fallon, you just worry about Amos Fallon and I'll worry about me."

He rode out of Winterset, with noon's shadowless brightness all around, traveling by stage road northward toward the steadily looming mountains. He had no very clear idea where he was going, only that he was still restless. The gunfight had not leached out any of that earlier annoyance and he had a feeling that he needed space and time and quiet.

He crossed a gravel ford and left the road, passing onward where the land began to swell up and break over into a series of long rolls. He struck a boiling white-water creek that obviously came plunging from those far-away mountain heights, and here he got down, let his animal drink, and moved upstream fifty feet from the horse to drink, also. The water was like melted ice. Then he pushed onward into that broken country where pine scent came on the afternoon air to token a nearness to foothills. Here, he found the same snow-water creek twisting and curving in a generally northward way, and finally stopped on a juniper hill where the soil was gravelly and shallow with sparse lupine and bunch grass furiously growing after winter's long coldness.

Here, he had an excellent view of the southward run of countryside. The grass was good, there was ample clear, cold water, and farther back behind him was a pine forest. Good cow country, he told himself, but for fattening critters, not for making up any big gathers to drive somewhere. He would ride on then, because he did not want to put down roots; he wanted to push the drag of some herd into new territory.

That damned Clancy, he said to himself savagely, and cut off the reflection abruptly. It hadn't been Clancy's fault; he himself had forced that fight. *What a mess, her uncle, of all the people to humble with a wing shot, her uncle!*

He got down from the saddle, rein-hobbled the livery horse, and moved into the spotted shade of a juniper to sit upon warm earth and savor the stillness, the bigness of this country, and let springtime's first warming heat winnow the troubled feeling from his heart.

Sometimes, regardless of how a man wills it, fate makes him do things that are pointless or senseless or just plain stupid. He squirmed on the ground, plucked away a grass stem, and stuck it between strong, white teeth. No, he said severely to himself, it wasn't fate's fault. He'd done that stupid thing all by himself and deliberately.

He threw away the grass stem, tossed his hat down in the shade, and rolled in the grass. It was good to lie here, to let his muscles turn loose against that warm and fecund springtime earth.

Well, it was done, and the Clancys who had treed a town would now come a-helling after him.

He could take Amos Fallon's wise advice, or he could be a fool and wait in Winterset for what came next. The odds, though, were rather sobering. Six to one. Even a topnotch gunman wouldn't see any great cowardice in fleeing from odds like those.

He squinted upward through juniper limbs where a flawless sky was blue-burnished and empty save for a solitary high-spiraling red-tailed hawk.

For what? his mind demanded of him. The answer came instantly. *For a tail-tucked damned town afraid of its own shadow.* Not because he had any grudge against the Clancys; he didn't even know them; most pointless of all was that everyone had told him the fight had been a fair one—so why had he jumped in like a fool going off half-cocked?

That red-tailed hawk spied him and swooped much lower in a long and graceful glide. He beat his wings to hang momentarily still in the air, cocking a downward look. Durango watched him, saw those double-edged sharp talons hanging and the sloping predatory head.

Because of Maryann, he said truthfully, forthrightly to himself. Because something had happened between them in that sparkling springtime morning brightness, something that had entirely altered him away from what he had always been, in that one moment of confusing and bewildering magic.

He blinked; the hawk was no longer there. He sat up and reached for his hat and swore aloud: "Hell, a lot of good it did to ride out here. A man can run from everything but his thoughts."

And because this was so true, he resolved not to run from those six-to-one odds, after all.

He rose up finally, went after the horse, and rode on northward down off the little juniper hill, heading toward those nearing mountainsides where the moving sun no longer shone and where graying slopes looked cold and uninviting.

He made scarcely any sound in passing along, except for the tiny music of rein chains and spurs and leather rubbing upon leather. The ground was not yet summer-dry and packed; each hoof fall of his mount was absorbed into it, leaving a clearly defined imprint.

Twice he came upon a wagon's course and at other times he passed the bedding grounds of cattle, but not until he was a long four miles northward of the juniper hill, where pine scent was stronger, did he actually encounter any critters. Then, on sighting him, these cattle precipitously fled into the forest's shelter, and he could only dimly make out their white faces peering back down at him.

The highest mountain peaks were briefly alight

with the sun's explosive red light, then they were plunged into full darkness, and very gradually that obscuring pall advanced down the mountain slopes. Durango turned back at this point; it would be full dark by the time he reëntered Winterset, which was exactly the way he wanted it to be.

Spring dusk came swiftly. He was still far from Winterset when that creeping dusk swept up to him, over him, and ran like a flooding dark sea to shroud the onward land. He thought, after a time, that he was not far from the gravelly ford where he'd earlier left the stage road, when he heard a rider coming swiftly in behind him. He'd heard this identical sound in the night many times under many circumstances, and always his immediate reaction had been a mingling of interest and caution. He changed course, rode steadily into the west for several minutes, then halted altogether, leaving no sound for that oncoming rider to place him. Then he dismounted, again rein-hobbled the livery beast, and went cat-footing over his westerly trail, seeking whoever was behind him.

Sound and rider came ahead toward him. Whoever it was had also altered course and that meant simply to Durango that he was being followed. He stood still, measuring that closing distance with both ears, then saw the horse and rider break clear of dusk's mantling and seem to hesitate, as though the person was straining for sounds, before continuing again at a slower pace.

"Hello," he said, when the horse's outline loomed up dead ahead, moving forward and keeping the animal's body between himself and the rider's right hand and arm.

"Hello yourself," came a woman's voice, showing no surprise at all, but sounding blunt and challenging.

Durango stopped stockstill. "Maryann . . . ?"

"Yes," came the reply, "and who are you?"

He went fully up into her sight and halted again, gazing upward. "I don't know how I knew it was you," he told her.

She sat still in the saddle, both hands lying upon the horn. He saw instantly that he had startled her and that she was regarding him now, not with fear exactly, or apprehension, but with a guarded expression, as though she did not want him to say anything that would rob her of the initiative.

"What are you doing out here?" she demanded finally, holding his gaze in that murky light as she'd also done hours before in Winterset.

"Just riding." He took two steps closer. "By the way, my name is Bent Ander."

"You're on Muleshoe range, Bent Ander," she said stiffly to him. "It's not a healthy place to be in the night. My father and uncles are sensitive about riders being on our range after nightfall."

When she mentioned her uncles, Durango was jarred by a thought. He said: "Are they all at home this evening?"

Maryann's brows rolled downward in a puzzled little frown. "I don't know. They weren't all there when I got back with the supplies. Why did you ask that?"

"Just wondered," mumbled Durango, and sought for something to say that would fit into the awkward silence that settled now between them.

"You'd better get back on your horse and head out of here," she said, sounding skeptical of him and a little suspicious. "If the others'd found you, I don't think. . . ."

"Will you tell me something, Maryann?"

". . . What?"

"What happened at the Lone Star night before last?"

Her gaze became flinty. "Does it concern you?" she asked thinly. "Because if it does. . . ."

"No, it doesn't concern me. Not exactly, anyway," Durango said, sounding lame in his own ears. "What caused it?"

"Rustling. We've been missing cattle for over a year now. My uncle Aaron said something in the Lone Star about the law hereabouts not caring . . . that maybe the law was even involved. . . ."

When she added nothing to this, Durango understood. It was not a new story and he could fill in from experience the parts she'd left out. Her uncle had been drinking; the town marshal probably had also been drinking.

"One of those senseless things," he murmured,

more to himself than to her. Then he looked upward and saw that she agreed with him. But her next words did not say this.

"Now you'd better move on, Bent Ander. And I'll give you a word of advice."

He groaned audibly. "Everybody's got advice."

"Don't ride on Muleshoe range after dark. The next time you just might not have any luck at all. Our riders have orders to shoot first and look afterward."

She whirled her horse and loped away. In a twinkling she was lost to him in the darkness.

He stood a moment, until the final far echo of her was gone, then went back, located his livery beast, untied it, got astride, and continued onward toward Winterset.

He struck the stage road two miles above town, saw the lights come up off the ground ahead and punch their orange brightness through darkness, and let his horse pick its own way homeward.

Overhead a raffish moon hung lopsidedly amid a clear wash of cold-shining stars and an enameled sky ran on to a far-out dim merging with sharply standing, blacker mountain peaks. The night air cooled out swiftly, bearing upon its layers of cold the distant sounds from Winterset.

He rode into town from the north and passed through patches of alternating light and darkness as far as the livery barn. There, he turned in past smoking carriage lamps on either side of the great, doorless opening, and at once saw five men lounging near the harness room door, doing nothing at all, but very obviously waiting for someone. Then the whiskery liveryman squinted up at Durango and cried out to the others: "Here he is!"

IV

To startle a suspicious, wary man in the night is an uncommonly risky thing to do. Durango was a stranger in Winterset and he'd only a few hours before shot a Clancy. Then the liveryman called out like that and Durango's gun came up in an arcing curve and halted upon those five moving figures. They kept right on moving until Durango thumbed back the cocking mechanism. That one little sound halted every one of those townsmen hard in his tracks. The liveryman, Amos Fallon, made a little squawk.

"Mister," he croaked at Durango, both eyes standing forth from his head, "this here is the city council. They only want to talk to you. That's all."

Durango nodded agreeably at the utterly still townsmen. "Talk," he said pleasantly enough, but that ugly black pistol barrel continued to cover them from its peeping position over the saddle fork. "Go ahead, boys, speak your piece, I'm listening."

A sturdy man with a respectable paunch and carefully combed mutton-chop side whiskers spoke forth: "Stranger, it's all over town how you outdrew Nate Clancy. Now, this afternoon the council got together, you see, because we've had a pressing problem since night before last, and we unanimously agreed to offer you the town marshal's job. All you have to do is keep the peace, you understand, and from time to time. . . ."

Durango listened, dumbfounded, as this man kept right on talking. He put up his gun, and, while those words flowed, he swung his attention back to Amos Fallon again, read in the liveryman's face both hope and uncertainty, then he got down from the saddle heavily, flung the reins to Fallon, and said: "Whoa, mister. Whoa up with that speech a minute." When silence came, Durango drew in a deep breath and said: "Gentlemen, I accept."

He was never afterward certain why he had accepted. He reasoned with himself later that night at the town marshal's little office as he lit a coal-oil lamp and looked around, it was partly because, since he'd decided not to run from the Clancys, he liked the idea of having a star on his shirt when they came for him. Also partly it was because, while the job would never make him wealthy, it was at least capable of supporting him, and his finances were not right then at any kind of a zenith. Then there was a third reason, also, but he did not permit himself to consider this right then. Instead, he dusted the office, examined the defunct town marshal's files, and eased down into the only padded chair this office possessed, and very slowly smiled at the far wall. In a matter of a few hours, since he'd risked coming up over the border out of Mexico, he'd changed from being a man with a price on his head somewhere else to the respectable town marshal of a thriving little cow town.

The paunchy man with those handsome muttonchop whiskers who owned the emporium and whose name was Charles F. Flagg looked in on Town Marshal Bent Ander shortly before 10:00 p.m. He beamed a kind of false goodwill as he said: "Town's quiet tonight, Marshal. It usually is, though." Then he departed, humming a little tune to himself.

Durango cocked a skeptical eye at his departing visitor's ample back and gravely said aloud— "Sure, it usually is quiet."—then got up, yawned, and passed over into the one little cell his office possessed, thumped the straw pallet on the wall bunk, and eased down upon it for a rest.

Beyond, in the round-about night there was the customary discord of a busy village, men called hootingly to one another, horses whinnied, dogs barked, and somewhere not far off a mother was calling in her child. Durango classified each of these sounds out of long habit. It was second nature for a man of his type to appraise every sound, every movement, and every face he encountered. He was lying comfortably there when a sudden shout came from up the roadway near the heart of town. This was followed by a rush of horsemen and the abrupt *jangle* they made when they drew down. Durango's drowsiness vanished. He sat up on the edge of the bunk and listened. There were no more sounds. In fact, the town became quite still. He stood up, moved out across the office as far as that coal-oil lamp, blew it out to plunge the office into full darkness, then he went onward to the door, opened it a crack, and waited. Nothing happened, so he opened it farther and took a step out onto the plank walk. A man sat on a bench in shadows under the office's boardwalk overhang. He seemed to be an old-timer.

"They're likely lookin' for you," he said to Durango. "Looked to me like Muleshoe men."

Durango twisted, put a glance on the old man, then started away. Ten feet onward, though, he reconsidered and turned back. The old man gazed up at him through the shadows. He said: "Funny thing happened to me few years back. I was down in Mexico with a freight outfit haulin' hardware an' someone come up and said to me . . . 'See that young feller yonder with the ivory-butted pistol? Well, his name's Durango. The best *Yanqui pistolero* in all *Méjico*.' "

The old man stopped speaking. He tone expressed sly humor. A quick warning struck through Durango. He watched the old man, wondering how much else he knew.

"You got good eyesight," he ultimately said to the old man, "to recognize a man in the dark."

"Oh, this ain't the first time I've seen you. I was in the Lone Star when you braced Nate Clancy. I didn't place you right off . . . not until you made your play . . . then I did."

"And . . . ?" said Durango.

"Pshaw, a feller gets to be my age, he sees a lot, he knows a little, but he don't tell things. If he has that habit, you see, he don't get to be my age." The old man chuckled. "They could've done worse," he said. "Them well-fed merchants of the city council. They could've done a lot worse. The last lawman they hired was a drunk and a bully and I ain't exactly sure when Aaron Clancy called him a part-time owlhoot he wasn't maybe a little right. But you done a tomfool thing this morning, Marshal. A feller ought to hang and rattle a little before he goes jumpin' headlong into other folks' battles."

Durango cast a look behind him up the roadway. There was no sight or sound of disturbance, so he moved in closer to the old man and said: "What's your name, old-timer?"

"Mose Clark. I used to be a buffler hunter. Before that I scouted for General Crook.

Afterward, I was a swamper and freighter and horse trader an' . . . you name it, Marshal, an' one time or another I've done it. But when a feller's got as much frost in his whiskers as I got now, there's no work for him. He's just another old-timer, waitin' around for the Grim Reaper to make his big cut with that scythe he carries."

Durango leaned there, considering this wizened and loquacious old man. He said: "You're plumb right about what happened this morning. I should've waited. When I rode in here, though, I got the impression these Clancys were trouble-makers on the prod."

"They're tough, all right," said Mose Clark. "An' they make a little trouble now and then. But they ain't exactly what you thought they was. One thing, though, Marshal, when they're your enemies, you got the best enemies a feller can get because they'll work at it. They're hot-tempered and sort of itchy around the trigger finger."

"Thanks for the warning," said Durango. "They just came into town."

"Naw," said Mose Clark. "That wasn't the Clancy brothers. Them three flannel-mouths was their riders. Asa Boyd, Tex Crockett, and Nevada Carson. But they're kind of dangerous, too, so, if you go down where they're tankin' up, Marshal, use that eye you got in the back o' your head."

"You going to be sitting here?" Durango asked.

"Yep, this here is my favorite spot. At night I

can see the whole town and can't no one see me."

"If anyone comes lookin' for me," said Durango, beginning to move away, "tell them I'm up at the Lone Star."

"Sure, Marshal. Sure thing."

Durango crossed the roadway and paused at the entrance to an alleyway. He put his back on a wood siding there and sniffed the night for trouble, his interest lifting little by little. Why had not the Clancys come themselves? By now they certainly knew he'd shot Nate.

A man shuffled past, threw Durango a nod. Perhaps he recognized him. Two riders came jogging up from the south. They were speaking back and forth as they went by, and Durango heard their casual words without particularly heeding them.

Then he started for the Lone Star Saloon. If there was trouble coming, he could not detect it in the attitude of the townsmen he saw.

Beyond the plank walk in front of the saloon stood three drowsing horses. One probably had belly worms because he wasn't shedding his winter hair either as rapidly as the other horses were, or as evenly. Durango could not make out the brand on this animal. But the horses on either side of him had readable brands. Muleshoe.

There was no excessive amount of stillness, or noise either for that matter, emanating from the Lone Star. Durango took this to mean the Clancy riders were still absorbed in their drinking, and he pushed on into the building and halted just beyond the door.

There were poker tables near the door, back along the wall so as not to interfere with men passing to and from the bar. Several players glanced up at Durango's entrance. Not all of them resumed their gaming right away. They spoke very quietly from the sides of their mouths, and other heads raised. It was as though a quiet sigh had permeated that smoky, warm atmosphere and two men abruptly cashed their chips in, arose, and without a second glance left the saloon.

Durango made his way to the bar where three men were standing shoulder to shoulder, solemnly engrossed in their drinking. They did not look around.

For a while the noise in the Lone Star did not noticeably diminish. There was the steady murmur of voices, the clatter of chips, the occasional ring of glass upon glass.

That dour bartender appeared directly across from Durango. He did not say a word but he was waiting. "Beer," said Durango, and half twisted to lean upon the bar and look out over the room.

A fresh current was now running through the saloon's atmosphere. When the barman came back with the beer, he leaned far over and said to Durango in a pleading way: "Please, Marshal . . . not tonight."

Durango drank and put down the glass. The man at his side, having heard what the barman had said, was gazing steadily at Durango from the backbar mirror. He was a lean man with calloused big hands and a strong, somewhat truculent face. Durango saw him in the mirror, drank off what remained of his beer, and gazed look for look into the mirror. The cowboy dropped his eyes; he also nudged the man on his far side with an elbow point. But this rider only grunted, missing the significance of that nudge entirely.

Durango had seen. He said to the lean cowboy: "Try again, harder this time."

The Muleshoe man did not obey, although his neck reddened.

Durango put forth a hand, reached around, and tapped the second man on the shoulder. When this rider turned finally, Durango smiled at him, saying: "I'm the town marshal."

All three riders heard his words and put their considering looks on him. They were hard men, rough and seasoned, and they did not misread that smile.

The second cowboy said only: "Is that so?" He waited a moment, then returned his attention to the shot glass in his right fist, and boomed out for the barman. "Refill," he ordered. "Refills all around."

Durango waited until the glasses were poured full, then he tossed a Mex silver dollar down.

"On me," he said, and watched the bartender hesitate before taking his money.

The Muleshoe men did not take up their glasses right away. They stood there, looking down at them, and each face held an identical expression. Finally the unshaven cowboy standing in the middle straightened up, lifted his glass, and downed the whiskey. As he put the glass down again, hard, he looked over at Durango. "Thanks, Marshal."

The other two men also drank and murmured.

Durango waited until he was sure the Muleshoe men were not going to stand the second treat, which was customary, then he said: "I'd like to meet your boss sometime. Tell him that for me, will you?"

"Yeah."

"Another thing, boys. After this don't come into Winterset wearing guns."

Three faces swung to bear. Durango put up that little smile again. "It's a new ordinance. No guns allowed within city limits. You can pass that along if you will."

Durango left the bar, passed outside into the night, and put an appraising look out over his town. Everything was quiet. A drunk was sitting cross-legged in the dirt just over the edge of the plank walk, rocking back and forth and humming to himself, and somewhere beyond the livery barn a dog fight was in progress, but otherwise Winterset was calm enough.

He stepped down into the hardening roadway, passed over to the yonder side, and turned south toward his office. He was thinking of something. There was a no sidearm ordinance in Winterset and actually he had no authority to make such a ruling. He'd have to see Charles Flagg in the morning and see to it that the city council passed such a ruling; otherwise, he was going to be embarrassed.

V

Durango met Charles Flagg at his enormous general store the following morning and made his request about the no-sidearms ordinance. Flagg was thoughtful about this. He said: "It might antagonize the cattlemen. That would be bad for business."

"It could be fatal for the businessmen if it's not passed," stated Durango, annoyance rising in him. "And as far as I'm concerned, you fellers either pass it or get yourselves another lawman."

He left the store and met Amos Fallon head on just outside. He would have brushed past but Fallon detained him with some hard words.

"The Clancys are coming, Marshal. Arch Holt who drives the stage saw 'em out on the plain north of town. Even Nate."

Durango moved off, was half across the road

when Charles Flagg's voice hit him in the back. "Marshal, come back." Durango turned. Flagg and Amos Fallon were standing side-by-side. It required only one glance to see that Fallon had given his information about the Clancys to Flagg, also. He returned to the east side of the road and halted just off the plank walk.

"We're calling a special meeting of the council," said Flagg a little breathlessly. "I'll move to have your ordinance adopted."

"Good."

"Marshal? The Clancys will be armed."

Durango dropped his glance to Amos Fallon. "How far out were they when the stage driver saw them?"

"South of the foothills. Maybe a two hour ride from town."

"Mister Flagg, how long will it take your council to get that ordinance passed?"

Flagg squirmed. He locked both hands over his paunch and pursed his lips. "If everyone's in town," he ultimately answered, "and willing, no more than half an hour."

"Then get your meeting started," said Durango, and started back across the roadway again. He stopped, though, and looked steadily at Flagg. "Send me word as soon as the ordinance is passed, and it better be passed before the Clancys arrive or you can have this badge back."

Within twenty minutes Durango noticed a

peculiar thing. Winterset appeared as deserted, as hushed and expectant, as it had been the first time he'd ever seen it. There were watchers sitting by windows and occasionally a scurrying figure darted from a building, along the walkway, and into another building.

He saw this from a slouching position in the doorway of his office and thought privately that the old ways of violence were never changing, rarely different. Those who feared, fled, those who had no fear, fought. The trouble was that the latter never stood in equal numbers with the former, men who had courage were usually, when the chips were down, quite alone.

"Care for a smoke?"

He turned. Mose Clark was there, easing down upon the wall bench. He had two cigars in his hand, and one of these he now held forth: "Old freighter friend of mine brang 'em back from Durango, Mexico, last fall. I ain't much of a smoker, but for special occasions I usually light one up."

Durango made no move to accept the cigar. His downward gaze was hard. "Is this a special occasion?" he asked.

"Yep." Old Clark nodded, pocketing the refused cigar and lighting the other one. "Ain't every day a man gets a close-by seat when there's a big fight brewing."

"Big fight?"

Clark's powdery gaze turned sly, turned knowing. "Burt Clancy ain't bringin' his brothers and his riders to town for no quiltin' bee, Marshal."

"The word gets around," murmured Durango, and returned his attention to that deserted roadway.

"It wasn't no surprise, though," stated Mose Clark. "Folks been talkin' about nothin' else since you winged Nate Clancy. It's only been a matter of time, and let me tell you something, Marshal, Burt Clancy picks the time. He's a cold and calculatin' man as don't fear critter or angel, either."

Mose blew out a heavy cloud of smoke and smacked his lips. "Good tobacco," he murmured, and seemed to be solely interested in the cigar.

Durango put his back on the old man, irritated by his cheerfulness. Around him the town lay still in midday sunshine, too peaceful-appearing, too quiet. He sighed. Behind him old Mose said: "Care for that cigar now, Marshal?"

Durango turned. The old man was smiling at him. "Sure," said Durango, and bent to light up from a match the old man held forth. He sucked back a rattling inhalation and let the smoke back out. "Pretty good," he said.

"Take your time," suggested Mose. "You got about an hour."

Durango studied that old, lined, and shrewd

face. He slowly smiled. "You've got everything figured," he said.

"Yep. Everything but the most important thing. Which one o' you fellers is going to come off top dog."

"Which *one?*"

Mose caught the emphasis and nodded. "Sure. Burt won't turn the hull crew loose on you. He ain't that kind. But afterward, if he comes out on top, he'll lead 'em on a tear through town that'll make history. He's like that, gets all steamed up inside, then, when the showdown's over, he just comes loose all over lettin' off steam." Old Mose fell thoughtfully silent for a while, then he said gravely: "It's too bad."

Durango, feeling this mood change, said: "What's too bad?"

"He ain't in your class with a pistol, Marshal. He's good and he's tolerably fast. But he's not in your class. That's what's too bad." The old man blew out smoke. "I ain't the only one that thinks that way, either." He looked upward, put a bird-like gaze on Durango. "You want to know who else doesn't?"

Durango shrugged; he did not really care.

"Go 'round the corner at the end of the square south o' here and you'll see who else thinks so."

Durango's expression gradually clouded over with perplexed interest; he sensed something here. "Don't tell me the townsmen have found their courage," he said, "and are going to back my play with guns."

Old Mose puffed silently, still with that bright and beady look on his face. "Nothin' like that," he finally said. "Go on, walk down there and turn the corner. You'll see."

Durango spoke a coarse word at the old man, but Mose ignored it to hold up his cigar and consider with critical approval its gray ash. After a long time he said: "Go on. They won't be here for an hour yet. You got plenty o' time."

Durango went. He crossed southward before old Mose and his echoing footfalls were the only solid sound for the length and breadth of Winterset's main roadway. He was not doing this out of curiosity; he was doing it out of annoyance; he wanted no excited storekeepers behind him with cocked guns when he had to walk out into the roadway and brace the Clancys. He wanted no one behind him at all.

There were faces at windows as he paced past. They were, as before, apprehensive, and this fixed on each of them a kind of unnatural ugliness. He saw them now and then brought to the window-panes by his footfalls, but he paid them no heed.

Overhead the sun was a gigantic yellow disc stuck in the center of an azure firmament. It seemed not to move at all. There was heat, but it was not as wilting as it had been the day before when rain puddles had reflected it upward. In fact, the roadway was hard again.

The last store southward before Durango reached that far corner was a gunsmith's shop. Here, a man in a soiled dark apron accosted him in the doorway, his eyes as steady as stone and his oil-stained, work-roughened hands calmly at his sides.

"I wouldn't try it alone," this man said quietly, arresting Durango with his quiet tone. "They'll give you an even break . . . but one at a time."

Durango looked into this man's unwavering eyes. "Would you like a hand in it?" he demanded, knowing in advance the answer to this.

"No. I got a wife and four kids. But I can give you some advice, Marshal."

Durango put an exasperated look on the gunsmith. "This is the damnedest place I was ever in for giving advice. Mister, I don't want your advice, but I'd appreciate your support . . . with a gun in your hands."

Silence settled between them. It drew out to its maximum length, then the gunsmith turned and slowly reëntered his shop. Without looking up again, he closed his door with quiet finality.

Durango moved on, came to the corner, and halted briefly before turning it, caution warning him of tricks. Old Mose had said, though, that Burt Clancy did not Indian fight; he came at a man with a warning and standing up in plain sight. Durango stepped forth and passed around the corner. He was putting a lot of faith in Mose Clark but did not right then think of this at all.

A familiar voice struck him with hard words. "Who do you think you are, forcing fights like this?"

He saw her standing there, holding the reins of a sweaty horse, but could think of nothing except how astonished he was at her presence.

She lashed him with words, saying irately: "Mose told me who you were and how fast you are. What are you trying to prove . . . that you can kill my father as easily as you shot my uncle?"

"What are you doing here?" he asked, and immediately understood how silly this sounded. He changed his tone. "Get on that horse and get out of Winterset."

"I will not! I came here to stop the fight and I'm not leaving until I do!"

"How? How can you stop it? Your menfolk are on their way. If you think you can turn them back, go on out and try it."

"I can't turn them back, Durango, but I can stop you."

He braced into her fiery glare, saying nothing, wondering how he must handle this. Then she was speaking again and he was very conscious of the way her breasts roughly rose and fell, and how her tawny eyes flamed an almost physical fire against him.

"Give me your gun!"

He made no move at all, except to gather his brows together in the beginning of a scowl.

"I said *give me your gun!*"

Now he drew back a little and fixed her with a laconic look. "Not likely," he replied very dryly. "Not with your pa's crew on the prod. Now listen to me, Maryann. . . ."

"Corey," she snapped in a loud tone. "Cock it!"

Durango stiffened. From somewhere behind Maryann someone unmistakably cocked both barrels of a shotgun; that was a sound, once heard, no one ever forgot.

"Keep him covered," said Maryann in the same loud tone, and moved forward and to one side, then, holding her breath, reached out firmly and jerked away Durango's holstered six-gun. He ignored the abrupt lightening of his holster and continued to probe the onward sheds and shadowed places for someone called Corey and a shotgun. He did not see that person until Maryann, holding his gun at her side, moved well back and spoke without looking away from him.

"All right, Corey. He's disarmed. Come on out now."

That lanky, smiling chore boy Durango had first seen the same time he'd initially seen Maryann Clancy crawled awkwardly from under a deserted hen house at the rear of a residence several hundred feet westward. He stood up, holding a shotgun with both hammers strained back, and now he was not smiling; he was white from his throat to his eyes but very steady; the trigger finger lay gently curved and business-like.

"Point that thing away," growled Durango. Then he looked at Maryann. "This doesn't solve anything. Your pa is still coming."

"Let him come," she retorted. "All right, Corey, give me the shotgun and go after the horses."

As the chore boy moved quickly to obey, Durango said to Maryann: "Dammit, as soon as you're gone, I'll get another gun. This was a foolish play, miss."

She very gently wagged her head at him but did not speak. The shotgun was not so steady in her hands, and Durango, seeing this, said: "You're far enough away so's I can't rush you. How about easing off with that thing. If it goes off by accident, I'm going to be a mess, lady."

She did not move the gun. Her eyes, he thought, were becoming unnaturally bright and shiny. Her chin quivered once, then was held rock-like by tightly clamped jaws.

Durango kept looking at her. It was impossible, even under these circumstances, for him not to feel the pull of her as a woman. Then Corey returned and Durango's eyes widened with understanding. The chore boy from Muleshoe had not only his mount and Maryann's animal; he also had Durango's horse, and it was saddled and bridled.

"Get astride," Maryann ordered.

"Damned if I do," responded Durango. "Your pa . . . everyone for miles around . . . will think I ran out on this fight."

"Damned if you won't," said Maryann, and leveled the shotgun. "If I pull these triggers, you'll be more than just damned. *Now get up there!*"

Durango moved finally to obey, his face as black as thunder.

VI

They took him west in a hard run for several miles, then north toward the far-away hills until the southerly run of that spill-way creek that he'd seen earlier was in sight, then they slowed.

Durango tried to remonstrate with Maryann Clancy with no success; she put the shotgun on him, and above it her face was as uncompromising as granite. After that one effort, he rode along silently fuming until, where willow shade diluted the sun's brightness, she pointed her mount inward and led them along until there was no chance of their being seen, and halted. Then he said to her: "This will only delay the meeting. You know that, don't you?"

She got down and motioned with the shotgun

for him to do likewise. "When it happens again, I'll think of something else," she said, and watched him from dappled shade as he hit the ground and put a calculating look upon Muleshoe's chore boy. She read his thoughts and said: "You can try it, if you're of a mind to, but it won't be easy. We'll always be on opposite sides of you. If one of us doesn't get you, the other one will."

Durango stepped deeper into shade, turned, and leaned upon an old willow tree. Thirty feet away the boy called Corey was grinning over at him as he took their horses back a way to tie them. Maryann moved a little, grounded the shotgun, and gazed at him. The way sunlight slanted into this secret place and touched her made the skin at her throat golden-yellow and warm. Her lips relaxed a little, changing in their way of expression to match the also altered gaze of her eyes; she was no longer tightly wound, but there remained as firm as ever that mistrust and reserve.

Below these things, though, Durango saw something else, a fullness waiting, a temptation that was as much a promise as a challenge, and his knowledge of this brought on a smile.

Maryann saw that smile and understood it; she did not blush but her face turned smooth and tight and defiant; her nostrils flared a little, but only for that brief moment when the warmth of a swift, common thought lay between them. Then she looked beyond him to Corey Smith.

"Keep watch," she ordered. "As soon as he comes into sight, let me know."

Corey moved off, still smiling, and Durango pushed back his hat. "Who comes?" he asked.

"None of your business," she snapped. Then, ashamed of her sharpness, said to him in a gentler tone: "You can sit down, if you want to."

"Thanks, miss. How long is this going to take . . . this scheme of yours, whatever it is?"

"Long enough to keep you out of Winterset until my pa and the others are gone."

"In that case," he said with a sigh, "I reckon I will sit down." From a position with his back to the old willow tree, he canted a sidelong glance upward at her. "You didn't know what had happened to your uncle Nate when we met last night, I take it."

"Not until I got back home after we met," she answered.

"Tell me something, Maryann, why didn't your pa and uncles come after me last night?"

"They weren't at the ranch when Uncle Nate got home. They were tracking cattle thieves who took a little bunch of finished steers out over the mountains northward. In fact, they didn't get back until about four o'clock this morning."

"Catch the rustlers?"

She shook her head.

He plucked a grass blade and popped it between his teeth. "Must not be very good trackers," he murmured. "It's pretty hard to make fast time and hide your tracks when you're driving fat beef."

She was displeased with him for this and said: "You'd probably know about something like that, Durango."

"I've tracked down a few rustlers in my time."

"I didn't mean it like that. I meant you probably were the rustler."

"I know how you meant it," he said. "But you don't believe that about me and you know it."

This statement brought a quick break of surprise to her face. She kept watching him with a close look and a gradually wondering expression. Then she leaned the shotgun against a willow close at hand and sat down. "They had too much of a head start," she told him, referring again to the cattle thieves.

"I understand they've hit Muleshoe before."

"Too often," she admitted with bitterness. "We're not the only outfit they raid, but it hurts just the same."

He chewed the blade of grass for a while, then turned to face her. "Is that why your pa and your uncles are so hot under the collar all the time?"

"Wouldn't you be, too?" she flared at him.

"Yes," he assented. "If you'd act sensible, maybe I could throw in with your folks and help them run these men to earth."

She said nothing for a moment, her expression looking for that brief moment hopeful, then clouding over with distrust again. "And while you were spying on the rustlers, Durango, who'd be keeping an eye on you?"

He considered her over a long interval of silence, then sighed and turned his back on her to lean loosely against his willow tree.

She was stung by this and showed it. "Well, what did you expect me to say . . . with a reputation like yours?"

He looked around. "What reputation? Who've you been talking to around here?"

Her expression closed down again; she only shook her head at him, saying nothing.

He turned fully and crossed over the intervening distance between them. She instantly caught up the shotgun and turned it belt buckle high on him. He stopped, looking down at her, then shrugged, and reseated himself upon the grass in front of that awesome double-barrel. For a time they looked at one another, then Durango very slowly put forth one hand until the fingers touched the gun barrel, and he very gently pushed it aside.

"You don't need that," he told her. "I'm here, and, if I figured to leave, I'd just get up and go get my horse. You wouldn't shoot."

"Do you want to try me?" she said, her eyes wide and steady.

"In the back?"

She held the gun a moment longer, then slowly put it aside. "Corey's out there anyway," she muttered, but they both understood she only said this because she had to.

"I was a fool, Maryann. I called your uncle Nate before I knew what was going on around here. I apologize for that."

"Tell him, don't tell me."

"I aim to, first chance I get."

"If you get the chance," she snapped, then shrugged as though she disliked herself for saying that. "I'm sorry. I guess misjudging people can work both ways." She looked at him with solemn eyes. "I wish. . . ." She didn't finish it. At that moment Corey came swiftly into the shade behind Durango and spoke.

"He's coming, Maryann. He's got his big-bore old carbine with him, too."

Maryann arose in a swift and supple movement, and Durango, watching both their faces, also got up off the ground. Corey Smith had Durango's ivory-butted six-gun stuck into the waistband of his trousers. To the boy he said: "Give me the gun. I don't mind meeting your friends, but I feel kind of naked unarmed."

Maryann's brows drew down. "No," she said stoutly, and started past. "Stay behind him," she told Corey, and Durango watched the chore boy go out and around and come in behind him.

"Follow her," the chore boy ordered.

Durango walked along in Maryann's tracks. Where they passed in and out of sunlight, he watched the reflecting glory of her hair. It was clubbed at the back of her head with a skimpy little green ribbon. She swung along with a good stride, her shoulders and arms rhythmically moving. From back there he said: "Maryann, I'll bet you're a good dancer."

She stopped and turned and he saw immediately that she had her own temper. He watched it come to her face and narrow her eyes, change her full mouth so that it lost all its warmth. But she said nothing, and after that freezing look went forward another 100 feet and halted with finality where a mounted man was getting down from the saddle and starting toward them in the willows. He was carrying a heavy-barreled, short and stubby carbine of ancient vintage in one fist. Because Maryann blocked his view, Durango did not recognize this man until he also stopped, lifted his head, and ran a sly look forward at the three of them.

"Mose!" he exclaimed. "Mose Clark!"

The old man ambled up closer and stopped to put a little smile on Durango. "A feller does what he figures is best," Mose stated, then shifted his attention to the girl. "They got to town 'bout half an hour ago. Your pa was fair frothin' at the mouth when he couldn't find this here wild and wooly Durango."

"Does he know who the town marshal really is?" she asked.

Mose inclined his head. "I told him. It didn't seem to make no difference, though. Him and your uncles, Aaron and Nate, was loaded for bear and spoilin' for a fight."

Durango heard this exchange and heeded it, but he was working something else out in his mind at the same time. Old Mose had deliberately trapped him; he'd known in advance what Maryann meant to do. It nettled him, this knowledge, and he put a bleak stare on the old man.

But Mose had earlier demonstrated to Durango that he was not easily ruffled, and he saw that glare now with much the same expression he'd worn back in town, a kind of half-wise, half-foolish smile. He understood it, too, because he said: "Marshal, she was plumb right. Her pa'd only kill you or get killed by you, and the real trouble would still exist. You understand?"

Durango growled: "And everyone in Winterset thinks their new town marshal tucked his tail and ran."

Mose shrugged. "Like she said when she come to my shack in the early hours this morning . . . it ain't really important what the townsfolk think, Marshal. What *is* important is that you and her pa team up some way and catch those cussed rustlers."

Durango absorbed these words and turned a

little to see how Maryann was standing there, looking steadily up at him. He wanted to say something to the waveringly hopeful look she presented to him, but could not, for the life of him, think of the correct words. He cleared his throat and turned. Corey Smith was smiling at him and holding out the ivory-handled six-gun, butt first.

VII

They returned to the deeper shade along the creekbank and Durango felt better now that he had his weapon back. When he stopped and turned, the others also halted. They were watching him, the beautiful girl, the lanky boy, and the rickety old buffalo hunter, Mose Clark. It was clear in each of their faces that they looked to him for leadership.

"*He* told you about me," Durango said to the girl, pointing at old Mose.

"Yes."

"Mose, darn you, what kind of lies did you tell her? She would've shot me, I think. You must've painted me pretty bad."

Before Mose answered, Maryann walked over, took up the shotgun, returned, and held it out for Durango to take it. She said nothing, but watched him heft the gun, then break it at the breach to withdraw its loads, and stand like stone, looking from the two empty barrels to her face.

No one said anything. Durango snapped the gun closed, and put it aside. His face was grave and disapproving. "That was a foolish thing to do," he barked at Maryann.

"No, it was a bluff and it worked. You said a little while ago I wouldn't shoot you in the back. Well, I never believed you would shoot a woman."

"I told her you wouldn't," piped up Mose Clark. "All the same, I was a mite uneasy about that unloaded shotgun."

Durango looked helplessly at the old man. Mose was wearing his smile again. He reminded Durango of a child—except for those sly and knowing old eyes.

"There wasn't any other way to do it," Maryann told him, drawing Durango's attention back to her. "We couldn't have asked you to leave town and we couldn't have ordered you to leave town. There was only this way."

Durango looked at her a moment before speaking. "You're a darned good actress," he stated. "To tell the truth, I figured you *would* shoot me, that's why I didn't try anything back in town. You sure acted like you hated the sight of me."

Corey Smith chuckled. "I could've told you she's real good at play-acting, mister. We grew up together an' she's. . . ."

"Never mind, Corey," Maryann said. "He's not interested."

He smiled, and then he laughed, and she watched him with her eyes half closed. He saw this and understood its meaning; she was still assessing him for his real worth, his real character. He shot a look upward where the sun was dropping off westerly and turning late afternoon red.

"Too late to head back now," he told them. "Let's sit down and you folks tell me about the cattle thefts."

Maryann dropped down at once. Old Mose sighed and put his buffalo gun beside a tree and gingerly eased his old bones to the ground.

"They come over the mountains," said Maryann, turning brisk toward him now. "Who they are we don't know. We never have any advance warning, either. Although this last raid, at least, seemed not to be as well-planned as the other raids were."

"What do you mean by that?" asked Durango.

"They struck in the early night, like always, but this time my uncles and father were close by. The other raids happened when the menfolk were either in town or out somewhere on the range."

"That's interesting," stated Durango, and put his reaching gaze on the distant peaks. "What's across those mountains?"

"Thirty miles of prairie, then more mountains."

"No ranches or towns?"

"Not until you get across the next range of mountains. Then the country is settled up. And there's a town called Ballester."

"Has your pa checked over there to see if anyone's been shipping out Muleshoe cattle?"

Maryann nodded. "Yes. And no one has."

"Then," opined Durango, "they're taking them to some cow range." He turned to Mose. "You've been around these parts long enough. Where's a likely place to get rid of rustled cattle?"

Mose sniffed. "East or west," he said. "There's nothing to stop rustlers from going in either direction as far as they want to go. It's all open range as far as a man can see in both directions, and a heap farther, too. And I'll tell you something else, too. Fat cattle bring a good price. Them fellers wouldn't have any trouble sellin' Muleshoe critters to any of the big cow outfits . . . after they'd blotched over the Muleshoe brand."

Durango was silent. Obviously it would be time-consuming to try locating whoever had bought those stolen cattle, and time, he thought, was the one commodity he did not have a lot of—not alone, anyway. He looked from Mose to Maryann, then on to lanky Corey Smith. Of his three allies, Corey was the most likely one to make a long ride. But he did not speak of this to the boy. Instead he said to Maryann: "Would your pa let Corey go off on his own for a week or two?"

She did not do what most women would have

done, ask the obvious question. She said simply: "I think he would."

"Corey," said Durango, looking at those mountains again, "take a bag of chuck, a stout saddle horse, and track this last rustled herd until you know which cañons the thieves take."

"Yes, sir."

"Wait a minute. I'm not finished. When you've found where they break clear of the mountains and hit the plains beyond, don't go any farther. Just locate a way to get atop one of those high peaks, make a camp near water, and stay there. It may take a week, it may take a month, but sooner or later, if those fellers feel the pinch for ready cash again, they'll come back, and this time you're going to be up where you can see them long before they get close."

"Yeah," said the chore boy exuberantly, "and I'll warn the ranch."

"No," contradicted Durango. "You'll ride hell for leather to Winterset and you'll warn *me*. Do you understand?"

Corey nodded, but Maryann said in puzzlement: "Why you? Why not my father and uncles?"

Durango uncoiled up off the ground. He said: "Because, it doesn't sound like an accident to me that whenever they strike, your menfolks aren't around the ranch."

Maryann gradually turned white. She, too, stood up. "Are you saying my uncles . . . ?"

"I'm saying you've got three cowboys working for Muleshoe," Durango cut across her words to say.

Mose, also, stood up. He reached for his buffalo gun and leaned upon it, his gaze drifting from one face to the others, then back to Durango again. "It makes sense," he told Maryann. "But you got to get your pa to let Corey go off like this without spillin' the beans to him."

Maryann turned reflective. She finally said: "I can do it. But he'll probably dock Corey's wages because we'll have to make out that he wants to go hunting . . . or something."

Durango looked at the youth. "I was told he got only room and board," he said.

Maryann flared at him for that. "What do you think my pa is?" she demanded. "He pays Corey chore boy wages."

Corey said nothing; he was grinning at Maryann's show of temper. Durango shrugged.

"A feller can sure pick up a lot of misinformation in this country," he said. "Nothing to get all hot about, anyway." He took Maryann's arm and turned her toward the deeper shade. Over his shoulder he said to Corey and old Mose: "Look after the horses, you two. I'll be along directly."

He led her far back where the shade broke up and the creek was visible, its tiny whitecaps glistening under sunlight. There, he halted and released her arm. Turning, she showed him an uncertain expression. He watched her eyes darken and noticed the round curving of her shoulders. One soft banner of light struck down and gleamed upon her hair, making a rich glowing. She had been angry at him and defiant and hopeful, all of them since coming to this white-water creek, and each of her moods had cut him hard under the heart. What he had to determine now was whether she could also be tender toward him.

Then she spoke and her lips, the lovely turnings of her body, and the richness of her voice brought to him the fullness of his longings, and, although he had never been in love, he could recognize in this warm and shady place that he now was.

"I didn't want you to dislike me," she said. "Maybe that was why I acted toward you as I did. Because I was sure you *did* dislike me, and I didn't know what to do about it. So . . . I was angry. Not angry exactly . . . hurt, I guess."

He felt a rise of quick heat to his face. She had thrown him off balance with this candor. He put out a hand to touch her. She came fully around at this touch and stood waiting, her face pale, her eyes more tawny and darkly gold-flecked than ever. She was uncertain and perhaps a little frightened and this softened her features and lent them a sweetness.

Then he put his hands on her waist and smiled, and her troubled look vanished so that her expression became lighter until she was smiling back. He swayed her up close; their bodies touched and blended. She held her lips up to him and he felt for them with his own mouth. It was not a forceful kiss, yet she shuddered at his touch and put her hands up to strain lightly against him. He did not at once release her though, and finally her hands went upward, around his neck to press his mouth closer to her lips and let her passion burn against him for a second.

When she got free from his hungry mouth and put her head against him, she had both eyes tightly closed and both fists knotted.

"I didn't do that to see if I could," he murmured.

"I know. I understand."

He would have held her out at arm's length, but she resisted, stayed up close so that he could not see her face, and he desisted, content to stand like that with the lowering red sun exploding in silent grandeur over the sharply cut yonder peaks and pinnacles, letting this sweet moment run its full course.

Finally she stepped clear of him and swung away, face averted, a pulse in her throat noticeably erratic in its constant pounding, and she said: "Please . . . don't fight my father. Please."

He touched her hair. "I won't. But in exchange I want a promise, too."

"What?"

"I want you to be here tomorrow again. Without Corey."

"I will be . . . Bent?"

"Yes."

"Please go now."

He left her there by the white-water creek. Went all the way back to his horse and encountered only Corey Smith when he got to his saddle.

"Mose went on back to town," the chore boy told him. "He said he can't ride fast any more and he wanted to get back before sundown."

Durango nodded. He considered the youth's cheerful smile. Then he pushed out his hand and gravely pumped Corey's hand, then turned and without a word also struck out for Winterset.

A half mile away from the willows he halted for a look back. Moving swiftly into the shadowy dusk of the foothill north, two riders ran along side-by-side. He watched them as long as light permitted, then resumed his own way. His thoughts were troubled and confused all the way back to Winterset's north-south stage road, while around him evening thickened and dusk came down to cover everything except those winking, onward lights.

A man, he thought wryly, did as old Mose had said, he did what he thought best for him to do. His original intention had been to rest at Winterset, then push on again northward. Now he had a solid hunch that he was never, in his life-time, going to get permanently any farther into the northwest than the town he was now marshal of because of a sturdy girl who could pull a man to her against his wishes. He thought of this. Against his wishes? No, not against them. Not against them at all because his wishes no longer included far-away places. They had solidly changed and now included nothing beyond this sturdy girl with the golden hair and heavy mouth.

He hauled back a half mile north of town and sat a moment, thinking how the chemistry of a man could be forever channeled into a fresh course by the sweet taste of a woman's lips. He had, in times past, witnessed how this had happened to other men. But never once had he considered how it could also happen to him.

Not that Maryann Clancy was the first girl he had kissed, far from it. But she was the first girl ever to lie easily in his arms and put a strangeness into his thoughts and an ache under his heart and in his arms as he held her.

He eased out the horse again. He thought that right this minute he'd give a handful of Mexican adobe dollars for one of Mose Clark's strong cigars, that this was one of those moments in a man's life when all that had gone before was obscured and something that had just happened was still happening to him, stood out starkly clear and unnerving, so that a man needed something. A release of some kind. He'd noticed this odd feeling in himself once before, the time he'd picked the fight with Nate Clancy. Then, he'd needed a fight, a strong drink, or a woman's kiss. He felt the same way now as he entered Winterset from the north and pushed steadily along to the livery barn, and there encountered Amos Fallon.

"My God," gasped the smaller man, "you shouldn't have come back yet."

VIII

Durango gazed silently at Fallon.

"They ain't left yet, Marshal. They're still in town!"

Durango dismounted with a quick eagerness running through him. "All of them?" he asked the liveryman.

"Yes, sir. Why are you dismounting? Nobody's seen you yet. You can still ride on back out and stay away until they're gone. They likely won't hang around much longer."

Durango looked at Amos Fallon and saw what he expected to see; the liveryman thought he had fled town to escape the Clancys. He said: "Have you seen Mose Clark tonight?"

"No, sir, I ain't. But he's usually on that bench down by your office."

Durango put a glance across the road where the Lone Star's lights were glowing lively orange.

"Go tell Mose I'm at the Lone Star. Also tell him the Clancys are still in town."

"Yes, sir. Marshal?"

"Yeah."

But Fallon did not say what was on his mind. He simply stood there, drawing the reins of Durango's horse back and forth through his hand, wearing a doleful expression.

Durango turned away. He passed over the dark roadway and stepped up onto the far walkway. There, two loiterers recognized him and their mouths fell open. It was obvious from this that these townsmen, too, believed he had deliberately left town to avoid a meeting. He teetered there in the plain sight of these two men, forming a plan. Then he abruptly turned southward and went along a distance, stopped, and turned to look back. Neither of the loiterers was in sight. He smiled with his mouth but not with his wary eyes. The loiterers had run into the saloon to spread word that the marshal was back in town.

Durango went back toward the Lone Star, stepped into a recessed doorway, and waited. It was not a very long wait. Three men came boiling out of the Lone Star. A moment later two more men came out. They all stopped on the boardwalk, looking up and down the roadway. One of them said a few short words and the original three men dashed to the hitch rail, got astride, and went pounding south in an excited search. The two remaining Muleshoe men also mounted up, but with less excitement, and they rode north along the roadway.

Durango left his doorway and moved swiftly along until he was near the Lone Star's entrance. There, as three more men came out, he faced them. The last two men saw him at once, and at once retreated back into the saloon. The other man was like stone; he stood and glared and did not move an inch.

"I'm sorry about the arm," Durango told this man, who was Nate Clancy. "I jumped to some conclusions."

"You better be real good at jumping," said Clancy, his sulphur gaze unafraid even though he wore his right arm in a sling made of a black neckerchief. "I'm not alone this time."

"I know. I watched the others fan out to look for me."

"They'll find you."

Durango nodded. "I reckon they will." He appraised the dark man before him. "A funny thing happened to me today. I walked head-on into a kind of conspiracy. Got taken out of town a few miles and held prisoner there."

Nate Clancy's lips drew down. "Likely story," he said. "That's not what they say here in town. They say you ran like a scalded cat when you heard we were coming."

Durango ignored this. "My captors were a

long-legged, grinning boy and a girl as handsome as a springtime moon."

Nate Clancy's heavy brows gathered over his eyes. He understood all right, but because he had not believed when Durango had spoken before, he was perplexed now.

"Yeah," said the marshal. "You guessed it. Maryann and Corey Smith."

"I don't believe you."

Durango shrugged. "I don't care whether you do or not. But if I was lyin', Nate, believe me, I wouldn't say it was someone you could verify it from that easy."

Clancy continued to study Durango from under his hat brim, and, while his hating look was still there, so also was an expression of thoughtfulness. Finally he said: "All right, suppose you're not lying. What then?"

"She made me promise not to fight her pa."

Nate's expression cleared at once. This was one thing he had no doubts about. "You won't be able to keep that promise, Marshal. Not in a million years. Burt'll find you and force a fight."

"He'll lose," said Durango quietly.

"If he does, there'll be Aaron. And if Aaron loses. . . ."

"There'll be you, Nate. I don't want to fight the Clancys. I made a bad mistake with you. I don't want to make that same damned mistake two more times. I said I was sorry about winging you. I meant it." Durango paused to draw a breath. "I don't fear any of you."

"I reckon you don't . . . Durango."

"The word gets around."

"Yeah."

"Nate, I want to ask a favor of you. Take your brothers and your riders and leave town."

Nate Clancy relaxed where he stood. He looked away from Durango for the first time, and he said in a quieter tone: "They won't go. Burt's been storing up steam all day." He looked back at Durango. "You're a strange fella," he said. And probably meant to say more, but at that moment a man's urgent cry rang out and Durango shifted his stance the slightest bit to see those three cowboys jogging back up the roadway from the south. He also caught a changing expression on Nate Clancy's face and his own countenance instantly hardened against Nate.

"Easy," he said. "Real easy, Nate. You're in no shape to sit in this time, and I won't be able to single out a man's shoulder."

"You could still run," said Nate, watching Durango.

"I'm too old to start doing that." Durango faced away a quarter turn to keep an eye on those oncoming riders. "One thing you can do, though. Tell your niece I tried."

"Tried what?"

"To keep from having to fight you fellers."

Nate Clancy continued to watch Durango. He looked troubled now and uncertain. Then he did an unexpected thing; he sprang off the plank walk into the path of those oncoming men and let off a loud, full call to them.

"Hold it! He's up here with me. Go get Burt and Aaron and tell them . . . !"

A gun exploded from dim shadows north up the roadway. Those slowing cowboys acted instinctively; they threw themselves clear of leather, struck dirt, and frantically rolled. Durango was turning to look behind him for the gunman when a second shot came. This one cut a white pine splinter eighteen inches long off the overhang upright not four inches in front of him. He dropped, scuttled sideways, and drew his handgun all in one fluid motion.

Out in the roadway Nate Clancy was cursing. At the top of his considerable lung power he was ordering the three Muleshoe riders not to fire. Then a third shot came from that hidden gunman to the north and Nate's words were instantly choked off. He took three wilting forward steps and folded over, slid down into the dirt, and lay there, turning soft all over.

Somewhere, off behind this main thoroughfare, there echoed the strong thunder of galloping horses. Durango heard them, knew who would be astride those animals, and had no time to speculate further because, as Nate went down, the three Muleshoe men south of him opened up. Bullets struck the front of the Lone Star Saloon. From within came the cries of men and the stampeding rush of their feet as they fled out the back way.

Durango dug in with his toes, waited a moment, then catapulted himself forward to strike the saloon doors and sprawl beyond them, rolling sideways. He glimpsed the chalk-white face of the barman, and saw also that the barman was holding aloft a sawed-off shotgun. He swung his pistol to bear as he came up onto one knee.

"Drop it!"

The shotgun fell with a loud *crash* and the barman strained upward with both hands. Durango got partially upright and moved away. "Put your hands down and don't touch that gun."

A bullet sang over the door, struck and demolished a full bottle of whiskey on the back-bar, and the shaking man standing close by dropped down behind his bar with a little squeak of fright. He did not reappear again.

Out of the dark roadway those oncoming riders were close now. Durango heard their mounts slide to a skittering halt and knew the men had left their saddles on the jump. He got to a window and risked a sidelong look outside. There were two sprinting dark shapes in good view. He broke the windowpane with his six-gun, pushed it out, drew a low, careful bead, and fired off one round. One of those sprinting figures stumbled and went down on all fours in the roadway. He saw that man's twisted face lift and turn toward the saloon. The man expected a final shot, knew instinctively he could not get away from it, and simply hung there.

Durango called to him, his voice interrupted by gunshots. "Come in here! Get up off your knees and walk into the saloon. Leave your damned gun out there."

The man did not immediately obey and to the south those three riders worried the Lone Star's siding with a heavy fusillade. Durango stood back from the window until the shots fell off to a steady pattering, then yelled at the man out in the roadway once more. This time he got up. A bull-bass roared at him from beyond Durango's sight and the rider hesitated, but only briefly because Durango pushed his gun out into this man's sight. He then started forward, got up onto the plank walk, and those southerly gunmen held their fire until he passed into the Lone Star. Even afterward they did not fire, for a time.

Durango was waiting, shoulders back to the saloon's wall. The rider turned; they exchanged a steady glance, and Durango saw something in this man's face that was in some vague way familiar.

"Who are you?" he demanded.

"Aaron Clancy."

Durango lowered his gun. Aaron Clancy looked a little like Maryann; he had the same shade hair and the same tawny eyes. He was a lank man with a massive jaw and a face that was almost square. He had no look of fear or apprehension at all, and now he said: "I thought you'd be a better shot, Durango. Your slug nicked the heel of my boot. It was 'way too low."

Durango looked across the bar. Two empty shot glasses were over there, one half full and both abandoned by those recent patrons who had stampeded out the back door. He shot once from the hip. A spray of amber liquor and glass particles exploded upward. He shot again. The second glass also burst into pieces. He put his glance back upon Aaron Clancy.

Out in the roadway where those two shots had been heard a thunderous voice cried out ragingly. Before Durango could move, Aaron Clancy, without taking his eyes off Durango, let out a bellow equally as loud and thunderous: "No harm done, Burt! Hold your fire for a minute!"

Durango waited. The gunfire ended abruptly. He flipped open the door of his pistol cylinder, punched out spent cartridges, and calmly plugged in fresh loads from his shell belt. He did not say a word or lift his eyes to Aaron Clancy's face until he was finished and had holstered the weapon. Then he said: "Satisfied I didn't mean to shoot any higher than your heel?"

Clancy said: "Satisfied." He stood still, as a man stands who is waiting for further speech.

"Who shot Nate?"

Aaron Clancy said in the same passionless way, "You, I reckon. Burt and me hadn't come up yet. We was lookin' for you in the byways east of town when the firing started."

"No," said Durango. "Not me. Someone up the roadway north of me. Do you know how bad he's hit?"

Aaron Clancy shook his head. "Burt'd know. You spilled me long before we got close."

"I told your brother I was sorry about that wing shot. That I misjudged him when we met."

Aaron Clancy stood stolidly looking at Durango and saying nothing. His gaze was uncompromisingly hard and speculative. Durango drew away from the wall under that steady regard.

"I promised your niece I wouldn't fight you. I want to keep that promise, Aaron. It's up to you. If you want to push it, I'll find you a gun. If you don't, call your brother in here."

Aaron shifted his weight; he looked away for the first time, over toward the bar where an abrasive scuttling sound came into the stillness.

"The bartender," murmured Durango, and raised his voice. "Hey!" he called. "Stand up from back there."

The barman came up very slowly; he was badly shaken and his lips were tightly locked with this fear. Aaron and Durango looked back at one another. They were roughly alike in size and build, and in other ways, too, in their slow thoughtfulness and in their total lack of fear. Aaron blew out a held-back breath.

"I'll call my brother," he said, and passed along the front of the room to that shattered window. There, he called out: "Burt! Come in here." Aaron paused, thought of something, and said: "Put up your gun."

Durango heard the solid sound of a heavy man's booted feet strike down on the outside board-walk. He could read into that strongly oncoming sound the wrath, the anger, and the sense of urgency that impelled Burt Clancy toward the Lone Star's battered doors.

On Durango's right Aaron Clancy turned inward, also facing the door. It was impossible to tell from his tough-set expression what his thoughts were, but one thing was evident enough: Aaron Clancy was perfectly collected, perfectly calm.

Burt Clancy slammed past the spindle doors and fetched up short just inside the room. He was also a big man, but a good deal older than his brothers. Also, he had that identical willful look up around the eyes that his daughter had. The same tawny eyes went instantly to Durango and stayed there. Burt Clancy's right hand, hanging loosely and easily within three inches of his holstered six-gun's graceful stock, gently opened and gently closed.

Durango had almost to lean into the wrathfulness that emanated from big Burt Clancy. He watched the bigger, older man's nostrils flare, his lips draw out thin, and his eyes darken with the wish to kill. It was a bad moment.

"How is Nate?" Durango asked, and heard Aaron, off on his right, draw back a long, slow breath in all that utter stillness.

"He'll live," said the elder Clancy, biting those words off sharply.

"I didn't do it."

Burt looked over at Aaron, held his brother's gaze for a second, then returned his attention to Durango, saying in that same lethal tone: "If I thought you had, Durango, I wouldn't be standing like this now."

"Do you know who the man was who did it? He was behind me, north up by the roadway. Your brother was telling your riders to hold their fire when whoever that feller was cut loose."

"I know. He told me that."

Aaron spoke for the first time. He sounded puzzled. "Could Durango have done it, Burt?"

The elder Clancy shook his head once savagely. "No. Nate was hit square in the back. Durango was over here by the saloon. Whoever downed Nate was either across the road, or north up the way, where he had a clean, straight, southward shot."

"Who, then?" asked Aaron. "How bad off is Nate?"

"I don't know who. If it was one of these damned townsmen, though, we're going to take Winterset apart board by board."

"How bad I asked."

"In the side. Plowed along his ribs. Maybe busted two or three of them. I sent him along to the doctor's house. We'll go see him after this . . . this is over with."

Burt Clancy hung his smoldering gaze back on Durango. He said nothing and he did not have to. His stare was enough.

Durango said: "I apologized to Nate for winging him."

The craggy older man did as Aaron had done earlier; he simply stood there, looking hard and waiting, saying nothing which might have made it easier for Durango.

"I misjudged him."

"You misjudged the lot of us," ground out Burt Clancy.

"Maybe," murmured Durango. "Maybe not. I don't want to fight you. I told Nate that and Aaron that. Now I'm telling you."

"I heard you."

"But I'll leave it up to you. You're armed and so am I. If you don't want it to end right here. . . ." Durango deliberately left the rest of it unsaid and kept his eyes steadily upon the angry older man.

The silence between them grew and grew. Obviously Burt Clancy was having a struggle with himself. He clearly wanted to fight, to lash out at something, to retaliate for Nate and for the way this calm-voiced man from Mexico had seized the initiative and had kept it in the face of Clancy wrath. Then Aaron spoke, dropping quiet words into the tight stillness.

"He could have shot me, Burt. He could have shot Nate, too, and I think he probably could out-shoot you right now. Ease off and let's listen to him."

But big Burt Clancy was not a man to turn his emotions on and off at a word or a glance or a thought. He did, though, let a little of the stiffness leave him, and with it went that teetering balance that tilted a fighting man in one direction or the other, and Durango saw this and recognized it and also relaxed a little. There would now be no shoot-out. Durango let a little pent-up breath pass his lips.

"I'll listen to nothing you have to say," spat the elder Clancy at Durango. "I don't give a damn what it is!" He jerked his head at his brother. "Outside," he commanded. "Go look in on Nate." Aaron moved reluctantly but he moved. As he passed around Burt and Durango, the craggy older man said bitingly to Durango: "You get on your horse, Mister Durango, and you ride out. And you keep on ridin' until the land looks completely different."

IX

Mose turned up at the town marshal's office some time after Durango arrived there from the Lone Star Saloon. He was still carrying his big-bore buffalo gun, but he now also had a huge horse pistol of a six-shooter stuck into his waistband. Its barrel was so long that Mose had to draw the thing forth and put it upon a table before he could bend over and sit down, facing Durango.

He was not wearing his customary half-foolish, half-sly smile. He was instead quite sober and thoughtful. "Can't for the life o' me figure out who 'twas that shot Nate. Can't figure out the why of it, either, Marshal."

Durango had two cigars he'd acquired at the Lone Star. He handed one to Mose and lit it, then lit the other one for himself. The smoke had a biting, sharp, and tangy taste that was very good.

"I can tell you who wasn't behind Nate," he said to Mose. "The three Muleshoe cowboys."

"Can you tell me who was up the road from him, Marshal?"

Durango smoked with eyes slitted from that lifting, fragrant cloud. "His two brothers. But they weren't actually in the roadway as far as I know. Still, it could have been one of them."

"Nonsense," Mose snorted, and darkly scowled

over at Durango. "I've known the lot of 'em since they were boys. The clan of 'em has always been closer'n a nest of ticks." Mose considered the cigar. He wrinkled his nose at it. "Ain't as good as mine, are they?" he asked.

Durango said: "Nowhere nearly as good. Mose, where were you?"

Those powdery old eyes shot upward and forward. Mose was startled and shocked. "You sayin' I did it?" he gasped. "Me? Why, Marshal, you ought to. . . ."

"Where were you?"

"If you got to know, I was across the road in Amos Fallon's doorway, stayin' back in the dark. An' I had m'guns, too."

"What were you doing over there?"

"Waiting. Just waiting. When Muleshoe rushed you in the saloon, I calculated to let loose a few buffler gun slugs at 'em and sort o' bust up the party." Mose kept his indignant and unwavering stare on Durango. "Damned if I'd do it now for you. Sittin' over there like Gawd A'mighty, accusin' me of. . . ."

"I didn't accuse you of anything. I just asked. . . ."

"You did so accuse me! You sat right there and the same as said I shot Nate."

"Mose, damn it all, I only asked where you were."

Old Clark got upright and stamped an angry

foot at Durango. "Yeah," he snapped, "you only asked me where I was . . . like you thought *I* shot him." Mose's pale eyes shone with indignation. He quivered with it. There were little flecks of spittle at the outsides of his bearded lips. When he could stand it no longer, he slammed over to the door, yanked it wide open, and glowered backward. "Fine how-de-do!" he exclaimed. "Fine way to treat them as befriends you." He stumped on out of the office and wispy parting sentences lingered in his wake: "Dad-burned ingrates folks raise nowadays. Help 'em an' they up and snap at the hands as feeds 'em. Fine cussed how-de-do. . . ."

Durango rose, crossed over, and closed the door. He stood a moment looking at the floor, then he sighed and shook his head, and went back to his chair. As he eased down, a little smile lifted the corners of his lips. An angry man spoke his exact thoughts and no one would have denied that Mose Clark had been angry. But old Mose had revealed himself as a friend, and that was, in Durango's eyes, the important thing. All he had to do now was placate the old man.

An idea of how to accomplish this was firming up in his thoughts when the door opened and the emporium's corpulent owner stepped into the room. He did not nod or smile at Durango, and he carefully closed the door after himself before moving over to take the chair Mose had recently vacated. Then he said from a pale and solemn face: "Marshal, we passed your no-sidearms ordinance. But after the firing started, two of the councilmen ran out the back door of the firehouse where we meet and forgot to affix their signatures."

Flagg brought forth a paper from his coat pocket and held it out. Durango took it, considered it through wreathing tobacco smoke, then flung it aside. He said: "I'll have copies made and post it around town."

"Marshal?" queried the merchant with some diffidence.

"Yes."

"Uh. There's a matter of fourteen dollars worth of damage to the Lone Star Saloon."

Durango thought a moment, then said: "That's too bad."

Flagg nodded, waiting for more. When Durango said no more, he murmured: "The council has no fund for that, Marshal."

Now Durango put aside his cigar and leaned back in his chair to spear Charles Flagg with a speculative look. "I think you're working up to asking about taking fourteen dollars out of my pay. Is that it, Mister Flagg?"

The owner of Winterset's emporium moved where he sat. He reached up dubiously to scratch the tip of his nose, and all the time he was studying Durango's expression. Finally he dropped his hand and sighed with resignation. "I'll pay it," he muttered, looking and sounding crestfallen. Then he said in a firmer voice: "But, Marshal, I think after this we ought to have some kind of a policy about these things. Don't you think so?"

Durango kept his face impassive. Inwardly he was delighted by Charles Flagg's discomfort. "Yes, indeed," he gravely agreed. "I think we should, too. Now, why don't you inaugurate such a policy right now by sending a bill for that fourteen dollars' worth of damage to Burt Clancy at the Muleshoe?"

Charles Flagg leaped to his feet as though he had been stung. "No!" he exclaimed swiftly. "No, that's all right. It's only fourteen dollars. That's quite all right." He went over to the door and hesitated there, one hand lying upon the latch. "Good night," he said. "The council sure hopes the ban on firearms will work, Marshal."

Durango said amiably: "I think it will, Mister Flagg. But I've got a request to make. I need a part-time jailer."

Flagg looked dumb. "A jailer, Marshal?"

"Yes. To keep the place clean and watch prisoners . . . when I have any to watch . . . and sort of back my play when there's trouble."

"But there won't be any trouble if no one carries sidearms, Marshal," protested the storekeeper.

Durango smiled flintily over at Charles Flagg. "It's not then," he said, "that I'm thinking about.

Sure, after everyone who comes to town knows they can't ride in armed, we probably won't have much trouble."

"Well . . . ?"

"Mister Flagg, it's not going to be that easy to enforce the no-sidearms regulation initially." Durango rose up to put a sardonic look at the merchant. "For instance," he said, "would you like to back me up the next time Muleshoe comes to town armed to the teeth, and I order them to get out of Winterset or give me their guns while they're here?"

Charles Flagg's hand on the door latch convulsively closed. "I see your point of view," he admitted, and brought up a sweaty smile. "By all means, Marshal, hire yourself a deputy town marshal. By the way, what would his wages be?"

"Forty a month and ammunition."

Flagg's smile slipped badly but he nodded. "I'll see that it's authorized by the council," he said, and fled out of the office.

Durango retrieved his cigar, lit it, then burst out laughing. He had successfully carried through his plan for placating old Mose Clark.

He went into the little cell his office contained, prodded the straw mattress until the larger lumps were flattened, and lay down fully clothed to finish the cigar. Afterward, he tilted up his hat to keep out lantern light and closed his eyes. He did not awaken until someone beyond the far door came around to knock on that panel from the outside. Then he sat up, blinked water from his eyes, yawned prodigiously, and arose. He did not recall barring the door, and, as he crossed out of the cell, he saw at once that it was not, in fact, barred. He scowled, wondering who had such exacting manners in Winterset that he would not enter the marshal's office without being invited to.

When he flung back the door, old Mose stood there, looking up at him from half-shy, half-smiling old eyes. "Time for breakfast," he said, then waited for Durango's reaction.

Without batting an eye or in any other way indicating that he recalled how the old man had stomped out of his office in great wrath the night before, Durango said casually: "So it is."

Mose instantly brightened, became his old self again. "I'll fetch it," he said, and, when Durango looked queerly at him, he broke into a grin that threatened to crack his face wide open. "I already told the cook over at the Shamrock Café to fix it for both o' us and that I'd be back for it."

Mose started swiftly away, scuttling out into the roadway. Durango frowned in the doorway and scratched his head. Then he shrugged, went to the wash basin, shaved, made himself presentable for this new day, and was beginning to feel quite human by the time old Mose came teetering into the office with his lips tightly pursed as he frowningly concentrated on carrying a heaping tray of hot food and coffee. He managed to rid himself of this burden and straighten up without spilling anything. Then he let off a great grunt of relief. "Steady as a rock," he crowed to Durango, and flexed a scrawny arm. "Steady as a rock and strong as a buffler bull."

Durango stood quietly near his desk, considering the old man. "Mose," he finally asked quietly, "what the hell's come over you?"

"Me? Nothing a-tall, Marshal." Mose blushed and ran a finger under his nose and looked down at the floor a moment. He said in an uncomfortable voice: " 'Bout last night, Marshal. I just sort of sounded off. You know how 'tis when a feller's a mite off his feed. Didn't mean nothing, of course, Marshal."

"Mose. . . ."

"Have some coffee, Marshal. Try them eggs, too. Fried in gen-u-wine sow fat."

"Mose. . . ."

"A man as big as you'd bound to get hungry as a bitch wolf when he ain't. . . ."

"Mose!"

The old man gave a little jump at that sharp-voiced exclamation. He looked up and he sniffled.

"What the hell's got into you this morning?" demanded Durango.

"Well," stated the old man, and sniffled again, "I was over at the emporium, you see, Marshal, and old 'possum-belly Charley Flagg was tellin' another councilman 'bout how he figured you needed a deputy town marshal and all, and I just naturally figured the first feller to get right over here an' qualify, as they say nowadays, would get the job. Now, Marshal, I been a lawman in my lifetime. Once down in Texas and once up at Spotted Tail Indian Agency in Montana, an' I naturally know a heap more'n some young whippersnapper'd know about apprehendin' outlaws and such-like, an' it so happens I got my own guns and horse an'. . . ."

"Whoa," protested Durango. "Shut up a minute, will you? Of course the job's yours. It never entered my mind to hire anyone else. Now then, how much is my share of this breakfast?"

Durango moved over to examine the food. Mose watched him with stunned surprise stamped upon his face.

"I said," repeated Durango, "how much is my share of this here breakfast?" He looked up, saw Mose rapidly blinking, and quickly looked down again. "That coffee looks almighty strong," he murmured in a quieter tone.

Mose lustily blew his nose, then peered over at the coffee. "Damned if it don't," he grumbled, and sniffled again quite loudly. "Damned if it don't, Marshal." Then he straightened up and put a look upon Durango that gradually turned troubled and anxious. Then he said gruffly:

"Hell, you didn't believe all them lies I just told you 'bout how strong and all I am, did you, Marshal?"

Durango looked up. "Sure I did," he said.

"Well, hell," muttered old Mose, embarrassed now, "they was pure wind, Marshal. Listen, I'm an old man. Hell's bells, you'd better give that job to some young feller as can ride hard and shoot straight." Mose watched Durango begin to eat. He hopped from one foot to the other and finally there was indignation in his voice as he resumed speaking. "Dang it, Marshal, listen to me for a minute, will you? I'm too cussed old. Anyway, my aim ain't so good any more. I was joshin' . . . I think I was anyway . . . 'bout me havin' this deputy's job. I. . . ."

"Mose," said Durango, looking up with a pained expression across his countenance, "for gosh sakes quit talkin' so much, will you? Fetch up a chair and let's eat. And after breakfast I got to ride out, and, when I get back, I want to see this office plumb free of dust and dirt and that one window in the road-side wall clean as new money." He watched the old man turn his back abruptly and grope for a chair. "For forty a month and shells I expect some work out o' you."

Mose came around. "Forty dollars a month?" he gasped.

Durango nodded and frowned. "Damned if you won't earn it, too." He looked downward again, feeling uncomfortable under the sudden rush of deep gratitude he saw in the old outcast's eyes. Around a mouthful of food he growled: "Now, dammit, let's eat!"

X

Durango left Winterset with morning brightness dulled a little by scudding gray clouds that swept in low from the west, dirty and ragged-looking and bringing with them a slightly metallic scent.

"Rain," he told his horse. "A wind'd better come up and blow those clouds away or we're in for another wet spell."

By the time he got out to the creek and commenced tracing it north toward his rendezvous with Maryann Clancy, the sun was losing its springtime warmth. The day did not turn cold; it was simply cool and a fish-belly color.

He reached the rendezvous an hour ahead of Maryann but this had been his wish, so, after he tied up, he made a little excursion round-about along the creekbank to familiarize himself with this spot and with what lay beyond it in all directions. When he was ultimately satisfied, he went down into the shade and waited.

It was not a long wait. He saw her coming in an easy lope, her body in rhythmic cadence with each movement of her horse. He arose and went forward. She saw him, reined down to a walk, and passed into the gloomier gray of the willows. He took her horse, tied it out of sight, and looked around at her. She was solemnly considering him.

She said: "My uncle Aaron told me about last night."

He waited, saying nothing, keeping his eyes fully upon her expression. It did not change. She had a quirt hanging from one wrist by a plaited thong. She swung it at the grass and turned away from him to sit down where her grave attention fell upon the tumbling creek.

"He said you did right."

Durango moved over to stand at her side, looking down. "What do you think?" he asked.

"You did right." She slanted him an upward look. She was near to smiling at him. "From what I heard at the ranch, you could've gotten killed . . . doing what you did. But I'm glad, I really am." She patted the grass at her side and he sank down, removed his hat, and tossed it aside.

"Your pa," he said, speaking quite slowly and picking the words, "well . . . he wasn't exactly friendly."

She seemed unconcerned about this. "Pa is hot-tempered. Besides, he was upset about Nate."

"He told me to leave the country, Maryann."

She looked over at him—beyond him, and her

steady gaze widened, her face lost its color, and her lips parted. Durango felt a sudden chill pass through him. He turned only his head to follow out her line of vision.

Her father was standing there.

For a terrible second no one moved or spoke. Then Burt Clancy said in a tone that was both quiet and knife-edged: "Girl, you get up from there. Get on your horse and get home." The eldest of the Clancy brothers let his breath out easy. "Followed you," he said to Maryann. "I figured it had to be something like this . . . and with him. He's the feller shot your uncle and tried to shoot the rest o' us."

"That's not true," protested Durango, rising up off the ground to face Burt Clancy's burning fury. "You know it isn't, too."

Clancy walked out until he was facing Durango. He was a solid shape there in that gun-metal day, hard and scarred by old fights and wanting trouble now.

"I'll talk with you in a minute," he said in that same oddly soft tone. His gaze went back to Maryann. She was on her feet now, at Durango's side. "Get!" he snapped to her. "Get along home, girl, or by God I'll take a quirt to you!"

Maryann was like rock; she made no move away from Durango's side nor uttered a sound.

Durango looked around and down. She was keeping her steady eyes on her father; there was courage in every line of her stiff and unnatural stance, but there was also anguish. "No, Pa," she said in a tone that was scarcely audible. "I'll not go. Why did you do this? Why did you sneak after me like I was committing some kind of a crime? I'm a grown woman. I come and go as I please."

"With the likes of him? Girl, we'll talk this over later. Right now you do as I say . . . get on your horse and ride for home. Nate's there and he needs some lookin' after."

Durango took a deep breath. He had words framed on his lips and he knew they would precipitate the fight for it was clear that Burt Clancy was hungering for battle; it was a shine in his stare and it was in the bloodless shape of his mouth.

"She stays, Clancy, if that's what she wants."

Clancy moved, his very thin restraint broken by Durango's words. He sprang in close and swung a fist all the way from his belt, missed, and kept right on coming, his arms slashing in scythe-like motion. Durango danced clear and forgot all about Maryann. He struck Burt Clancy a light blow under the ear; he stung him another little blow across the bridge of the nose. Clancy came about like a ship in a high wind, yawing wide. He blinked from the pain of those two strikes and started forward again. This time he had his head down behind one crooked forearm held high.

His face was protected. He pawed with his free hand and Durango moved away. Clancy dug in his toes and hurled himself forward. He flung out both arms and clawed at Durango's clothing, got cloth, and dragged himself in so that Durango's rapier blows could not hurt him.

Burt Clancy was a seasoned barroom brawler. He fought like a bear, using his weight, his strength, and his toughness to wear down or smother an adversary. He had the strength of two ordinary men, too, and Durango learned this at once, for Clancy dropped both arms around Durango's middle and locked them for the straining squeeze that would force Durango's lungs to empty.

But Durango was not entirely a novice. He got one forearm between his own chest and Clancy's gullet so that the older man could not press his face into Durango's chest for protection. Then, with Clancy's terrible grip tightening, Durango forced his head back, and with his right fist he smashed him again and again in the face.

Somewhere in the dingy gloom Maryann screamed.

Claret sprayed from her father's nose, from his split lips. He closed his eyes and strained the tighter. Durango did not want to hit his face again, but the air was being strangled out of him. He used all his dwindling power to force the older man's head farther back. Then he chopped a savage blow into Clancy's face, and those steel-cable arms suddenly fell away, and Durango staggered clear.

He could see through the mist before his eyes that Maryann's father was badly off. He ambled backward like a drunk man, put up a hand to his face, and dashed away both sweat and blood. Durango could have finished him then, but he had not the strength.

He gulped in air and kept watching Clancy as the older man's eyes slowly cleared to their fierce brightness again. Clancy's face was a swelling, purple shambles. He came at Durango once more and this time landed a solid uppercut. This blow roared and echoed in Durango's brain. He felt his knees softening. He knew he had to get away but the best he could do was go sideways and put up an arm to keep a second blow from striking his jaw.

Clancy struck him solidly in the ribs. He was standing, flat-footed now, and getting every ounce of his weight into these blows. Durango felt a stealing numbness come into his side; it threatened to pass over his entire body. He gave ground; he moved first one way, then another way, desperately trading space for time. Clancy followed him. He was eager and his worst strikes missed but he kept coming. Then he tried another hurtling attack, and Durango, knowing this was coming, squared fully around, dropped his right shoulder low behind a cocked fist, and fired as Clancy swept up. The pain of that strike passed like an electric shock all the way up Durango's arm to the shoulder.

Clancy stopped as though he had run into a stone wall. He shuddered from head to heel and his mouth dropped open for an abrupt passage of pumped-out breath. Durango waited for him to fall, but he did not fall. He hung there, half conscious, half unconscious, looking stupid and helpless. Then he began to bring up his torn fists again, but the co-ordination was gone from his movements. Durango danced around him, caught Clancy's shoulder, and whirled him. He swung a downward-sledging blow that slammed meatily into the back of Burt Clancy's neck with all the might he was yet capable of, and that was enough. Maryann's father's eyes went awry; he winced and dropped in a curling fall to the ground.

Durango stood over him, gasping for breath. The wild sloshing of his own heart was like roaring rain in his ears. He stepped away, went to the creekbank, and knelt there in mud to sluice his face with cold water. It took time for his thoughts to clear and his eyes to focus without a mistiness. Then he twisted for a backward look. Maryann was down beside her father. She was not crying but her eyes were almost black and her skin was the color of putty. She did not put a glance upon Durango at all.

He got up, tasting blood in his mouth. He spat and put up one battered hand to feel his lips. They did not appear to be split. He felt, with the dimming-out of his primeval urges, the beginnings of a considerable pain in his left side. He probed for broken ribs, found none, and moved to kneel opposite Maryann over her father.

She looked over at him, saying nothing, and he could not right then understand the peculiarly wild and chaotic expression on her face. "Take his hat," he told her, "and fill it at the creek and fetch it back here to wash his face."

She went, doing as he'd said, and Durango then noticed how badly cut up Burt Clancy's face really was. When she returned, he used the unconscious man's own handkerchief to wash away the blood gently. He spoke to Maryann without looking up as he did this trying mightily to make his voice sound normal.

"As soon as he moves or flickers his eyelids, I'll go. It's up to you whether you want to go with him or come with me. If you figure he'll make good on that threat about using the quirt on you, then I reckon you'd better come with me."

"No," she said, shaking her head and also gazing unwaveringly on her father's raw features. "He's said that before. But he's never struck me in his life. I'll take him home."

Durango rocked back on his heels and looked

over at her. "It looks like I wanted to hurt him, doesn't it?"

They both understood why he'd said that. She shook her head and for the first time there were scalding tears to trouble her vision. "No. No, I understand. I'm not angry at you."

Burt Clancy groaned and feebly moved.

Durango passed the handkerchief over to Maryann and put real effort into standing up. She watched him do this. "Are you injured?" she asked, seeing how shallowly he was breathing and how bone-wearily he moved.

"No, a little sore here and there is about all." Durango glanced soberly down at her father. "Do you think you can get him home all right?"

"Yes," she murmured, looking down again. "You had better go now."

He nodded at this and watched Burt Clancy's slow and reluctant return to consciousness. "I kind of had an idea our meeting here would be different, Maryann."

"Yes, me, too."

"I'd give a lot if your pa didn't hate me so."

She nodded again at this, but did not speak or look up at him. Her steady hand sponged away the last of her father's blood, and she sat back, both hands on her upper legs, critically examining the downed man's battered features. In appearance it seemed that her entire attention was absorbed in this steady gazing, but when next

255

she spoke, it was obvious that this was not so at all. "I want to see you again," she said very solemnly. "I don't want you to leave the country."

He bent a little and put forth his right hand. She reached up to grasp it, still without looking at him. Then she suddenly sprang up and put her full, bright stare on his face and gradually increased the strength of her fingers upon his hand until he returned this pressure. It was for both of them a confused and confusing moment, full of pain and uncertainty and strong longing. Then she dropped his hand.

"You had better go now," she murmured.

He left then, moving back down to his horse where he untied and got astride and looked back once. But she had her back to him and was bending low over Burt again.

He reined out through willows and struck open range. Here, again, the unique fragrance of coming rain, fresh, clean, metallic-smelling, struck him on that ruffling little breeze from the west. It felt good with its shades of coolness. He rode downcountry through it, scarcely thinking how the sun was quite gone now and a lowering, big-bellied leaden sky hung directly overhead from horizon to horizon.

He ached in the body and rode troubled in the mind. He had fairly and severely beaten big Burt Clancy, but that thought did not occur to him at all. His actual thoughts were bewilderingly jumbled. There yet lingered much of that smoky light of battle in his gaze; it did not lessen much, either, when he turned to look back, an instinctive urge compelling him to do this, and saw, coming on in a hard run, a solitary racing horseman with the darkening backdrop mountains making recognition impossible.

XI

Durango reined up to await the racing stranger. He thought it might be Aaron Clancy; otherwise, he had no idea who it was, although clearly that swift-riding horseman had seen him and was coming directly for him.

Then he recognized that shock-head, hatless and straining on ahead of the running horse, and those extra-long shanks and bony shoulders. An impulse ran out along his nerves to their tips and he pulled around to ride toward this fresh meeting.

Still yards out the oncoming rider yelled forward in full-voice excitement: "They're coming, Marshal! They're about to the mountain pass by now!"

It was Corey Smith, Muleshoe's chore boy.

Durango's weariness fell away instantly; his aches were forgotten as understanding rushed over him. He let Corey draw down and sit his excited horse. "How long ago did you see them?"

he sharply demanded, some of Corey's excitement going from the boy into him, too.

" 'Bout nine o'clock this morning, Marshal. I lit out as soon as I figured they were the rustlers."

"How many?"

"Eight, Marshal."

"You didn't recognize any of them by any chance, did you?"

"No!" exclaimed the lad. "They were a long way out and I only stayed up there watching 'em until I was plumb certain they were making for the pass through the hills to Muleshoe range."

"Pretty soon for another raid," murmured Durango. Then an idea came to him and he fixed a wondering gaze upon Corey. "It's going to rain," he said, and let this sink in before adding to it: "Corey, the last time they hit Muleshoe it rained, didn't it?"

Corey thought a moment, then his face brightened. "Yes. Come to think on it, Marshal, that's plumb right, and what's more, as I recollect back now, it always rained 'bout the time they hit somebody's herd."

Durango flexed a smarting hand. Corey Smith's eyes saw the battered, skinned, and swollen condition of those fingers and his eyes gradually widened. He lifted them swiftly to Durango's face, but he said nothing at all about the flood of questions that came now to fill his eyes.

Durango recognized Corey's rising interest and headed it off before the youth could speak. He said: "I want you to tell me exactly how they'll come through those mountains. Exactly."

"Yes, sir. Well, there's a sort of winding pass that cuts from the north an' where it enters the mountains there's a funnel-like big opening as though, maybe, one time a river run there. There's got to be a spring there, too, 'cause a grove of cottonwoods are at that northerly mouth o' the cañon an' they're the only trees as far as I know on that side of the mountains, low down to the plain, anyway. And there's. . . ."

"That's enough," cut in Durango. "The trees are enough."

"Sir?"

"The trees. Now listen Corey, I want you to ride to Winterset, explain to Mose Clark exactly where that northerly mouth of the pass is, and be dead certain that Mose knows the spot."

"Yes, sir, Marshal."

"Then you tell Mose I said for him to make up a posse and go around through the mountains to that spot and block it off."

Corey's expression gradually reflected complete understanding. "Sure, Marshal. You figure to run them fellers back the way they came."

"I don't figure anything," contradicted Durango. "I just want to be plumb sure that, if they do make a run for it back that way, they won't escape.

Corey, do you think a posse can get through the mountains to that spot?"

"Oh, yes, I could lead 'em through myself. I've had plenty o' time to get to know those mountains real well, keepin' watch up on top for these fellers."

Durango considered. Mose Clark was old and unfit for hard riding. He might even, in fact, slow a posse down. He said: "I've changed my mind, Corey. You tell Mose to round up at least ten men . . . and *you* lead through the mountains to that pass. Tell them everything you've told me, and also explain to them that I don't want them coming south through that pass . . . I want them to stay at its northerly mouth. That's all they're to do. Stay up there and stop those rustlers if I don't stop them on this side of the hills. You got that clear?"

"Yes, Marshal, only old Mose won't want to be left out o' this, I don't expect."

"You tell him I said to stay out of it. You tell him I said to keep order in town until I get back."

Corey made a little frown. "Marshal, you're not goin' to try and catch them fellers in the mountains by yourself, are you? I mean . . . well . . . the odds are. . . ."

"I know what the odds are, Corey. Now you skedaddle to town and do what I told you."

"Marshal . . . ?"

Durango felt annoyance. He frowned, his wintry eyes hardened against the youth. "Now what? Dammit, boy, time is important."

"There's no place hereabouts to get help 'cepting. . . ."

"Ride," snapped Durango. "Get going and let me do the worrying."

Muleshoe's chore boy bobbed his head, hooked his mount, and went careening downcountry in the direction of Winterset. Durango watched him for a moment, then swung his own animal north and a little west, in the direction of the Muleshoe outfit, and put him into a long-legged lope. He saw no one the first mile, and in fact was not certain he'd even find Muleshoe's buildings since he'd never before been to the ranch. Then, loping swiftly side-by-side and passing along his front from west to east, he spotted three riders. These men did not see him until, at long last, a set of ranch buildings rose up close to the foothills, then, sighting him, the cowboys slowed to an onward trot, riding twisted in the saddle to speculate on his identity. They did not recognize him until the buildings were close enough to be easily distinguishable. Then they sharply halted and let him rush up to them.

The first rider to speak was the cold-eyed man Durango had exchanged words with at the Lone Star Saloon prior to the subsequent gunfight, and this man, like his companions, put an unfriendly gaze on Durango as he drew down to ride the balance of that short distance with them.

"Who's at the ranch?" Durango asked, and his answer was slow coming and sullen.

"Aaron. Nate's there, too, only he's down in bed . . . as you ought to know, Marshal."

Hostility was a new and bristling substance in the lead-gray day as Durango rode along with these Muleshoe range men.

"Burt was around when we rode out, but he was actin' like he was goin' somewheres," stated one of the cowboys, his gaze fixed stonily ahead on the buildings looming up.

They came into Muleshoe's yard all in a bunch and Durango cut off from the riders, who went in a long walk toward the barn. He left his horse near the main house, stepped onto the old porch, and the door opened to show Aaron Clancy's smooth, impassive, and studying face. Aaron said nothing; neither did he nod nor offer any kind of salutation. He simply did as he'd done before; he stood there motionlessly, waiting.

Durango said what Corey had told him in quick, minimal sentences. Aaron's expression subtly changed, became eager and interested and vengeful. "Burt isn't here," he finally said. "Nate's a-bed and Maryann's gone, too."

Durango said nothing to this. His face was smoothly unreadable. This was not the time to tell Aaron of Burt's condition or how it had come about. He needed riders, and he needed them immediately.

"You, your men, and I, will make five guns. It might be enough, Aaron."

"I guess it's got to be enough, Marshal," agreed Aaron, and put his onward glance out over the yard where those three cowboys were emerging from the barn. "Hey!" he called. "Saddle fresh horses for yourselves and for me an' the Marshal here. Get your carbines and all the loose ammunition you can find. And make it fast. I think our cattle-stealin' friends from over the mountains're fixin' to pay us another visit."

One of those three cowboys emitted a little — "Yip!"—and thumped the rider nearest him upon the back, saying: "See, Tex, I *told* you we'd get some 'citement before this here business was settled."

"That ain't the business I was talkin' about," complained the cowboy called Tex, and went hurrying back into the barn with his companions.

"They'll do," said Aaron Clancy succinctly. "They've been in a fight or two before."

Durango nodded. He was half turned away from Aaron, looking up at those black-cut mountains. As he looked, he described the northerly cañon-mouth as Corey had described it to him. Then he turned and put a questioning gaze on Aaron Clancy. "You know where that place is?" he asked.

"Sure. We've always called it Big Rock Cañon because about halfway up it there's a bunch of boulders bigger'n a man on horseback."

"Then you also know where it comes out of the mountains on your range."

"I reckon," agreed Aaron laconically. "It's the same way those fellers drove out the last cut they made of our beef."

"In the rain," stated Durango.

Aaron looked at him and nodded, repeating those words: "In the rain."

Durango looked skyward where those billowing great dark clouds were steadily growing heavier, more swollen with each passing moment. Aaron Clancy followed the lawman's gaze and his eyes brightened with understanding. "Be damned," he murmured. Then asked: "What's the significance?"

"You've never been able to track them, have you?" asked Durango with obvious meaning. "Rain's better at hiding tracks than Indians are." He moved down off the porch and put an impatient glance on the barn. He growled: "What the hell are they doing over there . . . making the saddles they figure to ride?"

Aaron took several forward steps and raised his powerful voice. "Hey, what the hell you fellers doing? Hurry up!" He then said to Durango: "I got to take a last look at my brother and get my carbine. Be right back."

"How is your brother?" Durango asked as Aaron started toward the doorway.

"He'll do. Be right back."

Muleshoe's riders came from the barn leading fresh horses. Durango met them halfway in the yard, took the reins of a hammer-headed, snake-eyed, big and powerful and ewe-necked grullo gelding, and put his thoughtful gaze on the watching cowboys. "If this is a prank," he said, meaning that this ugly horse was obviously ornery, "it'd better be an awfully good one because, if he dumps me, one of you boys is going to ride him."

The cowboys shook their heads at him. One of them said: "Naw, he's not really mean. He's the toughest critter on the Muleshoe, Marshal. That's why we got him for you." The rider smiled. "You're sort of tough yourself."

Durango stepped across leather and eased down gently expecting the mean-eyed grullo to explode under him. He did nothing of the sort. He just batted his ears back and forth and continued to survey the world from his unfriendly and jaundiced little eyes.

Moments later Aaron Clancy crossed from the house on the run with a carbine in his hand. He got hastily astride with the others and said —"Let's go!"—then led the swift rush out of Muleshoe's yard.

A cowboy edged up beside Durango and

smiled genially enough. His words said plainly that the animosity was no longer in him. "Marshal, we tied a slicker behind the cantle in case it rains."

Durango looked around and down. The slicker was there as the rider had said. He put a little grin on this man and said: "Thanks."

"Don't mention it," responded the rider, and they hurried along behind Aaron Clancy, riding side-by-side. They were half a mile out when one of the men said loudly, his gauging glance upon those swollen skies: "Goin' to rain like Noah's flood, directly." No one answered him.

On ahead, Aaron Clancy was riding a deliberate course toward the mountains rising up on their right. Durango watched the crumpled foothills for a clue as to where that debouching pass from the northward plain would touch Muleshoe's range. He had to give this up, though, for there seemed to be many cañon mouths intersecting the eroded land.

A cowboy sang out: "Hey, that there looks like Miss Maryann ridin' with Burt."

Durango's heart flopped over and he swung a quick look outward where a brace of riders were making their onward way at a painfully slow gait. He swore under his breath, watched Aaron alter his course to meet his brother and his brother's daughter, then drew the grullo horse in just a little so that the others, unsuspecting, all passed him by in a rush to meet those slowly riding oncoming figures.

He was well back when the others slowed, swirled around Maryann and her father, and stayed that way, his gun hand hanging loosely and easily within quick-draw reach of his hip holster.

XII

"What in the devil," cried Aaron at sight of his badly beaten brother, "happened to you?"

Burt Clancy's eyes were swollen completely closed. As soon as he saw that this was so, Durango ignored the older man and looked straight at Maryann. She did not at once recognize him, then, when she did, her mouth dropped open.

Durango said to her: "Corey came out of the hills. There is a band of men coming toward Muleshoe range from over the mountains. We're going to intercept them."

He hoped she would recognize his urgent need not to be troubled now. She did; she drew her glance away from Durango and put it on her uncle.

"Pa will be all right," she said. "Go on, you'd better hurry, hadn't you?"

But Aaron's black scowl was unheeding. He leaned over to put a hand on Burt's arm and say:

"Can you hear me, Burt? What happened? Who did this to you?"

Burt Clancy's badly swollen lips parted, he said something that was not distinguishable, and Maryann broke in before he spoke again. Her tone to Aaron was sharp now, to match the flare-up of her impatient gaze. "Go on! Catch them this time. I'll take Pa home and look after him. He's going to be all right, Uncle Aaron."

"But who did . . . ?"

"Go on!" she cried out, and guided her own and her father's mount on through and past those stunned men. As she passed Durango, she gave him a full, head-on look. He nodded to her and booted out his grullo horse. The others then swung away, too. But for a long while afterward they called back and forth in awe-struck tones. Only Aaron did not join this talk. He rode up ahead with his head low and his expression grimly and thunderously dark and thoughtful.

Durango kept back, and even after Aaron resumed his hurrying gait he made no attempt to get near that leading rider who had a Winchester carbine balanced over his thighs. Leave Aaron with his thoughts, with his dark speculations, he reasoned to himself. It would all come out eventually, but there was neither the need nor the wish for that to be now. He swept along with them while the sky steadily blackened until afternoon was like dusk and a rippling, warm breeze came down cañons on their right to blow against them.

Aaron slowed after a time, oriented himself with a studying look along the northerly hills, then cut hard right and walked his horse to a place where the plain ended abruptly and a cañon's widening mouth showed its deeper, narrowing, and darker depths. Here, Aaron halted altogether and held up a hand. The others piled up behind him, also stopping. Durango dismounted and went stiffly ahead a little way, leading his horse, watching the ground.

There were no discernible shod-horse tracks here, which meant whoever those oncoming riders were, they had not yet gotten this far through the hills. He turned, saw Aaron watching him, and said: "Let's go. They haven't come out yet."

Without a word or a second glance, Aaron gigged his animal and moved onward, riding slow and easy now, and pushing a probing glance on ahead.

When Durango re-mounted, the cowboy at his side said: "Darker'n the hubs of hell in there. We could stumble right into them."

Another rider, hearing this, showed his familiarity with this cañon. "No place to get clear, either," he muttered. "Cussed walls are near straight up 'n' down. Leastwise, until we get halfway through . . . then there's them big rocks."

Durango was third in line behind Aaron Clancy. He was trying to estimate how much time had elapsed since Corey'd seen the rustlers, and he, along with Muleshoe, had gotten up here. It did not appear to him that a meeting between the two parties could be far off unless. . . .

He waited for a wide place to come up, then went around the rider ahead of him and came in behind Aaron to ask a question: "Any place they could turn off and go around us down some side cañon?"

Aaron shook his head. He twisted in the saddle to put his measuring look on Durango, and, when he spoke, his voice was cold and impersonal, as though something had recently occurred to change his mind about Durango.

"No place for a man to get out of here at all," he said, "unless he goes due north or due south."

They were riding in a dark world where a steady breeze came down to blow hard against their faces, to ruffle the manes of their animals, and splay horses' tails with static electricity. It was an eerie ride. The deeper they got into the cañon, the less Durango liked it. If that threatening sky opened up with a flashflood, they'd be in real danger. Springtime flashfloods had a way of dumping tons of water into cañons such as this one in minutes, until they were full from wall to wall with a horse-high wall of rushing water.

As he rode, Durango sought to estimate ways out, if such a flood occurred. He could see on both sides of him fairly well, but because of that leaden gloom overhead he was unable to see up the cañon's sides very far. There was a kind of hanging mist directly overhead that obscured the heights. The air through which they rode was troubled by that constant little wind, but it had a definite metallic scent and taste to it. He said to Aaron: "This'd be a poor place to get caught in a bad rain."

Aaron rode on, saying nothing until he came to some crooked trees. The trail widened to a width of not less than 100 feet, and dead ahead stood some huge gray monoliths of eroded granite. Here, Aaron reined down and let the others come up on either side of him.

"It won't be any picnic for the rustlers, either," he told Durango, and got down from his saddle. "It's the only wide place in the trail. We'll wait for them here, yonder in those rocks." He held forth his reins and a cowboy took them, leading Aaron's horse away.

Durango, likewise, dismounted and permitted a Muleshoe man to lead off his animal. Aaron was viewing him from a distance of some twenty feet. Around them the others were moving off toward the big rocks. Durango understood Aaron's expression and said what had to be said: "It was me. I met Maryann along the creek. Your brother had followed her. He came onto us in stealth and there was a fight."

"Must've been quite a fight," stated Aaron, his face as usual impassive.

"It wasn't my choosing."

"Probably it wasn't," said Aaron. "I noticed your hands back at the ranch. Only then I had no idea it was Burt you'd met." Aaron fell momentarily silent, then he said: "Maryann, eh? Why?"

"What do you mean . . . why?"

"Do you like her? Does she like you? Is that how it is?"

"You should've figured that out during the fight in town," said Durango. "I told you then she didn't want us to get into a battle."

Aaron grounded his carbine; he leaned upon it and kept weighing and probing Durango. Finally he said, with a little shrug: "I reckon she's a woman now. I reckon it's about time she was noticing fellers."

"Tell that to Burt," muttered Durango.

Aaron slowly wagged his head. There was no indication of humor in his look at all when he said: "Won't have to. Neither of us will, Durango. Maryann'll tell him. He's sort of busted up and she'll give him no rest while she's nursin' him. You see, Maryann's got a lot of Burt in her. You maybe don't know that yet. I watched her grow up. She don't take anything sitting down, if she thinks she's right." Aaron's steady eyes twinkled the slightest bit. "I wouldn't want to be in Burt's boots right now for all the grass in Texas. He can't talk back and she won't give him a moment's peace." Aaron sighed; he fell silent and continued to examine Durango with his critical eyes. "It's your bed," he murmured in dry conclusion. "You made it, and you're goin' to have to sleep in it." He straightened up off the carbine and looked around him. Only one Muleshoe man was visible in the leaden gloom. "All set?" Aaron asked of this man, and got back a strong head nod. He turned his back on Durango and strolled over into the boulders.

Durango, not as phlegmatic as Aaron Clancy, went among the boulders on both sides of the trail, checking on the Muleshoe men. He found them divided and commanding both sides of the trail. It was, in his view, an excellent ambush. He sought out Aaron Clancy and sat down beside him, both their backs resting on an immense granite slab, both their hands curled around Winchester carbines.

"Shouldn't be long, now," Aaron said. "You reckon that posse from town's had time enough to get around us?"

Durango shook his head. "Not a chance," he said. "Your chore boy had to ride to town, wait for a posse to be formed, then lead it back up here, on around us by some other trail, and out onto the plain beyond."

"Well," said Aaron laconically, "since we got

the drop on these fellers, we likely won't need no damned posse anyway."

Durango looked around. "They won't be simple cowboys," he warned. "A rustler's got only one thing to lose in a trap . . . his life. He gets hung to a tree limb if he surrenders, or gets salted down with lead if he fights. With a choice like that, I don't think many men would surrender. If you go out fighting, at least you might take someone else with you."

"Then let 'em fight," said Aaron indifferently. "I personally don't give a copper-colored damn what they do. We've lost a lot of beef to those fellers and I'd be the first to pull a rope or a trigger where they're concerned."

Time passed. The men in the rocks, from time to time, made little restless, abrasive sounds. Once, someone's carbine barrel scratched over stone making an unmistakable sound, and promptly came several growled protests about this. The sound was not repeated.

The wind rose fitfully now, pushing along the cañon like it was being forced through a too-small funnel. It had a strong dampness to it.

Durango looked uncomfortably at the blacked-out heavens; there was a strong uneasiness stirring in him. He felt confined. Bringing his gaze downward along the dimly discernible slopes that shouldered in on both sides of the cañon here, he made out some trees, some red-barked manzanita, a few madroña clumps, and the ubiquitous sagebrush, tough and wiry and unkempt-looking. In a pinch a man could scuttle up those side hills, but it would take a bit of doing, for the footing was largely shale and talus rock. Still, Durango comforted himself with at least the feasibility of getting out of the cañon this way, if he desperately had to.

At his side Aaron Clancy said quietly: "Durango, we had to come only about four miles. Those rustlers had at least a six-mile ride. We came fast and they didn't." He held forth a tobacco sack. "Care for a smoke?"

Durango made no move to accept the offer. He looked hard at Clancy, saying: "No, I don't want a smoke. And neither do you. Whether we've time for a smoke or not isn't the point, Aaron. We're risking our necks by being here and you're not going to increase that risk by smoking . . . so maybe the rustlers smell the tobacco before they get here."

Aaron kept his tobacco sack dangling and his tawny gaze upon Durango. Then he slowly put the sack back into a shirt pocket and said: "All right." For a while longer he was silent, then he said: "You know, I'm the only Clancy you haven't beaten yet, one way or another." He let it lie between them, partly a statement of fact, partly a challenge.

Durango said nothing. He raised the carbine,

checked it carefully, and got to his feet to put a rummaging look as far up the trail as he could see. The way he stood, listening, he might not have heard Aaron at all. Then, as Clancy also rose to stand with his back to their boulder, Durango said: "You call it, Aaron. Only I'll ask that you postpone it until this other thing is over with."

Aaron's smooth expression cracked a little at the edges. Something was inwardly amusing him. He, too, spoke aside while considering that fading-out northward stretch of cañon trail. "What's there to fight about between us?" He brought his gaze back and settled it on Durango's face. "Besides, if I whupped you . . . gun or claw . . . Maryann'd give me no peace the rest o' my life." Aaron gravely wagged his head. "It wouldn't be worth it," he murmured, and swung back to look up the trail.

Presently, with darkness coming stealthily down into the cañon, Durango heard the steady echo of ridden horses passing down from the north, sometimes loud, sometimes soft. Overhead a trembling glow of watery star shine momentarily showed, then was layered over again by those dirty dark clouds. The sounds came again, faint at first, as though the oncoming riders were passing around a bend, then stronger, a sound as of someone dribbling pebbles over a corrugated tin of a barn roof.

Durango brushed Aaron Clancy's arm with his

fingers. "Go warn the others in case they didn't hear."

Aaron at once moved off, trailing his carbine.

A big, fat drop of water struck stone beside Durango. Another big drop hit sun-dried dust at his feet and hissed. Now that constant breeze died out entirely and in its wake came a ponderous silence deeper than the night would have been; every sound carried a great distance in this oppressive stillness, and something age-old stirred in Durango to make him restive and apprehensive.

XIII

When Aaron returned to Durango's side, those intermittent raindrops were striking with cadenced irregularity. He brought with him two black slickers from behind their saddles. Handing Durango one of these garments, Aaron put aside his carbine and donned the other one. He said: "Everyone's ready."

The rain, though, made it difficult to hear those riders. Then the wind came again, sweeping in from the northwest and causing a turbulence deep in the cañon. Durango swore about this and moved ahead to seek those sounds of ridden horses again. Aaron Clancy strode along in his wake, big, solid, and shimmering-wet in his raincoat.

Durango was well north of the last boulder when he caught the oncoming sound again. This time, there was a man's voice, too, but that whipping wind sucked it away before Durango could make out words. Another voice, though, raised to buck that soughing air, called forcefully: "It helps us in one way an' hinders us in another!"

Durango thought the rustlers were referring to the rain. He turned to go back and bumped into Aaron. They moved off together, careless of being seen because, if they could not discern the outlaws, neither could the outlaws see them.

Back again in the rocks, Durango put his mouth close to Aaron's ear: "They've got to be given a chance," he said.

Aaron thought otherwise. "They'll turn tail and run north. That posse won't be in position and they'll get away. Durango, us cattlemen've suffered a helluva lot from these men. We want 'em dead or alive."

"Not murdered, though," stated Durango, and drew off a little. Aaron's face was mantled by an angry scowl. He did not say what he was thinking, but it was obvious even in that misty gloom that he would prefer murdering the thieves to risk having them escape to continue their raids on Muleshoe herds.

"When they're close to the rocks, I'll hail them," stated Durango. "I'll give them one chance. You cover me. You tell the others to cover me, too. Go on, Aaron."

"You'll be wasting your breath an' they'll kill you for it," growled Clancy.

"It's my life. Go on."

Aaron moved off in a gliding fashion. Durango turned back facing the north. Now, despite the big drops of water, he easily made out the *jangle* and *squeak* of riders in the murky cañon depths. He stood quietly listening to these sounds, gauging the closeness, the numbers of those riders. A little later he found the spot where he meant to deliver his ultimatum, and here he waited until he sighted the first bulky shapes. He raised the carbine, settled it over a boulder, cocked it, and lowered his head, drawing that initial horseman to him down the rain-wet barrel. Then he called out: "Stop right where you are! Don't a one of you make a move!"

That foremost horseman sucked back on his reins sharply and, without locating Durango at all, threw himself sideways off his saddle. Instantly there came the crashing break of ragged gunfire from those dark horsemen; muzzle blasts lit up a scene of confusion, blurred movement, and plunging animals. Durango sought his target and fired when he thought he might score a hit. But rain, coming now in a steady downpour, the swirling mists that accompanied it in this gusty cañon, and the instinctive agility of those cow thieves, made his bullet sing wide, strike stone, and go whistling off skyward.

Men's wild shouts up the cañon greeted a fusillade from behind Durango where the Muleshoe opened up. One word rose shrilly over the others: "Ambush! Ambush!"

Durango levered up another bullet and waited. He was wholly calm in this riotous bedlam, waiting for a good shot. Aaron Clancy came slipping up behind him to call out: "I told you, they're like a bunch of antelope! Make a sound and they break all up, running for cover."

Aaron's tone was gratingly excited. Durango put a brief glance upon him. Aaron's hat brim was dripping water; it glistened from his slicker and dripped from his nose and chin. "God damn' rain," snarled Aaron, squinting ahead. "Can't see nothing!"

"The horses!" called Durango. "Keep 'em off those horses." He raised his voice and sang this out over and over again until he was sure all the Muleshoe men had heard and understood.

Gunshots burst ahead out of the northward downpour, little red-orange lights that winked on and winked off, their sounds coming thunderously on a little wind to make faint flutters in the turbulence. The firing stayed brisk; no one joined in another volley; it was every man for himself, and the fighters understood this as they lay in sticky mud with water hitting them, flinging water from their faces, and seeking through slitted eyes to find targets.

A bewildered horse with his reins broken and hanging loose came into Durango's sight. He winced each time gun flame erupted near him. A man swirled up off the ground under this animal's feet and lunged to get astride. The horse whirled as that cow thief made his jump. Durango and Aaron Clancy fired simultaneously as the rustler rose up the side of the horse. Both bullets hit him hard. He gave a great bound out into the rain, away from the horse, and fell like stone, and bounced. Water beat mercilessly on his upturned face. He did not close his eyes against this drenching, or his mouth, either. He was dead.

Aaron let off a fierce war whoop, and in anticipation of their location being revealed by this, Durango swiftly dropped down on the ground. He swore at Aaron, saw Clancy turn a white face toward him, then they both felt water running under their bodies, gnawing at the soil there. Bullets came from both sides of the trail to strike with shuddering force against their granite shelter. Durango called to Aaron—"You muddle-headed idiot!"—and ran out of breath.

The rain was increasing with a vengeance. It had a rather frightening roar to it now, and it did not descend in drops but came in sheets of water, wave after wave of them pushing in from the north and getting steadily colder as they moved along.

Durango spluttered and got to his knees. Beneath the slicker his clothing was wet and he was covered with a slimy coating of mud. He peered ahead, saw those winking gun blasts, and threw several shots northward at them. At his elbow Aaron Clancy gasped as a rivulet of icy water funneled down his neck. Aaron said: "If it's any comfort . . . they got even less protection than we have."

"Keep firing," said Durango, "and watch their horses."

It was not a wise thing to say because the horses were not now in sight. Durango was aware of this; it bothered him very much. He thought that as soon as they could, the rustlers would wiggle backward so that they would not be pinned down by Muleshoe gunfire, then get astride and ride northward back the way they had come as swiftly as the treacherous footing would permit. He knew, with five guns, he could not prevent this, but he hoped with Muleshoe's lively fire to keep the outlaws pinned down as long as possible in order that the Winterset posse men might get through and be in position at the cañon's far-away mouth, when the rustlers finally made their dash.

A ragged burst of shots came from the rocks east of the trail. Durango flung water off his eyelids to look in that direction. It came to him that the rustlers might be attempting to flank him and Aaron and that one other Muleshoe man who was west of the trail, by eliminating the two men across the way.

"Stay here," he ordered Aaron. "I'm going across to see who's doing all the shooting over there."

Aaron said something that might have been a protest, but Durango neither heard nor heeded him. He slipped and stumbled to the last large rock east of the trail and hunkered there in mud, gauging the number and position of guns across from him. Five men were over there; no more than two of them could be Muleshoe. As he studied conditions, he saw that three men were seeking to get above two other men. This was evident from the changing positions of their muzzle blasts. He was certain these would be outlaws, but what interested him was this aggressiveness. He had thought the rustlers would want to break this fight off, to get back astride and get clear of Muleshoe's ambush. He shrugged and put his carbine in a stone crack, waited for muzzle blast, then fired instantly. He did this several times, tracking those climbing men by their flashes, and eventually drove them back down into the northward cañon's depths. From across the trail, deep in among rocks, a man's voice called out dryly: "Thanks!"

Durango considered crossing over, but he now

saw no real need to risk exposing himself and began to make his way back to Aaron at the latter's forward position. This was hard; the cañon floor was awash with a deluging flow of water, some of it coming on from the tilted north, some of it pouring from those closed-in side hills. Mud was like paste making his boots and spurs weigh ten pounds each, and he could not now see five feet ahead. Only when he turned to look northward on up the trail was there enough wet iron-like light to see by.

A Muleshoe rider he recognized stepped across swiftly from one boulder to another in front of him. Durango said: "Try and keep them pinned down. How's your ammunition holding out?"

"Got plenty!" called this man, and the wind whipped away something else he said.

Durango nodded and continued his way onward. Now, for some reason he could not at once fathom, the firing on ahead where the outlaws lay in liquid mud increased to a fierce and booming crescendo. Bullets struck around about with singing fury and drove everyone, Durango included, down low. He listened to this racket for a moment and understood it. Their enemies could not see enough Muleshoe men to warrant such stepped-up gunfire, and that left only one plausible explanation for it. They were pouring lead into the rocks to keep the Muleshoe men down while they made a rush for their horses.

Durango let himself fully down into the mud and peered around the base of a boulder with his chin resting in three inches of hissing water. By skylining the northerly distances, he could dimly make out moving shapes. He fired at them, levered up, and fired again. He yelled over the rising howl of rainfall and whipped-up wind: "Fire! Shoot! Muleshoe, give it to them!" He called out much more, saying frantically what the rustlers were up to, but at that moment the wind swooped down into the cañon with stinging force and carried his words away down the cañon with it.

Aaron made another triumphant whoop. On both sides of the trail gunfire increased until it rivaled the rain's own constant roaring. Flashes lashed out among the rocks; men moved and fired and moved on again. The Muleshoe men had understood at last the purpose of that fierce volley and were moving up desperately to prevent its purpose from being achieved.

Durango tried to get up, slipped and sprawled, and dirty, thick water filled his mouth and nose. He spat and swore and got to one knee. His carbine was shot out. By feeling under the slicker he was able to locate another set of re-loads, but these bullets were all he had with him.

He got up finally, when the Winchester was ready to be fired again, and continued onward until he found Aaron Clancy. There, exhausted by the arduous trip, he sank down on his heels and sucked in air, then stood up and leaned on Aaron's granite bulwark.

"Can you see them?" he yelled.

Aaron wagged his head, looked around, and flung water from his face. "Can't see anything!" he cried out. "They didn't make it, though, because they're still shooting at us."

Durango's heart was pounding from that recent exertion. Normally that would have prevented him from firing; now it did not for the elemental reason that it could hardly impair his aim when he could see nothing to aim at anyway. He dumped four fast shots up along the northward trail, saw winking, red replies come back from the mud on either side of the trail, and stopped firing long enough to say to Aaron Clancy: "Listen, we're not strong enough to rush them and they're not able to dislodge us from these rocks. It's a Mexican stand-off."

"Then," yelled back Clancy, "we stay here until we pick 'em off one at a time!"

But Durango, listening to the steadily rising roar of rain around them, said: "No, we got to get our horses and make a run for it."

Aaron demanded: "You crazy? They'll get us and our horses, too."

Durango put forth a hand to touch Aaron. He said: "Listen, what do you hear?"

"Rain!" exclaimed Clancy. "Rain an' guns! What else?"

"That's not just rain, Aaron. You hear the tone of that water? It's building up northward in this damned cañon. It's coming south in a wall of water. If we stay in here any longer, it'll come raging down on us maybe twenty feet deep. Every manjack in here'll get drowned." Durango withdrew his hand and watched Aaron cock his head, listening. Then he brushed Aaron's arm again, saying: "Tell the others. Get the horses, drop south back down the cañon, and meet me there."

Aaron hesitated. He cried out: "What of them rustlers?"

"One thing is damned sure," stated Durango. "They can't go north now. Now get going!"

XIV

That steady roar was increasing so that, over the other sounds deep in the cañon, it forced its way into the awareness of the men trapped there. Durango, making his way toward their tuck-tailed horses, noticed that the pressure around his lower legs was greater in its swirling southward race. He stopped once to gauge this stream and was chilled at what he saw; that water was not only plunging downcountry, it was also increasing in depth each second.

He found one drenched Muleshoe cowboy

standing with his feet braced against the current dashing water from his face with his pistol hand. He caught this man roughly and pushed him away from his boulder.

"Go to the horses!" he yelled. "Hurry up!"

The rider stumbled off. Durango shepherded him along, caught his elbow when he was nearly swept off his feet, and got down where their animals were, moments ahead of the other Muleshoe men. By this time all gunfire had ceased, only that ominous and grinding roar of confined water plunging along its only outward course was audible. It drowned out even the pounding of that furious rain.

Aaron slipped and fell beside his horse. He got up with his lips angrily moving but his words were lost in that increasing roar. Somewhere northward, over this frightening rumble, came the keening, thin cry of a man. They got astride, spun their mounts, and headed down the cañon. Their footing was made doubly treacherous by adobe mud and spuming water.

There was no use in calling back and forth; human vocal cords could not begin to ride over that other sound. Around them in their south-ward rush tons of mud sloughed off hillsides and oozed into the choked cañon's depths. Twice Durango had narrow escapes, once a gigantic stone came whistling from the overhead heights to crash behind him, and another time, when he was groping his way, nearly blinded by whipping rain, a fir tree, shallow-rooted and upended by wind, toppled across the cañon. His horse was stung by lashing-fingering limbs and gave a great bound, slipped, fell, and frantically recovered footing to push on rapidly in the wake of the men ahead.

Aaron Clancy led. He knew this cañon better than the others. All five of them rode along strung out single file, hunched up against rain and cold and wind, and that rearward roar. Twice Durango twisted to look backward, seeking some sign of the outlaws who he knew had to be following them. Visibility was less than ten feet and he saw no one. Once, though, he thought he heard a man's hoarse voice raised in a whipped-away cry, but immediately after this came a shattering *crash* of black thunder, the first thus far in this storm, and could not be sure that other noise had been man-made.

They came to one of the wider places in the trail and here Aaron halted to count noses. Durango pushed up beside him and flagged onward with his arm. He leaned from the saddle and yelled into the storm's teeth: "Don't stop! Head for the prairie! Get t'hell out of here!"

Aaron nodded and moved out. Water now swirled above the fetlocks of their horses, and the animals had caught some of the apprehension that gripped the men. They fought their bits, constantly bobbed their heads up and down and rolled their eyes in near panic.

That drowning rain never slackened; it hissed in torrents from the pressing-close side hills and sent thick rivulets of chocolate mud swirling downward to swell the rising river in the cañon's bottom. It brought with it constant impediments such as tree limbs, rocks, uprooted sage and manzanita bushes that harassed the fearful horses.

Durango thought he could make out, onward past Aaron's humped-up shape, a watery brightness that would be the cañon's mouth. He was concentrating upon this when without warning his horse gave a terrified whinny and went head over heels. Durango struck hard, choked as water filled his nostrils, and tried to sit up. He had struck his head and for a moment dizziness held him. He struggled for a clear head, and when it ultimately came, he got up unsteadily and looked for the others. They were gone. His horse had evidently regained his feet and had rushed along after them. He was quite alone.

He looked anxiously at the shimmering mud banks on either side of the trail knowing at once he could not hope for footing there to climb upward. He looked northward and saw a rush of horsemen coming at him, faces down against that hurting rain, bodies humped and clothing black with water. He had not the time for running after the Muleshoe riders and there was no place close by to hide, for that oncoming bunch of riders was a solid vague motion north of him.

He pressed back with his shoulders hard in the mud and let the first two or three riders pass, then he considered each following man until he found the last one. He moved out at once to a juncture with the head of this man's horse, caught the bridle, and jerked the beast to a snorting halt. The rider's lowered head whipped up. Durango's cocked six-gun was staring him in the face. The rustler blinked, flung away water, and stared. Then he opened blue lips and called out—"Will, hold it!"—but the onward horsemen did not slacken their gaits nor even turn to look back. They passed along phantom-like, hunched over, cold, drenched, and miserable.

Durango got up behind the cantle of his captive's saddle and put his lips close to this man's ear to say: "Get going, mister. You try calling out again and I'll cut you in two." By way of emphasis he jammed his gun barrel into the cow thief's kidneys.

Somewhere ahead a horse nickered. This was the only sound Durango could hear over that crashing, careening roar of a wall of water coming swiftly down behind them. He leaned far over to see how deep the water was underfoot. It was nearly to the knees of the horse he and his prisoner were astride. He straightened up again, trying to imagine how far down the cañon he was toward its ending. He thought there was perhaps a half mile yet to go. In seeking to judge his chances of beating that wall of water to the prairie, he concluded they would have to risk going faster or they would not make it.

The onward riders were dead ahead and slackening. His prisoner, saying nothing but with obvious intent, urged his own mount toward the nearest horseman ahead. Durango pushed that hard steel gun barrel into the rustler's spine again, saying: "Easy does it, mister. You get cute and this horse'll only have one rider . . . me. In fact, I think that might be best for the horse anyway."

The outlaw replied in a believing tone. "Just let's get out of here. That's all."

"Ride around them," said Durango. "If they call to you, don't answer, just act scairt and wave toward the cañon mouth."

"Act scairt!" exclaimed the rustler. "Who's acting? Pardner, I *am* scairt!"

They passed two slumped riders and Durango kept his face low and close to the cow thief's shoulders. From the corner of his eyes he watched those uncomfortable and fearful riders. They put resentful looks upon Durango's captive as he edged past but they said nothing aloud, or if they did it was indistinguishable in all that constant roaring.

They could not for a while do any more passing. Then, where another wide place appeared, Durango gouged his captive and once more they went around other slithering, lunging horses and men. Someone near the head of the column said: "Hey Ace, don't crowd, dammit all."

They got around this man, too, and were at last in the lead. "Now head out," ordered Durango, and the outlaw immediately protested.

"I das'n't, dammit, if this critter slips'n falls we're goners."

"We're goners if you don't get us to hell out of here."

These perilous alternatives struck home and the cow thief gigged his animal the slightest bit. The response, though, was sluggish. The horse was struggling through water that sloshed the bottom of his rider's stirrups. Although the current was traveling in the same direction, downcañon, it had so badly undercut the beast's invisible footing he was reluctant to hasten.

"Faster," said Durango, and twisted to look back for the other rustlers. They were back there coming unsteadily on through a drowning world. Water curled around the legs of the horses and over the boot toes of the riders. It came down from above in endless sheets and it washed over them in waves that the rising wind whipped and sawed and churned.

Durango's captive kneed his animal and got a

little more speed, but the animal was badly frightened now and very reluctant. As Durango leaned out and around for a fresh glimpse onward, his hand brushed something iron-like and cold. He felt it, curled his fingers around it, and drew forth the outlaw's six-gun and let it fall into the water. He had, in his apprehension, completely forgotten to disarm the man.

"It's lighter on ahead," said the rustler. "I think we're going to make it."

Durango strained to see. He could not fully open his eyes because of that whirling, stinging rain, but he, too, saw the brightening of the leaden sky dead ahead. He watched this hopeful distance with mistrust, at first, and finally with relief. It was the cañon mouth.

Somewhere in the unseen rear a man screamed.

Durango heard this knifing sound over all other sounds and heard it drown out in a deafening roar as tons of side hill came crashing down into the cañon far back. There rose, too, a terrible *hissing*, a boiling as of water being momentarily checked by this landslide and fighting around and over it, forcing that great mass of slime to give way, to mix with the flashflood's cresting tide and go hurtling down the cañon. He did not now tell the rustler to spur his beast, but used his own goads. The animal, cut hard in the flank, first tucked his tail as though to buck, then broke ahead instead, fighting through the rising water in grunting leaps.

In this fashion Durango and his prisoner came out of the cañon. Around them water dropped lower as it spread out over the range in a glittering, rusty river. The cow thief, until he was certain they were out of danger, had been occupied guiding his animal, now he turned without any warning and struck hard at Durango with an upraised elbow. Durango twisted clear of the full impact, caught the residue on one shoulder, and said tightly—"All right, you want it this way. . . ."—and swung his six-gun in a short, downward chopping arc that hit the rustler over his left ear. He wilted, slumped, and fell heavily from the saddle. Durango had no time to look down, the horse gave another big jump, and Durango was fully occupied getting over the cantle, into the empty saddle, and there he leaned down over the stampeding animal's neck, groping for the reins. He found them and hauled back. Gradually the horse came to a stop, he was quivering all over and could not stand still.

As Durango was turning to look for the other outlaws, a gun flashed redly at him from the west. He was not struck, the horse was fidgeting, but that slug came head-high close and he heard its lethal whine. Wasting no second glance up the cañon, he spun away eastward. Two more shots came out of the steely distance, forcing him to cut south and west. He tried yelling but that emerging great wall of water drowned out his best efforts. He knew the Muleshoe men were lying off in the east and had fired, believing him to be one of the renegades.

He rode west until well beyond that fanning-out sea of liquid mud that was gushing in a ten foot wave out of the cañon, and there he halted to peer around him. Not a horse or a man was anywhere in sight; he had the bizarre sensation of being the only human being left on earth.

Howling wind broke out of the cañon in the wake of the flashflood's first cresting gorge of water, and afterward both water and wind subsided, but the drowning downpour did not abate one whit.

Somewhere off to the east, during a capricious, sucked-back, sudden, and momentary hush of the wind, Durango heard a gunshot, then another gunshot, then eight or ten explosions fired at the same time. He thought Muleshoe, having emerged first from the cañon, was lying in the mud now, seeking targets of mounted men by skylining them. There was no other way to see a target, unless it was moving, and was limned against the steely horizon. A fierce break of shooting came on the increasing wind, born to Durango and as suddenly torn away and sent southward upon a shrieking whiplash of churned air. He struck out in the direction of that firing, and at long last the horse he rode seemed to have lost the major portion of his panic. The rain made him shake his head very often—water in the ears is anathema to horses—but otherwise the beast went willingly enough back into the slow-moving broad stream of water flowing from the cañon, which was now only about twelve inches deep where it was spending its heretofore confined power by rushing east and west over a glistening, fish-belly gray world of lost horizons and confused points of compass.

He had covered several hundred yards when a rider came out of the mist dead ahead and pushing westward. He had his head twisted to see over one shoulder and a Winchester carbine hung ready in his free hand.

Durango could not determine who this man was. He drew his six-gun and halted there, expecting the horseman to face around. But instead, the stranger suddenly reined up, strained backward a moment, then whirled his horse and threw up his carbine. Durango looked out along this man's sighting and instantly saw the second shape bulk mistily through the downpour. In a flash he recognized this second man's build and heft: Aaron Clancy. He fired a fraction of a second ahead of the outlaw. The shot man's horse gave a bound sideways, shying from the startling red burst of flame from Durango's gun. His rider also fired, but his body was sliding off as he did this and the slug struck wet mud with a flat sound.

Aaron Clancy's handgun was swinging when Durango yelled at him. Clancy hesitated, then kneed his animal forward, paused where the shot man lay, and let Durango come up to rub stirrups with him. Aaron peered closely, then said in a booming voice: "Damn' lucky you saw him. I sure didn't."

"Where are the others?" asked Durango.

Aaron shrugged. "Scattered. We was waitin' for 'em when they come out of the cañon. But they expected that I reckon, 'cause they sure broke up every which way. We started after 'em, that's how come I was over here." Aaron flung off water and spat. Then he said, "Hell, I thought you got drowned or something back in the cañon. Your horse came out but you weren't on it."

Durango holstered his gun. "Time for that tale later!" he exclaimed. "Let's try and locate the others, then go rustler-hunting."

They turned back, riding west. For a while the horse of the man Durango had shot ran along behind them not wishing to be left alone. Then it got side-tracked in the mud and went careening south, the stain upon its saddle being steadily diluted by rain.

XV

It was Durango who, after they were all together again in the ceaseless rain, came to a thoughtful conclusion and voiced a decision. They had by then been seeking rustlers without success for nearly an hour.

"Winterset," he told the Muleshoe men. "There's no way to track them but we've covered the land east and west for miles and seen nothing. They've got to be heading for Winterset."

Aaron agreed with this and gestured the others to follow him. They rushed along skiddingly until that broad flow of chocolate mud was finally left behind, and from there on, until they cut the north-south stage road, gravel in the soil made solider footing. But upon the road's smooth and packed surface the danger of falling became greater again, and they were forced to proceed with more caution. Around them the land laid cowed and drenched; run-off boiled from erosion gullies and tumbled with fierce power over natural obstacles. The stage road was twin serpentine ribbons of molten steel. They passed along it in a bunch, stirrups touching, slickers glistening, hat brims dripping a steady dirty trickle, five miserable men with tempers worn thin by adversity, hunger, and purest personal discomfort.

Aaron Clancy rode at Durango's side. He leaned out once to shout: "Thanks for saving my bacon back there!"

Durango said nothing but he nodded understanding of the other man's words.

A mile along toward town one of the cowboys called sharply to the others: "Hey! Yonder's a rider!"

They followed out the direction this rider indicated with his upflung arm and saw the horseman. He was east of them and traveling in the same direction. He had some kind of a scarf tied over the crown of his Stetson and knotted under his jaw, evidently to keep the hat from blowing away.

Durango gestured eastward and reined off in that direction. The others followed him, jogging as rapidly as they dared toward that lone rider. They were seen by the stranger when they were still beyond gun range, and he jerked back for one long searching look, then he leaned down over his animal's neck, hung in the hooks, and went racing toward town. Aaron Clancy and one of the other Muleshoe men started out in a lunging run. Durango yelled at them; they did not hear him. He drew his six-gun, fired off one shot, and saw Aaron straighten around in the saddle. He flagged him back with the handgun. To the others he called out: "We'll find him! He's heading for town, too!"

When Aaron got back and said something unpleasant, Durango told him the same thing in different words: "He's not going anywhere. We'll run across him in town."

"But he'll warn the other rustlers," protested Clancy.

Durango looked across at Clancy. He said in a scarcely audible tone: "You think they won't expect us? They know we got out of the cañon. They know we looked for them . . . didn't find them on the range, and they've guessed we'll be after them all the way to town."

Aaron subsided. He continued to watch the running horseman until he was lost in the swirling rain. He said no more until Winterset appeared shadowy ahead, low and sodden-looking upon the dim horizon. Then Aaron checked his weapons and called to the other Muleshoe men: "Look to your loads, boys! I got a feeling this fight's going to get worse before it gets better."

Durango, until Aaron said that about their loads, had been unconsciously aware of something familiar and unrelenting in its bulky hardness under the right fender of the saddle he was astride. He now looked down, located the booted carbine's jutting stock, and drew this weapon forth to examine it. There was a full load in the Winchester. He worked its action twice, let the hammer lightly down upon a ready cartridge, and pushed the gun back into its boot. He then made a groping inventory of his six-gun belt loops. He had enough handgun ammunition, he was sure, but if the rustlers were still in Winterset and put up a fight there, he'd have to find more ammunition for the Winchester.

Around him the others finished with their weapons. They had their interested glances fixed ahead on the town. Closer, well within sight of Winterset's main thoroughfare, the place seemed quite deserted. Here and there in the accumulating and compounded dark shone weak lamplight, but there was not a soul in the roadway and even the hitch racks were empty.

Durango cut in front of Aaron Clancy, heading out and around the town. The others followed him without a word. He led them west beyond sight in case the rustlers were watching for them, and approached Winterset from that direction keeping the backs of buildings between his companions and the town's main roadway. In this fashion they struck the refuse-littered back alley behind Amos Fallon's livery barn, and scuffed along it to ride into the stable. Here, for the first time since morning, rain did not pummel them. Here, too, as they dismounted in an atmosphere of sooty lamp glow, the overhead roar of the storm on Amos Fallon's tin roof was nearly as loud as that other roar they had survived back in the death-trap cañon.

Aaron stood at the head of his horse, watching

Durango. He had his carbine in his free hand, his reins in the other hand. Durango was calm; it seemed to Aaron that he was excessively calm. "Take care of the horses," said Winterset's town marshal, and plucked out the Winchester as a Muleshoe rider took his animal away. He turned and saw Aaron standing there in his customary impassive and considering way. He said to Clancy: "See if you can find the liveryman. We've got to have information before we go busting out of here."

Aaron went at once to the harness room and returned with Fallon. The liveryman explained that he had not heard them come in. He was pale in the face and patently fearful. He kept looking from the rain-scrubbed faces of Durango's companions to their filthy, limp, and sodden clothing, and back to their faces again.

"Some men rode into town a little while ago," said Durango. "Maybe eight of them, maybe less. Did you see them?"

Fallon shook his head. " 'Been sittin' the storm out in my harness room," he said loudly, over the thunder of that deluge on his tin roof. "You fellers after them?"

Durango did not reply to this question. He said instead, looking past Fallon to the roadway: "They need fresh horses. If they didn't come here at first, they still will." He dropped his glance to Fallon. "Turn out every animal you have. Turn them loose. Out in the road or in the back alley, I don't care where, only get rid of them."

Amos Fallon swallowed; he checked a rummaging look at the stalls on both sides of his barn's wide runway. He understood Durango's notion but he plainly was not favorable toward it. He said: "I could put 'em at the edge of town in the public corral." He said this hopefully, all the time watching Durango's expression.

"I don't want those men to have any chance to get fresh animals," said Durango, then stopped to view Amos Fallon's expression of resistance. He turned toward Aaron Clancy. "You do it," he ordered. "Have your men turn every critter loose that's in this barn and chouse them up the alley."

Aaron put a brief look of hard challenge upon Fallon, saw there would be no physical resistance, and wheeled away, calling for his cowboys to do as Town Marshal Bent Ander ordered.

Fallon craned his neck worriedly to watch this operation get into effect, then he said: "Marshal, you're responsible for them horses, you know. I aim to do my civic duty and all, but if anything happens to them. . . ." Fallon let his tone drop away in a steadily diminishing way; he was looking into the lawman's stormy gaze and it chilled him. He moved from one foot to the other, waiting for someone to speak.

"Your civic duty," stated Durango dryly, "includes helping us apprehend some rustlers.

They're the men we chased into town . . . the men you didn't see."

Fallon gasped and even in that flickering orange light his face went visibly pale and slack-muscled. "I'm no gunslinger!" he cried out to Durango. "Listen, Marshal, you got a posse. They went bustin' out o' town this morning with that kid from Muleshoe, Corey Smith, and there ain't many other fellers left here in town as would be any good about usin' guns against. . . ."

"Oh, shut up!" snapped a Muleshoe cowboy who was standing easy, off to one side, and glared his obvious disgust at the liveryman. "Fellers like you make me plumb sick, Fallon."

Amos Fallon's mouth was still open, but no additional words came from it. Durango removed his hat, struck water from it against his leg, and crushed it back shapelessly upon his head. To the liveryman he completed now what he had meant to say before: "Your civic duty includes trotting down to my office and telling Mose Clark I'm up here in your barn with the Muleshoe riders. Tell him to come up here at once . . . but use the alley, both of you. I've a feeling those cow thieves'll be watching the roadway." He scowled at Fallon. "Go on . . . what you waiting for?"

Fallon jerked his head up and down and went in an ungainly lope toward the rear opening of his barn. He stopped only once, and that was to peer

305

distastefully out, before he hurried on, spurred at once to greater speed by the coldness of the descending rain.

The same cowboy who had growled at Fallon now put his quiet look on Durango. "Old Mose and his buffler gun won't be much reinforcement for us," he stated, and waited.

Durango did not answer this man. Instead, he turned to Aaron Clancy. "Post a man up near the roadside entrance," he said. "Put another one back near the alley entrance." He paused until Clancy had given those orders, then he said: "Come on, you and I'll take a look around."

The two of them went up toward the roadway and at once saw what Durango thought they might find out there. Across the way and down several doors, at the Lone Star Saloon, two men were tying saddled horses that they had obviously just led up. At Durango's side Aaron Clancy, studying this, said quietly: "They're smart. Didn't even try to raid Fallon's barn. Must've figured they might run into trouble here. Raided back-yard sheds for those horses."

Durango was studying the two men. It was next to impossible to make them out in the deepening dusk of evening that was now compounded by the murkiness of the storm. The men worked fast and scampered up on to the plank walk in front of the Lone Star. They stood there under the protective overhang, momentarily facing outward, making a deliberate survey of that empty roadway.

"Do you recognize them?" asked Durango. "They might be townsmen or local cowmen."

"Naw," scoffed Aaron. "They aren't either."

"How can you be so sure?" asked the marshal. "You can't see their faces from here."

"Durango," stated Aaron with strong emphasis, "I was born hereabouts. I grew up here. I know everyone in this country by sight and I don't have to see their faces, either. I can tell who they are by the way they walk, or stand, or talk, and I'm telling you those two *hombres* are plumb strangers to Winterset."

Durango privately agreed that they had to be strangers. No local men would stand there, making such a meticulous study of the town. They would *know* what lay around them.

"We could drop them from here," murmured Aaron, straining forward to see the outlaws better. "Be no chore at all."

Durango was struck with a sudden idea, and to implement it on the spur of the moment he said to Clancy: "Stay here. Whatever happens out in the roadway, don't you walk out there."

Aaron started to twist about, to put a questioning glance on Durango, but the latter was moving past him out into the violent downpour. He paced slowly, carefully through ankle-deep mud, sloshing onward toward those two watching men. He slouched and kept his shapeless hat low to conceal his face until, some forty feet away, he risked looking up.

Both the outlaws were considering him with hands lying upon gun butts. They were clearly undecided about him. Durango now put into effect the solitary gamble of his scheme. He remembered two names he'd heard while the cow thieves were fleeing out of the cañon. He used them both now. Shaking water off, he called forth in a plaintive voice: "Hey, is that you, Will? This is Ace. What the hell did you fellers leave me for back in that gawd-damned cañon? I liked to drown. Hey, where's the others?"

The two men, standing motionlessly and silently looking down the roadway, eased off. One of them laughed carelessly and said: "Hell's bells, Ace. Last we seen of you, there was two fellers on the same horse an'. . . ."

The imitation outlaw broke over these words with a question: "Where is everybody? You fellers can't stay in this damned town. That posse or whatever it was that ambushed us will be along."

Now the other cow thief spoke, and he, too, sounded fully confident: "To hell with those farmers on horseback!" he called out. "And with these yellow-bellied townsmen, too. Ace, when we come bustin' in here, they broke and scattered like quail. I never seen such a cowardly town."

The other man chuckled again, and shook his head. "Ace," he said, "don't stand out there in the lousy rain like an idiot. Come on up here. The others are all inside, dryin' out. They got a stove in this here saloon and the drinks are on the house."

Both men laughed at this last statement.

Durango started onward again. He was enormously relieved. For one thing, the rain obviously made recognition of his voice as not actually belonging to one of the outlaws impossible. For another, the man he'd captured and knocked senseless back beyond the cañon's mouth, and set afoot back there, clearly had never found his friends. If he had, those two grinning men on the walkway in front of the saloon would have known Durango was an imposter.

As he continued to slip and slide, purposefully exaggerating this, Durango reached under the loose-hanging slicker, drew his handgun, and cocked it. When he was less than fifteen feet from the plank walk, he raised his head so that those two waiting renegades could see his face and at the same time he shoved forth the cocked gun.

The outlaws froze, staring out at him, their eyes widening and their amused looks winking out.

"Step down into the road," ordered Durango, "and walk right on across and into that yonder livery barn. Make one outcry or one move toward your guns and you'll be shot to hell by a dozen guns."

Durango gestured with his gun. The outlaws shot searching looks outward as though anticipating other guns and other cold-eyed men, then did exactly as they had been ordered. They walked out into the mud and, without deviating one whit from their course, made it to the entrance of Fallon's stable. There, just inside out of the deluge, they both halted.

Aaron Clancy came from the shadows, plucked away their six-guns, and wagged his head at Durango. He didn't say anything; he didn't have to; his face said it for him.

Durango put up his weapon and shook water off like a rat terrier shakes it off. "Turn around," he said. Both outlaws faced about and looked steadily at him. One of them, bolder than the other one, said: "Mister, that was pretty neat. But you had to know about Ace to do it. Where is he?"

"Darned if I know," answered Durango. "That was me riding out of the cañon with him. He tried to be cute after we got out, so I left him lying in the mud with a sore head."

"He's my brother," the outlaw said, his voice hardening against Durango. "For your sake I'd hate to think he's dead or hurt bad."

Aaron Clancy looked surprised. "You're talkin' awful big for a man who might never see the sun shine again, cow thief."

The outlaw had an answer for that, too. "Mister,

until I *am* dead, I'll go right on planning. Put that in your pipe and smoke it!"

Aaron looked for a moment as though he would strike the captive. Durango, though, turned toward the other man. "How many of you fellers got out of the cañon and down here to Winterset?" he asked.

This less communicative outlaw said: "I don't know. What I mean is . . . about fifteen minutes back another one o' us rode in. We got pretty badly scattered where you fellers dry-gulched us outside the cañon."

"How many were over there in the saloon?"

"Six."

Durango looked over at Aaron Clancy. "Four," he said. "These two don't count any more." He jerked his head. "Take 'em somewhere, tie 'em up, and put one of your boys to watching them."

XVI

Amos Fallon made his way back to the barn. He was shaking with cold and was drenched with rain water. He went up to Durango and said in an unsteady voice: "I found Mose an' I told him."

Durango looked back toward the alleyway. "Well," he exclaimed with a gathering frown, "where is he?"

Fallon raised his quivering shoulders and let

them fall. "I don't know, Marshal. I only did what you told me to do. I went down there and told the old devil what you said."

Aaron Clancy growled impatiently: "We can't stand around here all night waitin' for that old codger, Durango. Those fellers'll figure out pretty quick their two horse-stealing friends aren't going to come back. They'll light out and we'll have all that blamed ridin' to do over again."

Three Muleshoe cowboys came forth from the darkness to listen. One of them now murmured agreement with his boss and the other two solemnly nodded. Durango ignored these things. It troubled him that Mose had disobeyed his summons, but not in the sense that his companions were thinking. He thought he knew Mose better than that. Mose was just an old anachronism to everyone who knew him. He went unheeded in Winterset. But in Durango's eyes Mose Clark was more than just an old buffalo hunter and Indian scout; he was a man with pride who resented being passed over in all things because he was old.

"I wonder," he said out loud, "what the old devil is up to?"

Aaron growled something uncomplimentary under his breath and raised his head to stare on across the road where four humped-up saddled horses were standing at the Lone Star hitch rail. He shifted his stance and hefted his carbine;

impatience was making him edgy and resentful of delay.

Durango turned to gaze on the three cowboys. "I thought one of you was going to guard those two prisoners!" he exclaimed.

A Muleshoe rider said scornfully: "They couldn't get loose the way Aaron tied 'em if their lives depended upon it."

"Their lives *do* depend on it," snapped Durango, "and they damned well know that. Are they gagged?"

"No," replied the cowboy.

"Then you go back and watch them like a hawk," Durango directed this man. "When a feller's going to hang, he's not afraid to try anything . . . like chewing through his pardner's ropes. Get going, damn it! Stay with them, no matter what happens."

The cowboy departed sullenly. He looked at Aaron Clancy for confirmation of Durango's orders and got a curt nod. The other two riders stood back, watching Durango and saying nothing. They had just learned something about Winterset's new town marshal. When he told a man to jump, the man would be wise if all he said was how high?

"Stay here," Durango told these two Muleshoe men, and took Aaron Clancy forward with him to the barn's entrance again. There, the two of them resumed their earlier assessment of the Lone

Star Saloon. Not many of Winterset's store fronts showed lamplight, but the Lone Star was ablaze as though it were Saturday night with all the cowhands in town.

"I'm going over there and cut those saddled horses loose," said Durango. "You cover me."

Aaron had been thinking. When he now spoke, it was to reveal the trend of these thoughts: "They more'n likely figure our two prisoners are out getting the last two horses. I think you can walk right up and turn those critters loose."

Durango nodded, but he did not entirely share Clancy's confidence. "They're in a town with hunters after them. Whether they figure we're in town with them or not won't keep them from having a guard posted. You watch for him and don't give him a chance if he sees me."

Aaron raised his Winchester and cradled it across his body. "Go ahead," he said. "I won't let you down."

But Aaron did, for Durango had not gotten fifteen feet from Fallon's livery barn when not one, but two six-guns opened up on him from across the road. What kept him from being riddled at once was the shifting gloom of night and the obscuring downpour. Even so bullets splattered mud into his face and drove him belly down in a foot of rank mud. He got his gun up and working and over his head two more guns hurled lead into the Lone Star's door, tearing away one segment of it and putting those firing outlaws to flight. Durango used this respite in the fierce exchange to stagger upright, turn, and run awkwardly back into the barn's dark and damp interior.

He passed all the way back to a rear trough and there sluiced up a bucket of water to pour down the front of him, cutting away that cloying weight of mud. Aaron Clancy came hurriedly back to stand aside and say: "By golly, they must've figured something was wrong."

Durango lifted a sardonic gaze to Aaron's face. Very gently he said: "You reckon that's it, Aaron?" Then he finished his unique bathing process by dunking both booted feet into the trough, and afterward kicking free from muddy, adhering residue.

Up at the barn's doorway two Muleshoe riders were engaging the outlaws in the Lone Star in a furious exchange of gunfire. Aaron turned anxiously away from Durango to consider this briefly, then he departed from the barn's far depths in a trot to go forward and add his gunfire to that of his riders'.

Durango finished cleansing himself of the mud and went to Amos Fallon's harness room for a rag with which to wipe his six-gun. There, he found the liveryman sitting in abject dejection. He winced when slugs tore into his building and started up when Durango entered, his eyes profusely watering.

"Got a rag?" asked Durango calmly, and waited while Fallon brought forth several rags. He then methodically cleaned his gun, wiped his hands, plugged the bullets back into the cylinder, spun it, and cast a considering look over where Fallon sat huddled.

To one side of the liveryman was a bank messenger's reinforced and rivet-studded heavy leather pouch. Gathering dust on a nail directly above this was an old and rusty pair of handcuffs used by bank messengers in earlier times, before the advent of the Wells Fargo iron-bound strong-boxes for transporting large amounts of money.

Fallon saw Durango's measuring look and said: "I ain't brave and that's all there is to it, Marshal."

Durango said nothing. Very slowly an idea was forming in his mind. He walked closer to the liveryman and reached up to pluck away those old handcuffs. "Solid steel," he said, his tone musingly thoughtful. "Tempered steel at that, aren't they?"

Fallon looked impatiently at the cuffs. He nodded, clearly uninterested at this time in anything as obviously unrelated to his immediate peril as an old pair of handcuffs. "Yes," he croaked, "they're tempered steel. They used to make 'em like that so's fellers couldn't saw through 'em."

Durango turned the cuffs over in his hand.

"That's interesting," he mused. "Real interesting. They used to cuff the bank messenger to that reinforced pouch, didn't they, so neither he nor anyone who captured him could get the money without a lot of trouble?"

"Yes." Fallon nodded. "It'd take a man a long time to cut through the pouch. It's got steel plates inside two layers of back leather. It can't be cut with a knife and. . . ." Fallon winced as the gunfire up near the entrance to his barn suddenly increased. He bleated: "Marshal, forget them damned cuffs, will you? We'll all be killed in here. Marshal . . . !"

Durango had picked up the messenger's pouch. Its weight staggered him. He regained his balance and looked at the terrified liveryman. "Easy," he said. "You'll live to tell your grandchildren you were in a real honest-to-goodness gun battle, Fallon. Just rest easy."

Durango made a minute examination of the pouch and found it to be exactly as Amos Fallon had said. It was as nearly tamper-proof as the ingenuity of some wily saddle maker could make it. Even the lock and hasp had been constructed so that nothing short of dynamite could break them. "I'll be damned," he said. "Mister Fallon, I think you just gave me an idea of how to get those rustlers out of that saloon without anyone getting killed."

Fallon gasped. It appeared, from his blank

expression, that he neither understood nor was entirely convinced that Durango was serious.

"Do you have the keys to this pouch and these cuffs?" Durango asked, holding both items in his two hands. "If you haven't, it's all right."

"I have them," stated Fallon, and sidled to a battered old roll-top desk, rummaged there a moment, and brought back both keys. "That lock'll be rusty, though," he explained, handing forth both keys. "Marshal? Are you feeling all right?"

Durango solemnly nodded. "Never felt better," he said, "or wetter." He passed out of the harness room into the full slash and cut of flying lead. Overhead, the storm seemed to be diminishing in force. Fallon's tin roof, which magnified all sounds, no longer drowned out other sounds with its hearty rumblings.

Durango went along the side runway, staying well back from those blindly hurtling lead slugs from across the roadway, and got opposite Aaron Clancy at the stable's entrance.

"Aaron!" he called out, and, when Clancy turned, Durango motioned him back into the barn's far depths. Both men sidled along until they were safely beyond sight of the roadway, then Clancy made a dash over to where Durango was waiting. He gazed blankly at the handcuffs and messenger's pouch, then raised his widening eyes. "What the hell's that junk for?" he asked, his voice rising in puzzlement.

Instead of replying, Durango said: "What did you do with those prisoners?"

"Yonder," stated Aaron, making a careless motion toward a tie stall behind Durango. "Why? What you got in mind?"

"Find me some cotton or rags," instructed Winterset's town marshal. "Pour a little coal oil over them from one of Fallon's lamps. Then bring them back to me."

Aaron planted his legs widely and darkly scowled. "Listen," he said bleakly, "we're in a fight. This isn't any time for. . . ."

"Move, Clancy," snarled Durango. There was nothing amiable about his face now and Aaron Clancy moved. He did not look pleased or even understanding, but he moved.

Durango looked back into that dark tie stall Aaron had indicated. A man strode forward toward him; it was the sullen Muleshoe cowboy who had been detailed to guard the prisoners. He stopped and grounded his carbine and gave Durango look for look.

"That belligerent one in there," said Durango. "Bring him to the harness room."

"I got to untie his legs to do that," stated the unhappy cowboy, and Durango snarled at him in the same manner he'd used with Aaron Clancy: "Then untie them . . . and move!"

The cowboy moved; in fact, he sprang away as though he'd been hit.

Durango cast an assessing glance up where those two Muleshoe men were swapping bullets with the outlaws over in the Lone Star Saloon. He thought it unlikely that either side would score any hits; both bodies of defenders were too well protected by buildings. He started back up along the barn's secure south stall way toward Amos Fallon's harness room. Halfway up there he encountered Aaron Clancy with a handful of soiled rags that strongly smelled of coal oil. "Come with me," he said, and Aaron reversed himself and paced along to the harness room, entered it behind Durango, and said nothing, just stood back by the door watching Durango go to work with two old keys.

The pouch opened with little trouble. Durango turned, took the rags from Aaron, pushed them into the pouch, and used a hame strap off a set of work harness to hold the pouch's flap from entirely closing. He then re-locked the pouch, pocketed the key, and sat down at Amos Fallon's desk.

Both Aaron Clancy and the shivering liveryman watched Durango concentrate on writing something on a piece of paper. When he finished this chore, he turned and spoke to Clancy: "Go see what's keepin' that cowboy of yours I told to bring one of those rustlers up here."

While Clancy was gone, Durango gazed at Amos Fallon. "Don't happen to have a cigar, do you?" he mildly asked.

Fallon blinked and shook his head. His expression said very clearly that he thought Durango had been injured some way in the head.

Aaron and the Muleshoe rider came into Fallon's harness room with their bewildered captive. They shoved this man roughly toward Durango and blocked the door, waiting to see what would ensue. Durango arose from Fallon's desk without a word and cut the rustler's bonds. He then, still without even looking at the man, snapped one of the handcuffs around the cow thief's wrist, secured the other cuff to the messenger's heavy steel-reinforced pouch, and said: "Pick it up." The outlaw's bewildered expression deepened. He looked from the pouch to Durango then back to the pouch.

"I said pick it up!"

The outlaw grasped the pouch, was staggered as Durango had also been by its unsuspected weight, and he held it across his body with both arms. "What in the hell are you doing?" he asked, his tone rising in inflection and entirely without antagonism now.

Durango made no answer. He took up the letter he had written and pushed it forcefully into the rustler's shirt pocket. "That's for your friends over in the Lone Star," he said. "We're going to turn you loose, mister. You walk out of here, cross that road, and go into the saloon. You understand?"

"Sure I understand," commented the outlaw.

"Only I can't figure you fellers out. What's going on?"

"If you halt in the roadway," stated Durango, ignoring the cow thief's words, "we'll cut you down right where you stop. You keep right on walking and enter the saloon. Is that plumb clear?"

"Sure. But what . . . ?"

Durango bent forward and lit a match. The rustler stopped speaking. He and Aaron, Amos Fallon and the Muleshoe rider all watched this with uncomprehending eyes. A little puff of smoke rose up from the pouch. It was immediately followed by a licking hot tongue of pale flame. Durango yanked out that hame strap, which in turn allowed the pouch's heavy flap to fall and smother out the flame. Only oily smoke trickled from the pouch now. The outlaw let off a little squawk and would have flung the pouch away except that he could not rid himself of it. Durango watched this maneuver with ironically amused eyes and jerked his head. "Fetch him along," he told Aaron Clancy, and shouldered past to return to the runway.

Up near the roadway those two Muleshoe men were still dueling with their opposite counterparts in the yonder saloon. Durango watched them as he waited for Aaron and the protesting outlaw to come forth. When they finally did, Durango cried out for the Muleshoe cowboys to hold their fire.

Almost at once the men in the Lone Star also ceased firing. Sudden silence came. It was deafening in its own way and Durango looked upward. "Rain's stopped," he murmured. "I'll be damned." He smiled at Aaron and walked forward.

XVII

"Hold your fire!" called Durango to the men in the Lone Star Saloon. He waited a moment to be sure this was going to be done, then he called out again: "We're sending a friend of yours over to you. He's got a note for you boys to read!" He paused again, waiting, and, when only the sound of water dripping from eaves came back from across the way, he said a final sentence: "Did you boys understand me over there?"

A muffled, deep, and antagonistic voice answered up at once: "We heard you. Send him on over. If you want to make terms, we'll be reasonable."

Durango turned, caught the cocky cow thief by the shoulder, and gave him an impelling shove. "Remember now," he said. "Don't stop or try to go in any direction but toward that saloon because, if you do, you're as good as dead."

The outlaw was holding his head averted to escape that steady little upward trickle of smoke from the pouch he was clasping across his body. "I think you're crazy," he gasped, and went onward to slosh through ankle-deep roadway mud. As soon as this man had left them, Aaron Clancy said: "Durango, you aren't going to make terms with those thievin' whelps, are you?"

Durango shook his head but did not remove his gaze from the yonder outlaw. "Shut up," he murmured to Clancy. "Just watch and keep quiet."

A moment later, as the staggering, sliding outlaw gained that far walkway, Durango said to Clancy: "Get all your riders up here. Have them make damned sure their guns are fully loaded."

Aaron turned to throw a call back down the barn. Instantly the Muleshoe men rallied to him. He barked a further order and the cowboys bent at once to checking their weapons.

"He's inside," said Durango. His voice had sounded tight and a little breathless. Aaron Clancy looked around at him in mild surprise. This was the first time he'd seen Durango show any trace of excitement at all. "He's inside," Durango repeated in the same tone, "and you fellers keep a sharp watch now. All hell's going to bust loose."

But this did not happen right away, and Durango swore with considerable feeling in a soft tone.

From somewhere across the roadway, then, came a wild shout. Durango broke off cursing at once and held his breath. "Now," he said. "Now! Watch those doors!"

Almost before he had finished speaking that one sound door across the way burst wide open and a man came frantically running out, his pistol blazing. So abrupt and savage had been his emergence from the Lone Star that the watching men in Fallon's livery barn instinctively winced and ducked low as those flashing shots came toward them to strike solidly against wood.

Another man came plunging from the saloon. He, too, was throwing lead wildly and running. Durango glimpsed this man's face. It was twisted by fear and desperation. This man swung right and went fleeing northward. At Durango's side Aaron and his men were watching in bewilderment. They were slow bringing up their weapons, and before they accomplished this two more outlaws hurtled through the Lone Star's doorway. The foremost of these two men craned for a look over his shoulder, saw the man with the smoking pouch close behind, and threw aside his gun to make better time. He swung southward and went slithering and racing down the roadway.

A great burst of gunfire erupted northward. Durango recognized that hoarse and thunderous explosion and it dawned on him where Mose Clark was, and what he had been up to. The northward passage out of Winterset was effectively blocked by old Mose's buffalo gun. There were other guns up there, too. They also fired now, and that outlaw who had swung northward halted in his tracks, threw down his six-gun, and pushed up both arms straight overhead as high as he could reach.

Southward another ragged volley erupted. Durango poked his head far out to peer in that direction. He recognized the soiled apron of Winterset's gunsmith down there. Behind him was another strung-out force of armed and ready townsmen. The outlaws seeking a southerly escape followed the example of their companion who had run northward; they tossed away their weapons and surrendered.

Only one man was still running. Behind him, lumbering awkwardly and shaking one arm frantically to free himself of the smoking messenger's pouch, came the last cow thief.

The foremost outlaw raced straight into the livery barn and there he flung away his gun, saw the Muleshoe men and Durango watching, and screamed out at them: "Keep that damned fool out o' here! Don't let him bring that *thing* in here or we'll all be blown to hell!"

Aaron and his Muleshoe riders stood like stone, mouths agape. They made no move toward the wildly cursing outlaw with the pouch hand-cuffed to him who ran into the barn.

Durango caught this renegade as he swept up and was staggered by the cow thief's momentum. "Hold it!" he cried out. "Stand still!"

Aaron snapped out of his trance. He went

forward, laid hands on the other outlaw, and pushed him over near the man with the pouch. This outlaw bleated vehement protest. "No. No, dammit, not near *him*." The man stopped speaking abruptly as Durango unlocked the handcuff and freed the pouch from the renegade to whom it had been secured. Both outlaws began crying out at once for him to get rid of the pouch.

"Throw it outside!"

"Get out of here with that thing!"

Durango held the pouch and gazed at the two prisoners. He then turned his back and walked out into the roadway where two bands of armed and ready townsmen were closing in, one from the north, one from the south, on those two unarmed and badly shaken cow thieves standing to their ankles in roadway mud. He saw the gunsmith and old Mose Clark poke their prisoners, turn them about, and begin marching them toward him. Only when he was fully satisfied that each remaining outlaw was securely in custody did Durango stroll back into Amos Fallon's barn with the pouch. There, under the unblinking eyes of the prisoners, he knelt, unlocked the pouch, and dumped its smoldering rags onto the ground.

The first outlaw to understand said: "It wasn't no bomb?"

Durango looked up and shook his head. He smiled at this man. "No bomb," he said.

Aaron Clancy and the Muleshoe men frowned.

Aaron said: "What's he talking about . . . a bomb?"

Before Durango could reply, the outlaw spoke up. "He sent a note to us saying there was a bomb inside that damned pouch big enough to level this lousy town and blow all of us to Kingdom Come. The note said the fuse was just long enough to hold off detonating the bomb for sixty seconds."

Aaron blinked. He looked around as the townsmen herded their prisoners into the barn. Old Mose was there, grinning widely and prodding his prisoner with his big-bore buffalo gun. "What's all the ruckus?" he asked of Durango. "Them fellers come out o' the Lone Star like Old Nick was right behind 'em."

"They thought he was," said Aaron Clancy, and leaned over to burst out laughing.

Mose crossed over to stand beside Durango. He put both arms around his old musket and said: "I don't understand the rest o' this, Marshal, but I want you to know I didn't come up here an' join the fightin' 'cause I allowed, if them fellers busted clear o' the Lone Star, you'd need someone to sort of have their retreat out o' town cut off. Me an' the gunsmith took care o' that." Mose paused to sniffle, then he said: "You ain't mad, are you?"

Durango got up and put an arm around the old man's shoulders. "Best damned deputy town marshal this pretty tough little town ever had." He looked around. "What do you boys think?" he asked of the townsmen and the Muleshoe men. They agreed instantly and profanely. Old Mose sniffled and blushed crimson and moved out from under Durango's arm. He pushed away from the crowd with copiously watering eyes. He was confused and embarrassed and thoroughly delighted.

Aaron wiped his eyes. He considered the prisoners briefly, then said to his Muleshoe riders: "Take 'em along to the marshal's office and lock 'em up. Get Mose to go with you. He's got the keys." As the riders moved off with their prisoners, Aaron pursed his lips and made a silent whistle. "How'd you ever come to think of that?" he asked Durango, referring to the ruse that had resulted in the capture without bloodshed of the last of the cow thieves.

"It wasn't an original thought exactly," answered Winterset's town marshal. "I saw it done once down in Mexico. Only I reversed it. In Mexico they put in a live bomb in the pouch and it didn't smoke at all. Then they sent the man it was handcuffed to into a barracks of soldiers, and, when the smoke cleared away, there were twenty-seven dead men. The only part of the man with the pouch they ever found was his right arm with the handcuff on it. All I did was fake the bomb. The note did the rest."

Aaron smiled. Durango could not right then ever recall seeing him do that before. "Wait until Burt hears about this," Aaron crowed. "He'll die laughing." He took up his carbine and turned. To the returning Muleshoe riders he said: "All right boys, let's get our horses and head for home."

Durango stood aside, watching this, and, when the Muleshoe men rode out through the thinning crowd into the roadway beyond Fallon's livery barn, he followed them, and caught at Aaron Clancy's leg.

"Aaron, there's a favor you could do me . . . if you were of a mind to."

Clancy leaned from the saddle. He said earnestly: "Name it. Just you name it."

"It's about Maryann. I'd sort of like to come courtin' after I'm cleaned up."

Aaron put forth a big, grimy paw, let it lie heavily on Durango's shoulder. "You come. It won't matter a damn to her or to me whether you're cleaned up or not. You just come along."

"Well," murmured Durango, "I appreciate that, Aaron. But your brother Burt. . . ."

Aaron straightened up in his saddle and his tawny eyes flashed a quick and uncompromising flame. "You leave Burt to me. You come out tomorrow morning and I give you my word of honor Burt Clancy'll be the first one to offer you his hand."

Durango stepped back. The Muleshoe men

broke over into an exuberant lope, flinging up great gobbets of mud, and, just before they passed northward out of Winterset, they turned as one man and gave Durango a rousing yell.

About the Author

Lauran Paine who, under his own name and various pseudonyms has written over 1,000 books, was born in Duluth, Minnesota. His family moved to California when he was at a young age and his apprenticeship as a Western writer came about through the years he spent in the livestock trade, rodeos, and even motion pictures where he served as an extra because of his expert horsemanship in several films starring movie cowboy Johnny Mack Brown. In the late 1930s, Paine trapped wild horses in northern Arizona and even, for a time, worked as a professional farrier. Paine came to know the Old West through the eyes of many who had been born in the previous century, and he learned that Western life had been very different from the way it was portrayed on the screen. "I knew men who had killed other men," he later recalled. "But they were the exceptions. Prior to and during the Depression, people were just too busy eking out an existence to indulge in Saturday-night brawls." He served in the U.S. Navy in the Second World War and began writing for Western pulp magazines following his discharge. It is interesting to note that all of his earliest novels (written under his own name and the pseudonym

Mark Carrel) were published in the British market and he soon had as strong a following in that country as in the United States. Paine's Western fiction is characterized by strong plots, authenticity, an apparently effortless ability to construct situation and character, and a preference for building his stories upon a solid foundation of historical fact. *Adobe Empire* (1956), one of his best novels, is a fictionalized account of the last twenty years in the life of trader William Bent and, in an off-trail way, has a melancholy, bittersweet texture that is not easily forgotten. In later novels like *The White Bird* (Five Star Westerns, 1997) and *Cache Cañon* (Five Star Westerns, 1998), he showed that the special magic and power of his stories and characters had only matured along with his basic themes of changing times, changing attitudes, learning from experience, respecting Nature, and the yearning for a simpler, more moderate way of life.

Center Point Large Print
600 Brooks Road / PO Box 1
Thorndike ME 04986-0001 USA

(207) 568-3717

US & Canada:
1 800 929-9108
www.centerpointlargeprint.com